# LILY AND THE GHOST OF TILLIE BROWN

NP Haley

# GLOSSARY

| | |
|---|---|
| Struck out | Leave in a hurry |
| Bar | Bear |
| Beef-witted | Stupid or dull |
| Blackbirding | To kidnap grown men and force them to join the crew of a Pirate ship |
| Chaton | French for "Kitten" |
| Elf Locks | A tangled mass of hair |
| Fantôme noir | French for "black ghost" |
| Far | Fire |
| Farbug/farfly | Firebug/firefly/lightning Bug |
| Fer/fur | For |
| Haint | Restless spirit or ghost |
| Hit | It |
| Jargoggled | Befuddled or confused |
| Bushwacker | A surprise attacker with intent to do harm |
| Kindly | Sort of |
| Mudcat | Mississippi River catfisth |
| Mon Père | French for "my father" |
| Privy | Outside toilet |
| Shin-dig | Party |
| Skin-walker | A person with the ability to change into an animal |
| Vittles | Food |

In Memory of
*Dollie Violet Patterson*
*1901 - 1918*

Little is known about the life of Dollie Violet Patterson. She
was born April 25, 1901 in Perry, Illinois to Cora and George
Washington Patterson. March 15, 1917, at the age of 15, she married Audie Lee Fletcher and delivered a baby boy July 13, 1918. Five
months later on December 14, 1918 Dollie died in Parma, Missouri
during the great influenza epidemic of 1918.
Presumably, Dollie is buried in Parma, Missouri, but her burial site
is still unfound.
*"Lily and the Ghost of Tillie Brown"* is dedicated to you, Dollie
Patterson Fletcher.
You have not been forgotten.

*Life is but a vapr…here today and gone tomorrow.*

# 1

## THE BODIES

It was hot! The humid, oppressive heat of summer in southern Missouri hung thick in the air. Lily's pillow was hot, her sheet was hot, even the breeze coming in through the window was hot! The hot humidity stuck Lily's hair to the back of her neck and sides of her face. Sweat drops were seeping out of her body like out of a sieve, or so she imagined; she was quite sure the bottoms of her feet were dripping great globs of moisture onto her bed. Beads of sweat ran down behind her ears and soaked into the neckline of her nightshirt. The weak breeze coming through her window did little to lessen her suffering.

Lying there in horrible misery, Lily realized the only way to get relief from the unbearable heat would be to climb out the window and jump in the horse trough sitting between the house and the barn.

She pushed herself up and leaned her back against the metal bed frame as she thought about jumping in the cool water of the horse trough, all the while listening to a mosquito diving and buzzing enthusiastically around her head as it tried every angle it could to get a bite to eat.

"Why are mosquitoes so hard to slap?" she thought as she irritatingly slapped at the pest. The mosquito had managed to get through the new metal screen André, her brother-in-law, had put across her bedroom window earlier in the morning. This mosquito in particular was good - it was outmaneuvering each and every attempt Lily made to catch it and squash it. Around and around Lily's head it flew as it became braver and braver.

*Smack!*

She got it, but now there was a big blob of blood on her forehead. Getting grumpier by the minute, Lily leaned forward to get out of bed.

*Tap, tap, tap.* The sound of dull knocking made Lily quickly sit straight up, alarmed. "Did I hear somebody whispering?" she thought, holding her breath to listen.

Lily!" *Tap, tap, tap.* "Lily! Wake up, Lily!" Lily's best friend Ophelia was whispering loudly through the open window.

Lily's eyes darted to her window. The moonlight illuminated the crystal-clear sky; she could see everything. The bright moon behind Ophelia blocked out her facial features, but Lily recognized her voice.

"Ophelia, not so loud or you'll wake the dead along with everyone in this house," Lily whispered. "Pull the screen toward you and climb on in through the window."

Lily watched as Ophelia pushed herself up and over the window-sill, leaned into the room, fell through the window and landed on the floor with a loud thud. She jumped up immediately, rubbed her backside with one hand and quietly pulled the screen shut with the other, then immediately scrambled onto Lily's bed.

Ophelia kept darting her eyes back to the window as she nervously whispered, "We have to be very, very quiet. I don't want them to know I'm in here."

"Who?" Lily asked.

There was a long pause as Lily stared at Ophelia waiting for an answer; Ophelia kept staring out the window. Then Ophelia leaned very close to Lily's ear and softly whispered, "I found a dead body!"

She quickly covered her mouth with her hand, as if she had let an evil, forbidden statement escape from the depth of her soul.

"The body is out in the woods between the levee and the river. And, of all things," she paused. "There is a great-big, dead parrot sitting right on top of that dead body!" Ophelia sat back looking wide-eyed and frightened.

"Well," she whispered, "The parrot *was* sitting on top of the body but now it's *beside* the dead body because I knocked it off when I stumbled over it. *Now* it's just lying there on its back with its bright orange feet sticking straight up in the air. Its wings are spread out like two big, blue fans and it has a little crawfish net on its head like a hat. Its bright yellow beak is wide open and its little red tongue is hanging out the side of its beak. That's all I saw before I took off running. But that bird and that person are both dead, I tell ya. Just as dead as a body can get!" Ophelia was getting more agitated as each second passed. She jumped off Lily's bed and began pacing around the room in a circle. Abruptly, she stopped and turned back towards Lily with a jerk to say, "Neither one of them moaned, groaned or anything when I fell over them. They are dead for sure, and I've seen a lot of dead people - so I should know."

Lily sat there with her mouth hanging open staring at Ophelia. Never before had Lily heard of a dead body being dumped in the woods between the levee and the river.

Without waiting for a reply from Lily, Ophelia kept right on mumbling about the whole thing, almost as if she were replaying it to herself. "I was on my way out to the river-bottom pond to cool off since it was so hot and all in my bedroom. I thought about coming over here to get you, but then decided you were probably sound asleep so I just went on by myself and when I got a short ways down the path leading through the woods, I decided to take a short cut, and as I stepped off the main path than, BAM, I stumbled right over that dead body and knocked that big ol' dead parrot right off the top of that body. I purt-near landed smack on top of them! For the first few seconds I thought the parrot was still alive since it had been sitting up real straight-like. But when it fell over in a heap I knew it was a goner. It was dead," she paused again. "Just like that body! They are totally dead! There is no doubt about it. That person and that parrot are as dead as my pappy's old horse Penelope! But I didn't even take a gander at the person; I just jumped right up, without giving it a quick look-see, and took off running for your house! My skin was crawling right off my bones, I tell ya! I could feel haints chasing me. It was like they were breathing down the neck of my nightshirt. I could feel each breath they took. Every few seconds I felt an icy breeze take a swipe at my neck. It was as if they were just about to grab me but I was runnin' just too fast for them to catch me. Then just as I got onto your yard I felt a big sweep of icy air blow across my back, as if they were giving it one last try. I kept on shaking my arms and rubbing the back of my neck to keep them from snatchin' me right up and taking me over yonder into the spirit world. I never ran so fast in my life. Gives me the willies is what it does."

Ophelia was talking fast and wringing her hands.

"When I got to your window, I looked back and didn't see anything so I guess I must have gotten away in the nick of time." She stopped pacing and peered out the window as she kept shaking her hands and wiping at her arms. "I can't seem to get the feel of that dead bird off me!" she whispered.

Ophelia's full name is Ophelia Corina Willowmenia Callie Knudsen. When Ophelia was born, her parents wanted to christen her with the names of every important female member of their families. So, the name Ophelia comes from her Great-Great-Grandmother, Corina is her mother's name and Willowmenia is the name of her mother's great Aunt Willowmenia. Aunt Willowmenia, at the grand age of ninety-five, still lives on Sugar Cane Island off the coast of South Carolina, where she had once lived as an indentured servant. She was once imprisoned for spitting on a military officer after he voiced his crude opinion about her mistress, Mrs. Opal. The jailer finally released young Willow back to the care of Mrs. Opal after being given quite a fine amount of money as a bribe from the mistress. After a lengthy lecture, the jailor reluctantly released Willow to Mrs. Opal along with a long written list of how Mrs. Opal should control her servants. To make sure Mrs. Opal saw and read his list, the jailor pinned the list to the front of Willow's dress. Mrs. Opal never did beat any of her servants as the jailor had instructed her to. In fact, when Willow turned eighteen, Mrs. Opal gave her papers releasing her from indentured servitude, making Willow a member of her paid staff, as a gift and "to show that haughty military officer and that ignorant jailor", as Ms. Opal so aptly put it. Mrs. Opal also built Willow a fine little house and gave her the signed deed for the land on which the little house was built. When Mrs. Opal passed on, she left Willow a large sum of money which provides for Willow still today. Local gossip whispered about Willow being Mrs. Opal's true granddaughter; seeing that while Willow was supposedly an indentured servant, she did not have *one* duty to perform and never had a want for anything. Only Willow knows the true story and she is, to this day, not saying one word about that subject.

Callie was Ophelia's mama's older sister who passed away giving birth to her first child at the young age of sixteen. After the death of his wife and infant son, Callie's husband Virliss Hodges, went into a deep depression and walked away from his farm and everyone he knew. Gossip was passed around stating Virliss had joined up with a cut-throat pirate named Bully Hayes and his ship *The Rona* off the coast of a Caribbean island, but then Bully Hayes was killed by Dutch Pete, the ship's cook, and his body was tossed overboard by the cheering crew members. It seems Bully Hayes was a murdering tyrant of a man, blackbirding drunken men from the river port saloons. If they tried to escape, they would disappear without a clue; the rest of his crew never admitted knowing anything about those evil doings.

While the details of Virliss Hodges' disappearance were unknown, rumors in southern Missouri were that his body was last seen hanging from a tree in Port Royal, Jamaica. A few years later, some childhood friends and Virliss' own brother Erliss told of seeing and talking to him in St. Augustine, Florida, where Virliss told them of his magnificent adventures with the pirates and what a grand time it was. Only after Captain Hayes' murder did Virliss become edgy. When the new Captain Moze and some of his new crew took control, Virliss watched as other members of Captain Bully's old crew were being made to walk the plank straight into the open waters of the ocean for minor mistakes. That was when he decided it was time for him to make his escape. Virliss finally managed to make his getaway by hiding in an empty water barrel and scooting it off the side of the ship while they were docked fairly close to the shoreline of New Orleans. Eventually Virliss settled in the swamplands of Louisiana and lived among the Cajun people.

Ophelia's last name, Knudsen, was passed down from her Great-Great-Grandfather, Jansen George Knudsen; when he was a young boy living in the Netherlands, he was an indentured servant for the Wijhe-Knudsen family. When the Wijhe-Knudsens traveled from the Netherlands to America in hopes of finding great adventure, they brought Jansen George along with them; soon after their arrival in New York City, the Wijhe-Knudsens released Jansen George from his servitude and paid him for his years of service. In honor of the family he had grown to love dearly, Jansen George took part of their last name as his own.

As a freed man, Jansen George traveled across America enjoying the sights and going-ons of his new country. But when he arrived in Missouri he met and fell in love with Ophelia Belle Bogarie. It was love at first sight for both of them, so they quickly married and built a farm in the Ozark mountain wilderness where they raised their fifteen children.

Young Ophelia's family now lives in the small settlement called Kin Folks Ridge, which is only about half a mile away from Lily's house. And as it happened, Ophelia and Lily became best of friends the day they met.

Ophelia is twelve, just a year young than Lily, but a head taller. Her hair is long, white-blonde and her eyes are the same hue of green as Lily's litter sister, Tessa. Sometimes their eyes look like the lily pads in the pond behind Granny Tomason's house; at other times they look like the moss growing on the trunk of a tree. Ophelia's legs are long and thin, and she can "run like a deer" as her mama always says. Ophelia can beat Lily in a foot race without even trying. In fact, Lily is quite sure Ophelia is the fastest runner in Caruthersville, and most people seem to agree.

Lily, on the other hand had a much different family history. She lived with her oldest sister and brother-in-law, Caitlin and Sheriff André Beaumont, as well as her brother Benny and her little sister Tessa. Not too many months back, Caitlin had been kidnapped by their alleged Aunt Birdie who planned on taking Caitlin down the river to New Orleans where she would be sold into the Brazilian underground slave market.

It turned out Aunt Birdie wasn't Aunt Birdie after all. Her name was Maude Burbank, and she had killed their real Aunt Birdie along with Lily's parents and a few other people. Sheriff Beaumont, now Lily's brother-in-law, had put Maude and her band of river rats in the Caruthersville jail to wait until the judge made it into town. Maude later died from unknown causes while waiting for her trial to begin, or so Doc Pfeiffer said. There were a few questionable stories about Maude's death, but no one bothered checking them out. The band of rats and all the others involved had been sentenced to life in prison.

Lily thought of her brother and sisters. Caitlin had the same black hair, amber gold eyes, black eyebrows and long, black eyelashes she had but Tessa looked like their mama, with her red-blonde hair and green eyes. When Lily thought of her mama, sometimes she pictured her with very light red hair and other times with light golden blonde hair. It was as if God could not make up his mind whether to give Mama and Tessa red hair or blonde hair. Occasionally Pa would refer to them as his fortune and say their hair was part ruby and part spun gold. They both had fair skin, with a sprinkling of freckles across their noses, and expressive dark brown eyebrows that moved up and down with their thoughts and moods.

Benny looked like their Grandpappy H with his dark ginger hair and blue eyes. Mama had told them that Pappy H kept his freckles until the day he died, so Lily was quite sure Benny's freckles were on his face to stay. Benny's arms and legs seemed to belong on a much taller person, but Granny Tomason said Benny's body would eventually catch up with his arms and legs; Lily sure hoped so, because Benny looked rather strange at the moment.

"You want to go see it or not, Lily?" Ophelia's loud whisper interrupted Lily's thoughts and brought her back to the problem at hand. "It's pretty scary, I tell you!"

"Of course I want to see it," Lily whispered quickly, scrambling off her bed to get dressed. "There's no doubt about it, I want to see it tonight!"

Quickly putting on her clothes and shoes, Lily whispered, "Ok, I'm ready; let's go see that dead body. Wait, wait - before we go, put on a pair of Pappy H's old britches so bugs won't bite your legs. And here's one of Benny's old shirts. That way we'll be covered up from those pesky mosquitoes. Did you bring a lantern?"

"Yes," Ophelia replied, also changing quickly into different clothes. "Its right outside the window. But maybe we should wake up Sheriff Beaumont and let him take care of it. That's what sheriffs do."

Lily looked at Ophelia with open-mouthed astonishment, "No way. I'm not letting André take away that dead body before I get to see it. He'll make us stay right here in this room and then he'll wake Benny up and let him help cart the body back into town! Nope, that is not going to happen. You ready to go?"

"Well," Ophelia gave a big sigh, "I guess. Let's go and get this over with. But I'm telling you right now before we even get there, if a haint tries to snatch us I'm out of there fast and even though you are my best friend, I *will* leave you behind."

"Okay," Lily nodded. "That's a fair deal."

Lily walked quickly to the window as Ophelia slowly shuffled behind her; they climbed out and pushed the screen back into place so no more bugs would get into her room. Then they turned and started walking by moonlight through the damp grass toward the levee.

The night sky was clear and offered plenty of moonlight as they took off running toward the levee. The glow of the full moon distorted and lengthened the shadows of trees, transforming everything into creatures found only in one's imagination. A eerie feeling lay thick and heavy in the atmosphere as both girls darted their eyes back and forth, watching for strange movements.

It didn't take them long to reach the top of the levee, where they stopped and looked out toward the river. Most of the trees were too tall for them to see over, but through a big open clearing they were able to see all the way to the riverbank and beyond. They could make out several huge paddleboats anchored for the night, their lighted decks and windows creating sparkling reflections on the face of the calm, glassy water.

With the night being sultry and hot, critter noise along the levee was louder than usual; it seemed as if the critters were also complaining about the heat. Cicadas buzzed loudly; bullfrogs and crickets sang out their night songs and the hoot-owls called to their mates. Off in the distance, next to the riverbank, campfires blazed as small boats and rafts pulled up onto the shore for the night and built their fires high, letting them smolder throughout the night hoping the smoke would chase away the wretched swarming mosquitoes.

Something was amiss along the levee tonight. It felt as if spirits were lingering longer than need be after a soul is taken; were they waiting and watching for something to happen? The tingling of fear blanketed both girls as apprehension crept deep into the marrow of their bones. Neither girl spoke, but both knew the other one felt the same turbulent presence.

"We have to go see it now before someone else gets to it and maybe moves it. Its really creepy is all I have to say. I don't know about you, but I don't like dead bodies or haints and I'm thinking this person's haint is still hanging around just waiting for the killer to come back so they can spook 'em and snatch 'em into that spirit world. And I ain't wanting anything to do with that stuff," Ophelia whispered loudly.

"I reckon they are." Lily quietly whispered, keeping her voice low so it wouldn't carry across the forest and attract stray haints which may be aimlessly floating about. "I hear-tell that sort of thing will happen every time a body passes over and doesn't get its proper burial and all. The haints don't rightly know where to go. They say those haints are floating around us all the time but we can't be seeing 'em unless they want us to.

"One time I overheard two church ladies standing outside the church-house talking about old man Elmer Monroe and how he was found dead down in a Tennessee holler by some hunting fellas. They said his body had been there a mighty long time and his haint was still hanging right there by his body. Those ladies said old Elmer's haint scared those hunting fellas something awful, but then decided to throw a bucket of water on the haint and it finally left so they were able to cart Elmer's body out and take it to on to his family. Those ladies said they do believe Elmer's haint, to this day, is still looking for whoever did him in. They said if he would have had a proper burial and all, his haint would have been fine and dandy and gone on to the spirit world real peaceful-like. They even said some haints from un-found dead bodies are watching us all the time, just waiting around for a chance to find their killers. But they said its the law of heaven and earth that haints can't spook us unless we are doing something bad. Like robbing, stealing or killing, and then they can spook us all they want. But, if we're doing something good, like burying a body that needs burying, they won't spook us. And those two church ladies said they reckoned it was the gospel truth, seeing that a traveling preacher-man had one time declared it and he swore by it. One lady said the preacher-man told her he had actually seen it happen, not just once, but many, many times. But then the she also said that the traveling preacher-man told her if she didn't give him some money he would conjure up some haints and send the haints into her house. Well, that lady said she went ahead and gave him some money just to be on the safe side and the other lady said she did the smart thing, since nobody wants to be messing with haints in their house.

"So you're probably right about that haint still hanging around down there, Ophelia. I'm quite sure the haint is still in there some-where. But if we go down there and do a good deed for that dead person I don't think they will spook us. Also, I'm thinking maybe it's our duty as good neighbors to make sure they have a proper burial and all. That must be the reason why you couldn't sleep and wanted to go out to the pond. Something wanted us to come down here and help that dead person."

"Well I reckon that might be true," Ophelia whispered softly. "I suppose it is our duty, as good neighbors and all, but I would rather poke a fork in my noggin than touch a dead body—so I'm not touching it! And I sure do hope the good Lord gives us a lot of points for doing this here good deed. I don't like it one little bit!"

Lily nodded in agreement.

Even though they could see the familiar well-worn path leading down the levee and into the trees, the one they had walked many times before; they kept standing there quietly staring at the tree line.

"A whole lot of people use this path every day," Lily mumbled to Ophelia. "I'm kind of surprised the body was dumped so close to the footpath. I'm thinking it must have happened after dark."

Ophelia groaned, "I surely hope those killers aren't lurking around waiting for someone else to come along."

Lily leaned close to Ophelia's ear, and in a trembling whisper said, "Well, let's go and have a look-see. Ya ready?"

Ophelia looked back at Lily and whispered nervously, "I reckon I am, if we have to. Should we light the lantern now or should we wait until we get down to the tree line? What do you think?"

"Well, let's wait until we get off the top of the levee and a little closer to the woods. We don't want any of those folks over on the riverbank to come snooping around trying to find out what the light is, do we?"

"Nope, don't want that, that's for sure." Ophelia nodded her head. "Good idea."

Lily drew in a deep breath and Ophelia shuddered. After a couple false starts, they worked up their courage and slowly started shuffling down the path. Just as they did, Lily caught a glimpse of two big lanterns being carried into the trees from the river side of the woods. Even though the river side of the woods was more than a half-mile away, in the bright moonlight Lily was able to make out the shapes of what looked like two big men.

"Wait!" Lily stopped and grabbed Ophelia's arm. "Look! Over there," she said, pointing in the direction of the river. "Someone else is going into the trees! Let's get on down to the tree line and see if we can tell where they're going."

"Land o' Goshen!" Ophelia muttered frantically. "Let's hurry before they catch sight of us."

As fast as they could run without falling down the side of the levee, the two girls reached the mouth of the path and quickly stood behind a thick clump of spindly trees.

During the moonlight hours, the river bottom trees created sinister images in one's mind and transformed into perfect hiding places for those wanting to do evil.

Tangled vines and brush grew in abundance on most of the land. Dead vegetation and fish from the spring run-offs left the soil in the river bottom extremely fertile. Seeds from every kind of plant growing along the Mississippi washed downriver and were deposited into the river-bottom soil. Every spring, farmers would clear a plot of river bottom land, plant their crops and wait with anticipation, hoping the flooding river would not reach their crops. Most years the crops flourished and the farmer's profits were abundant. But occasionally there come a year when high floods surged down the river flooding the river bottom, washing away every tender new plant on its way to the Gulf of Mexico. The farmers would lose everything to the rushing river as it showed its unstoppable power by sweeping through the shoot with vengeance, scooping up everything in its path: plants, trees and sometimes houses, emptying everything into the Gulf.

Well before Lily and Ophelia got to the top of the levee, dense river fog had rolled into the woods and was now hanging in misty clumps from the branches and vines. Only a scattering of moonlight could be seen throughout the trees as it speckled the forest floor. Half broken tree limbs formed a canopy over the pathway leading through the woods. The foliage-covered canopy kept out the heat of the burning sun during the summer days and kept the forest cooler during the hot and humid summer nights.

Only an outline of trees in the distance could be seen through the shrouded forest. Peeking out from their hiding place, Lily and Ophelia tried to distinguish the glow of lanterns coming along the pathway, but no light rays could be distinguished through the fog covered trees.

Cautiously easing around the clump of trees, Lily and Ophelia stepped onto the footpath. A feeling of death and sadness hung heavy around them as they walked a little further into the woods. With each step they took, the fog swirled around their feet in big puffs of smoky haze; to Lily, it seemed to be turning into a living creature.

River fog always appeared to be alive - stretching out its misty damp tentacles, grasping everything within its reach and slipping its wet, opaque fingers around bushes and trees, slowly reaching for higher levels. Once the fog would reach the upper branches, it would begin drooping down in great clumps of wet mist, as if it were stretching back down to the ground. Even when there was no breeze to be felt, the drooping fog always swayed to and fro. Lily was almost positive the river fog had a soul hidden deep within the unseen black water of the river.

Goose bumps popped up on Lily's arms and the back of her neck began to tingle with anticipation. From experience, Lily knew too well how the river fog could swallow up a man or woman, allowing them to hide and surprise her.

Shaking the thoughts out of her mind, Lily continued following Ophelia down the path through the trees. About twenty steps into the woods Ophelia stopped and spoke so quietly it was hard for Lily to hear.

"This is the spot."

Lily stopped and both of them looked off to the side of the path.

"Do you see any other lanterns coming?" she whispered.

"Nope, not yet. Let's light our lantern." Squinting, Lily strained to see through the murky woods. Squatting down, Ophelia lifted the lantern globe as Lily reached into her own pocket and pulled out a match. Bending over, Lily used the side of her boot to strike the match and light the wick. Ophelia carefully replaced the globe and they both stood up.

"Okay," Ophelia solemnly whispered. "Here we go."

Cautiously, with Lily following close behind, Ophelia took a step off the well-worn path and stopped suddenly, causing Lily to bump into her with a thud.

"Don't push me, Lily," Ophelia said in a sharp whisper.

"Sorry, I didn't mean to."

With a jittery voice Ophelia whispered, "Here they are."

Slowly, Lily peeked around Ophelia and then stepped next to her. There the body lay. It was a woman with a big, dead parrot lying at her side. The parrot's large yellow feet were sticking straight up in the air. Large talons protruded out from each claw and the talons had been painted a bright red. Its huge iridescent blue, feathered wings were spread straight out; the tail feathers were the same blue with occasional red feathers mixed in. A crawfish catch-net had been jammed onto the parrots head with its draw string hanging along-side the parrot's beak. Someone had painted the tip of its large beak bright red. There were three lines of little black feathers swirled around the parrot's eyes and short little green feathers were sticking through the crawfish net like tufts of grass.

"Some of those tail feathers must be two feet long," Lily mumble-whispered. "And look, Ophelia, the wings and body are bright blue, but its head is green."

Ophelia looked at Lily. "That's what I told you, Lily."

"It's a beautiful bird!" Lily whispered, still looking down at the parrot.

Holding the lantern a bit higher to get a better look at the body, they could no longer notice the damp fog sliding its milky white fingers around their legs as if trying to enclose them in its web. They were too absorbed in looking at the body to realize what the fog was doing.

Fanning the fog away from her face, Lily tried to get a better look at the person's face. It was difficult to make out the facial features, but they could tell the body was that of a small woman dressed unlike any other woman they knew. She wore a bright red gypsy blouse and burlap bloomers. It looked as if she wore the burlap bloomers as every day britches since they were dirty and frayed around the edges. The body was slightly turned onto its right side revealing her left arm and etched into her skin between her wrist and her elbow was a drawing of a beautiful parrot in flight.

On her feet were black stockings and brown men's boots, covered in dirt. Her legs were so skinny the tops of her boots could not lace tightly around her ankles. Her hair was long, black and bushy; it looked like she had never pulled a comb through it. On her head was a frayed, old and floppy brown felt hat with blue parrot feathers pushed into the dirty hatband. In her hand she was clutching a smoke pipe. Her face and hands were dirty but her gypsy blouse looked new and fairly clean.

Motioning for Ophelia to lower their lantern, Lily used her foot to slowly push the body onto its back. Lily bent down and suddenly knew who the woman was.

"Wow," Lily whispered loudly. She stood up and continued fanning the fog away from her face. "I know who this is – it's Tillie Brown! She lives over on the riverbank and is a gambling boat-hopper. She slips onboard the gambling boats when no one is looking, then hides until the boat is out in the river and once the Captain sees her, he lets her stay until she takes too much money from the other gamblers, then he boots her off at the next stop. Some of the captains like Tillie Brown coming on board because the high-roller gamblers from down south are always wanting to get the bragging rights of being able to beat Tillie Brown in a game of poker. So they gamble more money than usual and the riverboat gets more money. The gamblers seldom beat Tillie, so it works out good for her too. That's what the gossips say at least, but I really don't know if that's a true story or just a rumor.

Sometimes, when the *New Orleans Sirene* passes by town, I see her on the deck calmly leaning over the railing, smoking her pipe with her parrot perched on her shoulder; all the while laughing at the town folk as they gawk at the boat. Her parrot's name is Duck." Lily bent down to get another good look before saying, "I wonder what happened to them?"

"Are ya sh- sh- sure about that Lily?" Ophelia stammered, also bending down to get a better look. "I don't think so. It doesn't look like Tillie Brown to me. Tillie Brown always looked a lot bigger, ya know?"

"Of course it's me, ya empty headed gal!" a voice yelled down from the trees. "Who do ya think it is, the King of Persia maybe?" The voice let out a loud laughing cackle and started coughing.

Lily and Ophelia jumped up and grabbed each other's arms as they looked up in the trees, trying to find where the voice was coming from.

On a tree branch not more than ten feet above them sat the ghost of Tillie Brown and her parrot. "*Aawk! Aawk!* Tillie Brown is dead!" the parrot squawked. "*Aawk! Aawk!* Tillie Brown is dead! *Aawk! aawk!* Til-"

SMACK!

"Shut-up, Duck," yelled Tillie's ghost as she smacked the ghost-parrot's chest. He flopped back and spun around the tree branch three times, all the while frantically flapping his large wings, before coming to a teetering stop. He wobbled a bit as he tried to stop himself from going around a fourth time.

Every time the parrot-ghost spun around the branch, he dropped ghost-parrot poo. Three times little white puffs of ghost-parrot poo floated down and - *poof!* - disappeared into thin air.

"-lie Brown is dead". Duck finished his sentence with a sputtering low whisper.

"He's ah own-ree ol' parrot, but I love 'em anyway," Tillie said firmly to Lily and Ophelia. "Ya'all want ah parrot carcass fer breakfast?" she laughed. "Go ahead. Take his old dead body. He ain't gonna use hit no more. Hit might be kindly tasty if ya beat his bones with a board afore cooking 'em up with some taters and grits. He's a tough ol' bird...that he is! And, by the way, *he* is really a *she* but I jest call 'em 'he' cuz hit bothers 'em," Tillie said with a chuckle.

"*Aawk!*" Duck shrieked. "*Aawk!*"

Duck's ghost head was all the way back and his beak was wide open with his little round tongue sticking straight out as he flapped his long transparent ghost wings and shuffled quickly away from Tillie's ghost until he was sitting snug against the main trunk of the tree.

"*Aawk! Aawk! Aawk...* " Duck's ghost kept muttering in a low mumble; all the while nodding his head and sticking his red round tongue out of his beak trying to catch the crawfish-net bead dangling in front of his face. He caught the bead with his tongue, swallowed it and started choking. Tillie's ghost reached over and gave him a sharp smack on the back and Duck hacked up the bead.

"*Aawk! Aawk!* Much obliged," squawked Duck as he continued nodding his head up and down. "*Aawk! Aawk!* Much obliged."

Lily could not believe her eyes. She squeezed her eyes shut and then opened them, thinking maybe she was imagining this whole thing. She was quite sure this was just a figment of her and Ophelia's imaginations. It must be the hot humid air mixed with the cool night fog from the river creating this whole vivid picture.

Lily swallowed down her fear and spoke to Tillie in a whispery voice, "Ah, what's going on, Tillie?"

"Humpf. If I know'd the answer to that thur question," Tillie huffed indignantly as if the mere question offended her, "Do ya think I'd be a'sittin here on this here tree branch chewing the fat with a couple empty-headed gals like the two of you? Of course not! I'd be out gettin' me some revenge! I'd be nabbin' me some Tillie Brown killers! That's what I'd be doin'. Yes sir'ee — that's jest what I'd be doin' and I'd be givin' them fellers such a powerful spookin' they'd run as fast as thur scrawny chicken-legs can carry 'em right into the Sheriff's hoosegow, they'd lock themselves in and throw the key out the winder!"

Tillie sighed deeply and continued on. "Well, I ain't knowin' jest *who* done hit, but… I *can* be tellin' ya how hit were done. Them thur low-down polecatin' thieves whacked me upside the head is what happened. I had me a poke full of gold here in my pocket." Tillie stopped talking, patted the back of her ghost bloomers and then said, "And hit's *all* gone!" Tillie tried yelling, but instead of yelling she went into a fit of coughing before she could continue. Coming around, she said, "All I know'd is they smell like last year's horse manure and is ugly as mud. I didn't actually see 'em, but I know'd they be ugly as mud. All them thieves is ugly as pig poop. I hear'd 'em though. Yep, jest afore they got ta me I hear'd 'em coming. I was over yonder-" Tillie cocked her thumb towards the river. "I was jest startin' in ta sneakin' up to that thur big ol' campfar' south o' here," Tillie stopped talking and pointed to the south before continuing. "Hit's over close by that thur river point. Thur was a big ol' far a'goin' and three men was sittin' round hit. They had that thur big ol' mountain man, Bushy-head, tied up to a big ol' tree and they was jest a'cluckin and a'cacklin' like a barn full of hen-chickens trying to figger out what they was a'gonna do with 'em.

"Well, let me jest back up here a bit. All's I went over thur fer, in the first place, was ta pinch me one of them thur bar hides ol' Bushy-head had tied on his packmule – will, he ain't got 'em no more," Tillie cackled loudly. "Cuz them thur thieves got 'em all. But that was all I wanted - just one miserable ol' bar hide so's I could trade hit in fer a lot of vittles and such. Well, them thur thieves couldn't decide iff'en they wanted ta kill old Bushy-head or jest beat on 'em some."

Tillie started having another coughing spell, and when she finally stopped, she lit her ghost-pipe, sucked some ghost-smoke into her ghost-lungs and sighed deeply as if the smoke felt wonderful. Every time she inhaled smoke, it seeped through her ghost shirt and vanished into thin air. Then she sighed and continued her story. "Wow! Looky that thur. I'm a'smokin' and hits comin' right on out ah me," she let out another laughing cackle before continuing. "I see'd 'em tie 'em up. Yep, I see'd the whole thin'. I see'd the whole kit-n-caboodle."

With that said, Tillie reached over and knocked Duck off the tree branch so she could lean her back against the tree trunk and rest her legs up on the branch; she crossed her ankles and settled in for a long story. Duck squawked as he jumped onto a different branch.

"Well," Tillie said as she drew in some more smoke from her pipe and leaned her head back against the tree, "I'd been follerin' ol' Bushy-head fer quite a ways. Jest me and my horse, Tally-Ho. We was jest a'waitin' fer him to take a snooze so's I could pinch me a hide, but hit was *me* who took the snooze." She cackled again.

"And when I finally citched up with him, he was already gettin' acquainted with them thur fellers. They was all jest a'fightin and a'scratchin' and a'rollin' around on the ground with each other and that bushy headed ol' mountain man was getting the best of 'em. They had 'em grounded ones't, or twices't, but ever time he jumped right up."

Tillie was acting out the fight as she told her story. Her arms were punching the air and her shoulders were jerking back and forth as she demonstrated how Bushy-head was fighting the three thieves.

"Then ol' Bushy-head grabbed one feller by the hair and another'n by his britches straps and started in a'swingin' 'em both around in a circle. That ol' Bushy-head is a mighty strong feller. He whirled them thur two fellers around about five or six times, real quick-like, and then he let 'em go, right smack into that thur third feller. Well, all three of them fellers went down with a big THUD!

"Then, ol' Bushy-head turned to run on out of thur, but that third feller pulled out his big ol' skinnin' knife and held it out as Bushy-head passed him and that thur knife cut right inta Bushy-head's leg real bad. Well, that thur stopped the whole ruckus. Ol' Bushy-head tried ta keep on a-runnin', but he went down like a mountain and them three fellers was on him in a farfly's flash. They grabbed 'em and dragged 'em—by his hacked up leg mind you—back to one of them thur big trees and wound him up tight as a pig-in-a-poke - if ya know what I mean.

"I was jest squattin' behind that thur bush, kindly fascinated with the whole hullabaloo, when all of a sudden-like I smell somethin' *bad* creepin' up on me. Ol' Duck here, he starts in a'flappin' his wings and a'squawkin' so I took off runnin' jest as fast as my legs could carry me. Well, I hear'd horses runnin' after us and them thur horses was gettin' mighty close when all of a sudden-like, WHACK! Duck goes flying past my head. Them thur thieves smacked my Duck with somethin' hard and he was a *goner*. Well, I couldn't jest leave my Duck thur now could I? So's I slow down to grab 'em up, and WHACK! That was it! I was a *goner* too! Next thin' I know'd is you two gals are bending down jest gawkin' at my dead body and Duck was squawkin'in my ear sayin, 'Aawk! *aawk*! make 'em stop! Make 'em stop! *Aawk*!'"

Tillie looked down at Lily and Ophelia with her eyes wide and a frown on her face. "Don't' know how me and Duck got on this here path, don't have any idee who did hit or why they did hit. Musta' been they wanted the gold I had in my bloomers pocket. All I know'd is I'm gonna find 'em! I'm thinkin' they din't want ta kill me, them thur river folk think I have a big ol' stash o' money hidden somers. But, they done kill't me and now they ain't got nothin' but a little ol' bag o'gold." Tillie cackle laughed and said, "Look at me. Do I look like I have a pile o' gold?"

"Well, no," Lily said hesitantly, 'what did this Bushy-head fella look like? Did he have real bushy red hair and beard?

"Yep, that's him," Tillie laughed, "Hit's that ol' Mr. Bushy, as everbody calls 'em. I'd know that thur ol' mountain feller anywhere! He never lets me pinch even one little-bitty ol' hide. Not even one big as a mouse turd! He's a selfish old coot! Well, to be honest—now's that I'm a *goner* and all—I'm guessin' I better be tellin' hit like hit is...I did do a lot of pinchin' his hides over the years. So's I guess he did have a good reason not ta trust me."

Tillie laughed so hard she fell off the tree branch and had to float back up.

Lily and Ophelia continued staring up at Tillie and her parrot with open-mouthed amazement. It looked as if half of Tillie's back teeth were pretty much gone, and those she did have were dirty and tobacco stained. Her pale eyes were sunken into her gaunt face and her eyebrows were as thick as a man's eyebrows. Lily didn't know if it was because Tillie was dead or if maybe she had looked the same when she was alive, but Tillie sure looked bad, and her fingers were stained yellow from tobacco. But, being that Tillie was a see-through ghost it was a little hard to tell just what she actually looked like.

"Tillie," Lily called up to her. "Who do you think killed you? Was it the three thieves who have Mr. Bushy? We need to go free Mr. Bushy and then we can help you find the people who killed you. How's that sound?"

"Ha!" Tillie shouted down. "Hit weren't them thur three heathens, I tell ya. I was a'watchin' 'em when I smelled them other heathen fellers a'comin' ta get me. And anyway, Ol' Bushy-head is a *goner* jest like me and ol' Duck! Them thur thieves done got rid of 'em I tell ya. His body is sur'nuf floatin' in that thur river." Tillie sighed and added, "Guess I'll be a'meetin' 'em up at the Pearly Gates standin' in front of Saint Pete. I be guessin' I'll have ta 'pologize fer all them hides I done pinched from him over the years. Yeah, I guess I'll be doin' a lot of 'please forgive me's' ta ol' Bushy-head as I stand in front of St Pete. I've done some mighty awful thins' in my life. But hit weren't ever ta hurt nobody. Hit was jest out of necessity that I ever did commit them thur thins'." Tillie seemed to be talking to herself more than she was to Lily and Ophelia.

"Iff'en my ma or pa knew what I done did hit would break thur hearts, God rest thur souls, they was honest up-right folk. I guess I'll have to be a'tellin' Ma and Pa how bad I was and all. I sure be hopin' I can be gettin'in ta see 'em."

Tillie looked down at Lily and Ophelia.

"Hit's a waste of time lookin' fer that ol' Bushy-head," Tillie said firmly, scratching her ghostly armpit. Giving Lily a firm look, she continued, "You gals do whatever ya be a'wantin to do, but I warn ya, don't go over thur snoopin' around them thur thieves. They'll string ya up and dump ya in that river jest as fast as a farfly flash, I tell ya."

She continued to glare at Lily for a couple seconds before scratching her armpit again and looking around at her surroundings.

"Well, I have some busy-ness of my own to be a'doin'. I'm gonna go find me some Tillie Brown killers, that's what I'm a'gonna do." She turned to face her parrot. "Come on Duck, let's get on outta here."

"*Aawk! Aawk!* Tillie Brown's ah cheatin' gambler. Tillie Brown's ah cheatin' gambler!" Duck's ghost was standing straight up on stretched-out legs, bobbing his head and flapping his large, see-through ghost wings back and forth with his beak wide open as he squawked. "*Aawk!* Tillie Brown's ah cheat-"

"Shut up, Duck!" Tillie smacked Duck on the chest, sending him flopping around the branch again. "You're a looney bird! I won my money straight as an arrow."

"*Aawk!* Don't think so," Duck squawked again, still bobbing his head up and down with his beak wide open. His little round tongue was still wandering out of his beak once again trying to catch the drawstring bead on his crawfish net hat.

Tillie reached out to smack him again, but he took off flying; Tillie whisked herself away chasing after him, yelling at him to shut-up.

*Whoosh!* Tillie was back in front of them.

"Hey. You two girls take my locket. You, Lily Quinn, you keep it forever and never let anyone else have it." Lily noticed Tillie's accent had mostly disappeared. "That's a precious part of my life and I don't want nary a soul to have it except someone who knows the true value of it. Unless you find my Pa still alive, which is not very likely, hit's yours ta keep forever. Treasure it and keep it safe. It's the only thing left in this whole world of my family."

*Whoosh!* Tillie was off again. The two ghosts melted away into the woods, leaving Lily and Ophelia standing alone, staring at the empty branch and listening to the fading echoes of Duck's squawking and Tillie's reprimands. Lily and Ophelia looked at each other.

"Woah," Lily said. "Did you notice the change in the way she was speaking, Ophelia? I *knew* she was well educated! She dropped that river slang, didn't she!"

"Yes she did. That was a surprise."

Ophelia looked quite shaken and her face was an ashy grey.

"You okay, Ophelia? You don't look okay."

"Yeah… I'll be okay now that they're gone. That was the strangest thing I've ever experienced." Ophelia whispered a little baffled.

"Well, let's get Tillie's locket and get out of here," Lily said. "We need to go see if we can help Mr. Bushy."

"Nope, I'm *not* touching no dead body and anyways, Tillie told *you* to take it, not me!"

Both girls stood looking down at Tillie's dead body until Lily reached down and lifted Tillie's hair away from her neck, looking for the locket chain.

"There it is, Ophelia. Can you help me unlock the clasp?"

"Nope." Ophelia didn't move.

"Come on, just hold her hair up."

"Nope."

"Ophelia. Just lift her hair a bit!"

"Nope."

"Ophelia, I can't do this by myself! Will you please help me here?"

"Nope".

"What's wrong with you?" Lily stood up and frowned at her friend.

"Nothing's wrong with me. I'm just not gonna touch no dead body! I told you that before we left to come down here. I'm not touching no dead body, no dead bird and I'm not touching no dead hair either."

"Oh, for criminy sakes Ophelia, you're being a nincompoop." Lily's eyebrows furrowed as she looked her friend in the eye, then she sighed and looked down. "Alright, I'll do it by myself."

"Yep you will cuz I'm not touching no dead hair or no dead body!"

"Can you at least hold the lantern so I can see a bit better?"

Ophelia stretched her hand out to take the lantern, and Lily glared at her as she passed it to her. Ophelia walked around the body and held the lantern a foot above Tillie's neck.

With great care, Lily pushed Tillie hair back and found the chain-clasp. She carefully unhooked and pulled the locket away from Tillie's neck, admiring its beauty as she brought it closer to the lantern. It was a beautiful gold locket -- possibly two inches long and three inches wide. Engravingsof small flowers bordered the edges of the front, encircling the scripted letters *TB*.

"I don't feel right taking this locket, Ophelia."

"Well, if you don't, someone else is going to steal it from her dead body and sell it. Tillie wanted you to take it."

"Well, I guess you're right, but it just doesn't feel like a decent thing to do."

"It's okay Lily. Maybe someday we can find a distant relative of hers and you can give it to them."

"Okay… that sounds like a plan."

Lily slipped the locket into her pocket; the girls stood still, silently looking down at Tillie and Duck, their hands resting on their hips.

"It doesn't feel right just leaving them here either, does it Lily?" Ophelia said sighing loudly.

"Nope, it doesn't."

Ophelia sighed loudly again. "Well, chicken poo… let's drag 'em on out of here. Where should we drag 'em to?"

"Okay. I guess we could cart them into our barn, go help Mr. Bushy, then crawl back into my bedroom window until daybreak when I'll tell Andre and he'll take care of them. Tillie needs a proper burial and all, and Duck does too."

"Lily, I don't think I can do it. As soon as I touch that dead body I'm afraid I'll fall right over in a faint and then you will have to cart me, Tillie *and* the Duck back to the barn all by yourself."

Lily looked at Ophelia with open-mouth disbelief. "You're really serious, aren't you Ophelia?"

"Yes, I am. I can't touch a dead body. I couldn't even give my Granpappy Pake a kiss on his cheek when he died. My mama was so mad she gave me a whoopin' in the woodshed for being so disrespectful. I just get the sweats and start in shakin' and fall over in a faint. I can't do it. Nope, I just can't do it," she said, rubbing her upper arms and cringing. "The thought of it makes me a bit woozy."

"Ophelia, you don't have to kiss her!"

"I know."

"All you have to do is hold onto her pant legs and lift. You have to touch the body a'tall. I'll do all the touching. I'll stuff the Duck into her shirt and neither one of us will have to tote him. Come on Ophelia, we have to do this."

Ophelia thought about it for a few seconds, frowning and opening and closing her hands. Lily could hear the crickets and cicadas again in the silence, waiting for Ophelia to say something.

"Nope! I can't do it."

*Whoosh!*

Duck was whipping around in circles above the girls' heads. "*Aawk!* Run fer the hills! *Aawk!* Run fer the hills!" As Tillie reappeared, Duck continued. "*Aawk! Aawk!* Grab 'em and run!"

Tillie started yelling over Duck's squawking. "Grab the bodies and take off a-runnin'! Run fast and run fur as you can ta hide our bodies. They're a'comin', and they're a'comin' fast! They want to rob me of my locket and they can't have it. RUN! They're a'comin', and they're a'comin' quick!"

"*Aawk! Aawk!* Get a hustle in ur bustle! *Aawk!* Hustle in your bustle!"

"Who's coming?" Lily asked in amazement.

Tillie came up close to the girls. "Hit's the killers! They're comin' and thur a'comin' fast. Get on outta here!" She pointed away, jumping up and down.

"Ophelia," Lily said, looking her in the eyes. "Come on Ophelia, you can do this. Just grab ahold of her bloomers and pick up her legs and I will do the rest."

Ophelia's face was dripping with sweat; she was breathing shallow. She took a breath and stooped down to grab Tillie's bloomers.

Lily grabbed Duck's body, stuffed him down the front of Tillie's blouse, grabbed Tillie's arms and lifted her up. Tillie's head was hanging down almost touching the groun and her hair was gathering dirt and twigs as they took off.

With each running step, Tillie's head would thud against the ground and they picked up speed when Lily glanced back and saw an orb of yellow light coming toward them through the foggy path.

"Oh no, Ophelia, I can see their lantern coming!"

*Bump. Bump. Bump.* Tillie head was banging on the ground.

"Hey! Yur a'bangin' my head on the ground! Be careful!" Tillie's ghost yelled out.

"You're dead Tillie," Lily yelled back. "You can't feel it!"

"Oh yeah... I forgot. Well then, keep on runnin' like a mad-man. I wish I could help! I ain't wantin' them to touch my dead body!"

"*Aawk! Aawk!* Run faster, ya slugs!" Ducks voice took a pirate tone. "*Aawk! Aawk!* Slugs!"

"Shut... up... Duck!" Lily yelled as he buzzed past her head.

"Lily, we can't make it to your barn," Ophelia panted when they reached the end of the path. Between breaths, she said, "but look... over there, let's stuff them in... that old hollow tree and hide. I think... we can all fit inside."

"Good idea!" Lily was panting too.

*Whoosh!* Duck dove over the girls one last time before the two ghosts disappeared.

The hollow tree was large and could easily hold all three of them. Huffing and puffing, Lily and Ophelia stopped in front of the tree. With no time to catch her breath, Lily got inside and tugged on Tillie's body as Ophelia pushed from the outside. Lily could almost stand straight up inside the hollow tree, so she pulled Tillie further inside. Ophelia shoved Tillie's legs into the tree then squeezed herself in beside Lily. It was a tight fit, but there was enough room for the three of them. Lily turned around and – sure enough – there were a few holes in the tree trunk which were perfect for Lily to look out and watch for the killers as they came out of the woods. Luckily, the large, open side of the hollow tree was not facing the path, so the killers would not be able to see them unless they came all the way around the tree. She prayed that they would not.

Ophelia's face was pale and sweat was running down her neck. Not only was it hot and humid inside the hollow tree, but it smelled of rotted moss and dead animals, and with Tillie's dead body pushed right up against Ophelia's legs, it was quickly becoming overwhelming. She squeezed her eyes shut and tried thinking of something other than the dead body pressed against her legs.

Lily was peeking out of the hole when she heard Ophelia whisper, "Oh..."

*Thud. Plop.* Ophelia slumped down over Tillie's body in a faint.

"Ophelia! Ophelia! Wake up!" Lily whispered frantically, giving Ophelia a sharp shake.

No answer from Ophelia.

"Well," Lily whispered softly, "I can't help her now. I'll just have to leave her be for a bit until I see what happens."

As Lily silently stood in the tree, peering out for the coming trouble, her mind replayed the stories of Tillie Brown she had heard in the past. They were quite interesting. Tillie was a pretty, young girl living in a grand house in the Garden District of New Orleans. Her father, Dannistov T. Brantov, was the essence of success. When Dannistov and his wife Natasha arrived in America from Russia, years before their two girls were born, Dannistov changed his name from Dannistov T. Brantov to Dannison T. Brown so it would blend in with other American names. Dannison was the sole owner of *Cimarron Tradewinds Importers of New Orleans*, an importer of spices, beautiful woods and other exotic items from the East Indies. When the War Between the States broke out, Dannison T. Brown lost everything he owned. His warehouses were burned to the ground; his ships were seized and sent to the northern army and his bank accounts were frozen and ultimately taken by the northern banks under false pretense of one kind or another.

One dark summer night, when a family friend of the Browns fired three shots through the back door of the Browns home — to alert

Dannison of approaching danger — the Browns left New Orleans in a hurry. The gunshots were a prearranged signal he and his friends had made between themselves should Union soldiers approach their homes. Dannison, his now pregnant wife Natasha and their two children Tillie and little Macy fled out the back of their beautiful home just as soldiers stormed the front door with torches and set the house ablaze. As the Browns fled, they could see their neighbor's homes already burning in the dark night.

Weeks before the soldiers stormed their home, Dannison and Natasha devised a well-thought-out plan on how to safely escape with their children. They and their children always kept worn-out clothes ready to put on and each one of them had a small bag stuffed with bare necessities ready to snatch up as they fled. Natasha had sewn coins and all her expensive jewelry into the hems of her skirts, along with coins in the hems of her husbands and the two children's pant legs since both Tillie and little Macy were to be dressed as boys to keep their identity unknown.

As soon as Dannison heard the gunshots come through his back door, Natasha ran into the girl's rooms, cut off their long braided hair and threw the braids into the fireplace, snatched up both her girl's hands and ran out to meet her husband where he had readied their horses.

All four members of the Brown family knew how to ride bareback, so they were able to leave before the Union soldiers noticed they had disappeared.

Unfortunately, all of them did not make it to safety. Three days after escaping their burning home, Dannison was caught sneaking into Natchez, Mississippi in his search to buy food for his family. Natasha and the girls, who were hiding in an abandoned shack deep in the woods along the Mississippi River, never saw or heard from Dannison again; they assumed he had been caught and sent to prison, or worse yet – killed. Natasha then disguised herself, as best she could, by wearing her husband's clothes, cutting off her long hair and pulling an old hat low on her head. Even though it was hot summertime, she wore Dannison's old worn-out coat so she could turn up the collar and hide most of her lower face. Then she and her two daughters found their way into the small river town of Reed, Mississippi, where, for the price of a ruby earring Natasha claimed she had found, distant relatives allowed her and her daughters to live in an old abandoned shack at the edge of their back forest. Natasha scrubbed floors, cooked, and chopped cotton alongside her two daughters in order to stay alive. The three of them lived in the small run-down shack for seven months until Natasha died along with her baby daughter as she was giving birth. Natasha and her baby were buried the next day. That afternoon, the relatives decided Tillie and little Macy were going to be too much trouble, so the girls were taken to an orphanage in Natchez and lifted off the wagon at the end of the path leading up to the orphanage; the two little girls were forced to approach the orphanage scared and alone.

A few years after being placed in the orphanage, during an influenza epidemic, little Macy died with Tillie hugging her close. This left Tillie alone in the rough orphanage to fend for herself. Knowing the orphanage had very little food for the children and what food she did manage to get was usually taken away by an older orphan, Tillie took an old mule and struck out on her own, once again dressed as a boy.

She never looked back.

Fortunately, before her mother died, the two of them had taken the small amount of coins and jewelry still hidden in their clothes, put it all in a cloth bag and buried it under a large tree behind the shack. The first thing Tillie did after leaving the orphanage was return to the old abandoned shack and found the buried old bag. She then hid in the shack and watched the relatives from a distance. After a few days, she soon discovered Martha, the mother, was no longer living there. Only Eustice, the father, and his five sons went in and out of the house. By the time Tillie ran out of the food she had taken from the orphanage, she had a plan on how to pay back the relatives for their cruelty.

After eating her last insignificant bits of food and waiting until the night grew thick with darkness and she knew the men would all be sound asleep, Tillie put her plan into action. First, to make sure all the relatives knew who had taken revenge on them, Tillie wrote her name with a smoldering piece of log on the four walls of the shack.

She then slipped silently into the relative's barn, quietly walked all the horses into the back woods – except the finest horse, which she left in the barn – where she tied them to a tree branch and then she returned to open the gates to the goat pens so the goats would wander away. Quietly, she shooed them into the planted fields where they began munching on the newly spouted plants. Before shooing all the chickens out of the hen house, Tillie grabbed herself one chicken, wrung its neck and stuffed it into a gunny sack taken from the barn, along with a ham from their smokehouse. Using a skinning knife from the barn, she whacked all the remaining meat in the smokehouse into pieces and threw it into the empty pig sty with the rest of the pig slop. Going back into the barn, she took the big skinning knife, a hatchet, some rope and a tarp to keep the rain away. She found a good size box of matches and stuffed it into her gunny sack. She also put a nice saddle on the horse she was taking.

In the middle of the barn floor she placed a small pile of dry hay and formed a line with the hay leading to the other hay-bales along the sides of the barn. Quickly she lit the small mound of hay and watched to make sure it would burn. As the flames began to crawl across the floor towards the bales of hay, Tillie swiftly rode her horse out of the barn.

With the barn now smoldering, she ran her horse around in circles across their fields of planted crops until most of the plants were ruined. When she finished destroying their crops, she walked her horse into the woods and quietly sat there watching the fire expand and consume the barn. As she turned her horse to walk away, she cut the ropes tying the other horses to branches and gave them all a slap. She could hear the relatives yelling as they discovered their barn burning and beyond hope.

Now she was satisfied.

"Sleep well, my little sister. And may they always remember their evil deeds." With a smile, Tillie vanished into the dense Missouri woods and headed north.

Tillie wore a locket around her neck which contained a picture of her family taken in happier days. Every person Tillie met—since the day she struck out on her own—she would, with great pride, tell them the story of her family and show them her picture. Dannison and Natasha had been a handsome young couple with dark hair and light blue eyes. Natasha's features were small and feminine while Dannison were masculine. Natasha was tall for a woman, coming just a couple inches shorter than her husband, who himself was a tall man. Tillie and Macy looked almost like twins with their matching dresses. Tillie was a smidgen taller than Macy but much thinner and both girls had the same dark hair and light blue eyes of their parents. The picture had been taken at their mansion in the Garden District of New Orleans as they sat in their parlor. Behind the seated family were twin hand-carved circular staircases leading up to the second floor. Huge urns of flowers graced both sides of the staircases and a roaring fire was brightly burning in the fireplace behind them. The stones on the fireplace went to the top of the second level - the parlor's ceiling was two stories high. It was a beautiful, faded picture and Tillie would talk for hours about her lost family if given the chance. Lily was sure Tillie had received the best education possible when she was a young girl, but as the years passed and she had to fend for herself, her language had slipped into the slang of the river folk, and probably out of necessity. No one lived among the river folk and used proper English, or they would not live with them for long.

"Whur'd da body go?!?" Lily heard a deep, raspy voice call out, snapping her focus back to the here-and-now. "They said hit was right cheer! They said twenty paces from da mouth o' the path, ain't that right, Cletus? Did ya count yur steps, Cletus? I cain't count ta twenty but I was a'thinkin' you could. What happened to hit, Cletus?"

"How in a mule's mustache would I be knowin' that, Jedidiah? Maybe hit jest up and walked away! Maybe hit weren't dead after all!" Cletus snapped.

Lily peeked through the hole and saw two men standing at the mouth of the path, spinning around, and looking as if maybe the body was close. Cletus, the leader, was almost six feet tall and skinny as a stick. His hair was long, stringy, and in the darkness, looked light blond. His floppy hat was pulled down low on his head, which shadowed his facial features from Lily's vision. He wore dirty work pants and a wrinkled, dirty, white shirt full of small holes, hanging halfway out the top of his britches. He was carrying a shotgun with both hands and had quite a bit of rope coiled around his waist.

The other man was not much taller than Lily herself – almost a foot shorter than Cletus but looked to be nearly seventy pounds heavier. He had a round face with puffy cheeks and tobacco juice running out the side of his mouth. A little black derby hat was sitting on top of his bald head, he was wearing ragged overalls with no shirt, and he was barefoot. A pistol was stuck into the pocket of his overalls, and his rope was draped around his chunky neck.

"Dem fellers was da one's who plunked 'er down here. How we 'pose to know whur ta look? What we gonna tell Clem and Gus, Cletus? They gonna be powerful mad iff'en we don't bring 'em back that locket."

"We ain't a'tellin' 'em nothin'. We gonna find that locket an I ain't goin' home!"

"Whatcha mean, Cletus? What iff'en we don't find hit? Whur we gonna go?"

"I don't know whur yur a'goin', but I'm headin' west. I always did have a hankerin' ta go west and find me a big 'ol gold nugget. Anyway's, I only toll Clem I would come on back here so's I could steal that thur gold locket and head west ta Californy with hit. I ain't a'takin' hit back to Clem. He ain't gonna give us none of the money from hit anyways."

"What? You ain't a'goin' back ta Clem and Gus? They gonna be powerful mad. How ya gonna live? Whatcha gonna eat? Whur ya gonna sleep?" he paused, thinking, then spoke softer – "Can I go wit ya, Cletus?"

"Hit don't matta none atall ta me whatcha do, Jedidiah. Iff'en ya want ta come on along with me, that's fine an dandy. But I ain't a'goin' back. That thur life o' workin' our tails off fer Clem and Gus is done and over fer me."

"Well, ok Cletus. Hits fine an dandy. Now what we gonna do 'bout findin' that thur gold locket? An whur is P Joe?"

"I ain't knowin' whur P Joe be at, he prolly be a'sittin' in the woods som'ers takin' a sleep I s'pose. But, let me think on this here thin' a mite, Jeddy." Cletus started scratching his bearded chin.

"Iff'en she ain't here and iff'en that thur dead bird ain't here, whur are they? Might be thur haints done took 'em away," Cletus said with a slight hesitation in his voice and a nervous little laugh. "Thur' here som'ers. I'm mighty sure o'that and ain't no haints 'round here that I can see."

Lily watched as Jedidiah stood up a little straighter and stretched his neck around as he looked towards the tree line.

"Ya think so, Cletus? Ya think hit might be them thur haints done come and took 'em away ta da promis land? I don't like this here feelin' I'm a'gettin', Cletus."

"Oh shucks, Jeddy, I'm jest pullin' yur leg. Ain't no haints out here no how. They all be a'hangin' out at the old boney-yards. Let's build us a far ta chase away these here bittin' skitters and have us a sit-down while we wait fer P Joe."

"Okay, Cletus," Jedidiah said, glancing over his shoulder at the tree line. He started gathering small branches to use as kindling. In a couple minutes he had a good-sized pile of kindling; he put some larger branches on top and lit the fire.

"Hey Cletus, here comes P Joe," Jedidiah called from where he stood by the fire.

"Hey P Joe, whur ya been?" Cletus called out. "Ya been takin' a nap in the woods?"

"Yep."

P Joe looked a foot taller than Cletus and almost as wide as he was tall – a mountain of a man. He had on bib overalls and an old red shirt. His ears stood straight out from the sides of his bald head, and his skin was milky white. He slowly shuffled out of the woods, stooped over and leisurely swinging his long arms back and forth with each step. His big, bare feet stirred up black dust from the pathway with each unhurried step. In the light from the fire, Lily could see his whiskers and eyebrows were as white as his skin. Except for the beady-black eyes staring out at Jedidiah and Cletus, his facial features seemed to blend together.

"P Joe, ya see any haints a' floatin' around in thur?" yelled Jedidiah.

P Joe must have been somewhat hard of hearing – both Jedidiah and Cletus yelled whenever they spoke to the poor fella.

"Yep," P Joe said, still calmly shuffling toward the fire.

"Ya did?" Cletus yelled back, sounding a little alarmed.

"Yep," he said, nodding and nonchalantly slapping mosquitoes off his arms.

"Well, what'd they look like?"

"Haints."

"What *kind* a' haints, P Joe?"

P Joe stopped and looked at the other two men as if they had asked him a senseless question. "Jest reg'lar ol' haints," he said, holding out his arms in confusion. "What other kind is there?"

"Well," Cletus let out a big sigh and then yelled, "was they a woman and a big ol' bird?"

"Yep." P Joe was *still* making his way to the fire.

"Did they spook ya?"

"Nope."

"Did they try?"

"Yep."

"Was they a'follerin' ya?"

"Yep."

"Was ya scare't?"

"Nope... I weren't scare't a'tall. Haints don't scare me," P Joe shouted out annoyingly.

"A'right, P Joe," Cletus said quietly, to calm him down. "We believe ya, jest checkin' ta make sure."

P Joe finally plopped down on a broken log by the fire, and all three men were silent for a few minutes. P Joe stared at the fire; Cletus and Jedidiah stared into the woods.

"Well Jeddy," Cletus said quietly after a moment or two, "sometimes P Joe sees thin's nobody else sees, so let's not worry 'bout them haints right now, alright?"

"Ok," Jedidiah said, looking down and fidgeting.

"Not true," P Joe said emphatically. "I see everthin' I say I do."

"One time," Cletus said, ignoring P Joe's comment and sitting down by the fire to make himself comfortable, "when we was young'uns, I see'd this here haint peekin' inta my winder during the night. Hit was a big ol' haint with wild, long, red hair jest a'floatin' around hit's head like ah cloud and a big ol' long, white beard stretchin' down almost to the ground. Hit was tryin' ta climb right inta my winder. Hit had hit's big ol' foot half way inta my winder and hit's hand was jest startin' in ta push hitself up. So I jumped right up, kicked hit's foot outta my winder and slammed that thur winder shut afore hit could crawl in. Hit jest stood thur a'lookin' at me through the winder with hit's fingers stuck and then hit starts in a'cryin' big 'ol croc'dile tears. The more hit cried, the bigger hit's fingers puffed up. Kindly like one o' them thur new fang-dangled bay-loons. All of a sudden-like, hits fingers jest exploded and went right on back down to normal haint fingers! Hit jest kept right on a'bawlin' with hit's mouth wide open and them thur tears jest rollin' down hit's face. Hit was a pit'ful sight, is what hit was; seein' such a big ol' haint a'bawlin' like a little bitty baby, so I starts in laughin' cuz I couldn't do nuttin' else.

I weren't even scare't atall. I jest stood thur at that winder lookin' at hit and a'laughin'. Well, after a bit, hit starts in gettin' real mad cuz I'm jest laughin'. Hit starts in making a mad face at me. Hit's eyes was a'buggin' out and hit's nose growed as big as a horse nose and hit's mouth, all of a sudden-like, turns into a big ol' evil smile and hit's teeth was real big and yeller, and hit's smile went from the top of one ear clean over ta the top o' the other'n. Hit had one gold tooth in the front and a big ol' red tongue was stickin' out at me. Hit starts in lickin' at my winder and then, all of a sudden-like, hit's tongue curled up like ma's rollin' pin and starts in shootin' globs o'spit on my winder! Hit were big o' globs o' spit and they was all green an yeller an was runnin' down my winder pane! Well, I start in gettin' pretty mad at that thur haint a'spittin' on my winder, so's I goes over and picks up ma's old pitcher full o' water; throws my winder open and throws that thur water all over that thur big o' haint."

Cletus laughed loudly as he continued. "That thur haint takes off in a loud *whoosh*, jest a'yellin' and a'screamin' and a'cussin' and hit was the last I ever did see of that thur big o' ugly haint. I tol' Pa about hit the next mornin' and Pa said them thur haints with red hair on thur heads and white whiskers are haints coming down here from way up north and they be some mean 'uns. Pa said ta stay away from them thur red-headed haints cuz they be huntin' fur some good southern boys ta snatch up and take up ta them thur Northern states and make 'em work in the salt mines. I ain't never heard o' no salt mines up thur, but that's what Pappy said."

Cletus was laughing uproariously at his own story, but Jedidiah and P Joe were staring at him with their mouths hanging open.

"I got that ol' booger good." Laughing, Cletus fell over on his side and rolled around a couple times before stopping. When he finally stopped laughing and rolling around, facing the hollow tree.

All of a sudden, Cletus got an irritated look on his face and yelled out, "Hit's the truth, so don't be a'lookin' at me like that, you two buzzard-brains! And you two better be watchin' out fer that thur haint. I always did think hit was the haint of old Pappy Monroe's. He's prolly still mad at Pa fur stealin' Ma away from him. Well, maybe not any-more since Pa is over in the Glory Land with 'em. Maybe now they be good friends."

Jedediah spoke up. "I'm believin' ya, Cletus. I'm jest a'wonderin' why ah big o' haint wouldn't jest come right on in through yur winder glass like ever other haint?"

"I ain't never thought about that thur, Jeddy," Cletus said, scratch-ing his chin deep in thought. "Yep... now I'm really a'wonderin' 'bout that thur myself."

"That thur is migh-tee strange, Cletus."

"Yeah, hit tis, Jeddy. That thur's a migh-tee strange thin'. Hits a'gettin' stranger and stranger the more I ponder hit." Cletus kept on scratching his chin in bewilderment.

"I hear'd tell them thur haints can go right on through a body – if'fen they want to, that is," Jedidiah said. "Putt Knott *himself* tol' me he once'st see'd a haint poke a feller in the ear with hit's finger and jest in a flash that haints whole hand was flappin' out the other ear and starts in a'wavin' at Putt. They be migh-tee powerful is what I hear'd. Migh-tee powerful! Ol' man Roscoe Wilkes says once'st he went inta ah boney-yard down in Na-Orlin's and was jest a'standin' thur mindin' his own busy-ness when all of a sudden-like he see'd this here haint jump right up outta that thur ground and leap in front of a feller who was puttin' some flare's on a young-un's grave. Roscoe says the haint grabbed aholt of that feller's hands and starts in dancin' and a'shakin' that thur feller around like a cyclone and one of that feller's legs started in jumpin' an a'hoppin' up and down like ah rabbit doin' a jig. He said the feller was jest clappin' his hands and a'flappin' his arms up and down kindly like a chicken on a hot stove, all over that thur boney-yard with that ol' haint itself dancin' an a'laughin' like a looney-bird. Finally, the feller falls ta the ground and last thin' Roscoe sees is that thur' haint whoosh right on outta that boney-yard and take off inta the night, all the whiles laughin' an havin' a good ol' time'. He says the feller gets right up, looks around at Roscoe and says 'Woo-hoo mister, that thur was more fun than I had in a month-o-Sundays. Now I'm gonna have ta go talk ta the old Reverand and be askin' fur furgivness fur dancin' with a haint and enjoyin' hit!' Roscoe says that thur feller gives 'em a big ol' hug an takes off a'skippin' an a'hoppin' right on out of the bony-yard, jest as happy as a pig in slop!"

"Ya know Granny Wilkes, that church-goin' preachin'woman?" P Joe asked, scratching his armpit. "Them thur haints be scare't o' her. Hanson Knott tol' me he once'st was out in his field plowin' when he hear'd some racket coming down the road and looks up an see'd a haint a'runnin' down the road with hit's legs goin' so fast hit were wor-kin' up some smoke. Granny Wilkes was right behind that ol' haint in her buggy an she was snappin' her whip at that thur haint. But that haint jumped right inta a big ol' crawdad mudhole in Hanson's field and disappeared down that thur hole with the crawdads. She ain't a'fear'd o' no haints a'tall. She says 'the good Lord ain't a'fear'd o' no haints so she ain't gonna be a'fear'd.' She even says she ain't a'feared o' no devil either cuz the good Lord done told her she don't have ta be a'fear'd. Another thin' is, I see'd Hayseed Monroe's granpappy's haint da same night Cletus did. Hit climbed right inta *my* winder and was jest a'standin' thur starin' at me whils't I was in my bed. I wrestled hit back outta my winder an see'd 'em take off and go on over ta Cletus' winder. I ain't a'fear'd o' no haints."

"How'd ja wrestle a ghost, P Joe? Thur ain't nothin' ta hold on ta," Jedidiah asked.

"Yep, I did. Yep, I sure 'nuf did," was all P Joe replied, nodding his head.

"Well," Cletus whispered kind of low, "Let me be a'tellin' ya about the time me and Clem was doin' some graverobbin'. We was over in ah boney-yard down Nat-chez way and the night was clear and the moon was a-shinin'. Hit was hot – jest as hot as hit is right heer tonight, and thur weren't nary a breeze blowin' a'tall. Skitters was a'swarmin' everwhere an we was a'diggin' inta a big o' grave of some ol' man Clem said was rich. Well, we was getting pretty close to reachin' the box when all of a sudden-like, this here foot comes a'poppin' right on out of that thur ground beside us an hit starts in a'wigglin' hit's toe bones at us. Well, me and Clem just stand thur watchin' hit fur a minute or two and all the while hit's just a'playin' a tune with hit's toe-bones. Clem said hit sounded kindly like Yankee-Doodle Dandy ta him, but ta me hit sounded like When Johnny Comes Marchin' Home! Hit were the strangest thin' I ever did see. We jest stood thur a'starin' at hit and tryin' ta figger out what song hit were a'playin', when that thur foot bone starts in coming outta that thur ground and perty soon we can see hit's leg bone and then hit's knee bone! When that thigh bone starts a'showin', Clem starts in a'whackin' hit with his shovel as I claw my way outta that thur hole and take off a'runnin' like ah lightnin' bug. Well, after a spell, Clem yells at me ta come on back: he said hit was gone. So I go a'creepin', real slow-like, back and shur'nuf, that thur bone is gone back inta the ground. So, real shaky-like we start in diggin again and all of a sudden we hear'd this here groan. Hit was like a body was a'moanin' and a'groanin' in pain. Well, me and Clem, we stop diggin' and gets real still. We turn our ears an lean in towards that thur coffin and sure'nuf; that thur moanin' and groanin' was comin' from inside that thur old coffin. I start in ta shakin' again and Clem starts in backin' up outta that thur hole. Next thin' I knew'd, Clem done climbed outta that thur hole and is reachin' down ta help me out. Well, once'st we get outta that thur coffin-hole, we turn around and look back down. That thur moon was bright and we could see the top of that ol' man's coffin."

Cletus's voice grew lower and Lily had to push her ear against the hole in the tree to make out what he was saying:

Jedidiah and P Joe were leaning so far over the fire Lily was surprised they weren't catching fire.

"All of a sudden-like, that thur coffin starts in a'creakin' and hit's lid slowly starts ta open." Cletus was whispering so low Lily could barely hear what he was saying.

Cletus starts raising one of his arms to demonstrate how the coffin lid was slowly opening. "*Creeeak — creeeak,*" he whispered softly.

With shaking hands, Jedidiah kept wiping his mouth and P Joe was chompping a twig so hard the twig was flopping up and down.

Cletus sat in silence for a second with his arms raised before continuing his tale. He cleared his throat and spoke in a gravelly, nervous voice.

"We was so scare't we was froze right thur by that buryin' hole and couldn't move a muscle. I kept on tryin' ta make my legs move, but my eyeballs was glued ta that thur coffin. I jest couldn't tear my eyes away from hit. With a loud THUD the coffin lid slammed open and low-and-behold, thur laid that thur dead man's skel'ton! Them dead bones was white as snow and had some long, gray hair hangin' down in front of hit's eye holes and hit was a'sittin' right up in hit's coffin and hit's head was turned to look up at us. Hit's eyes was bright red and piercin' right inta the deep of our souls, I tell ya, right inta our souls. Hit didn't say nary a word, hit jest kept right on moanin' and a'groanin'. After a few seconds, hit's jawbones start in snappin' like a snappin' turtle and hit's teeth was a'choppin so hard some of 'em fell right out inta that thur coffin."

At this point, Cletus jumped up and started acting out his story.

"Hit's arms started in movin' real squeaky-like, like hit was gonna get on up outta that thur hole. Well, me and Clem finally get our legs movin' and we take on out of thur. We din't even bother pickin' up our shovels; we just ran. We get on back ta camp, grabbed onta our blanket an take off inta the woods ta find us a place ta hide. Finally we find a hidey-hole and climb inside. Hit weren't nuttin' but a bunch o' old trees that done falled down, but hit made a fine hidey-hole fur us. Well, we crawled inside an real quiet-like sat thur a'listenin' and a'peepin'out through them branches."

At this point, Cletus squatted down and cocked his heads to one side as he showed Jedidiah and P Joe how he and Clem had watched for the skeleton.

"And, shur'nuf, in jest ah shake we hear'd some moaning and a'groaning an some clinkin' and clackin' of ol' bones comein' through them thur woods. Well, we kept right on sittin' real quiet-like, peepin' out through them branches... and then we see'd 'em comin'. He was a big 'un. Musta been near on seven foot tall, if an inch, and he creaked 'round them thur woods fur nigh on an hour. Ever so often hit stop walkin' an turn hits head all the way around in a circle, an snap hit's jawbones a couple times. Skel'ton bones was a'fallin' off'en hit's body the whole time. Finally hit must o' got tired cuz hit up an clanked away. Me and Clem fell asleep inside that thur brush pile and when we gets up in the morning hit was bright and sunny so we decide to go on back and check out that thur boneyard. So, we do that and low-and-behold that thur grave looks jest like hit did afore we started diggin'. Weren't even a blade o' grass moved I tell ya. Hit was durn spooky is all I got ta say. Durn spooky.

"Well, boys, I'm a'feeling kindly edgy-like. I got some shivers going up and down my backbone," Cletus whispered, sitting back down a little closer to Jedidiah and P Joe. "How 'bout you?"

"Me too Cletus, me too..." Jedidiah replied. "And I'm a'thinkin' that thur Tillie Brown gal's haint might shur'nuf have some o' that gypsy blood. I hear tell she be from some country called Romany or somethin' like that. Might be she had some powers we ain't knowin' bout. I tell ya, Cletus - she was a mean'un back when they was staying in that old shack. She weren't bigger'n a button, but I member her starin' at me real spooky-like when she caught me in the woods spying on 'em. I was jest tryin' to see iff'en they was hidin' anythin' from Ma and Pa. But that Tillie gal never let me get close enough to see anythin'. Evertime I be out thur she'd come after me with a big ol' stick and chase me down till she citched me and gived me a whoopin' with that big stick. She was a mean 'un. I know'd we should'ah sent them thur women packin' instead of lettin' 'em stay in that shack.

Then, when she comed back an burned our barn down, Pa was purty scare't. I could tell. He said she must o' had some gypsy powers we din't know about cuz we din't hear one little thin' when she did hit. I know'd that were the reason he din't bother goin' after her.

I be thinkin' we best be leavin' that thur body alone and be gettin' out o' here. Whatcha think, Cletus?"

"Listen," Cletus held up his hand to stop Jedidiah from talking. "I hear'd a voice callin' out. You hear it?"

"Hear'd what, Cletus?"

"Hit's whisperin' in the wind."

"What's a'whisperin' in the wind, Cletus? And what's hit whisperin'?"

"I think hit's a haint and hit's callin' me!"

"Hit is? What's hit a'callin' ya?" Jedidiah cocked his head to one side.

"Iff'en hit's a'callin ya ah ugl-butt, hit's got the right feller." Jedidiah laughed.

"Be serious, Jeddy. Hit's a'callin' out my name!"

Jedidiah stopped laughing as all three of them cocked their heads to one side as they strained to listen.

"Yep... Yep, I hear'd hit," P Joe spoke up.

Lily tried her best to hear what the three men were hearing, but all she could hear was Ophelia snoring.

"Ya sure yur a'hearin' sumpin 'cause I ain't hearin' nuttin' a'tall," Jedidiah whispered.

"Wait," Jedidiah said a little louder. He held up his hand—as if to silence the night creatures—and the woods actually quieted as an eerie feeling of unease flooded the river bottom.

"I hear'd some moanin'. Hit sounds kindly like that skel-ton you was tellin bout," Jedidiah whispered to the other two.

"Ooohhh..." Ophelia moaned, waking up.

"Hit's a'comin' from that thur ol' hollered out tree!" Cletus whispered unsteadily as he jumped to his feet and stared at the hollow tree where Lily, Ophelia and the dead bodies were unknowingly sitting.

In a split second, Jedidiah and P Joe were on their feet beside Cletus, and they all began to slowly back away from their campfire.

"Jed-a-di-ah..." Lily moaned slowly. "Cleee-tuuusss..."

"Hit's a'callin' me too Cletus, hit's a'callin' us by our names! Hit's the haints. That thur's a woman haint. I know'd hit! They be after them thur killers and thur a'thinkin' hits us! I be feelin' hit in my bones, Cletus," Jedidiah whispered, pointing to the hollow tree with a shaking hand and taking a step backwards.

"Yep, Yep, hit's them same haints! I ain't scare't though!" P Joe yelled out loudly.

Inside the tree, Lily looked down at Ophelia just as she gave a moan, jerked her head up and knocked a head-sized hole into the side of the old, hollow tree; out through the hole popped her snowy, white hair. She moaned again, this time in pain.

"Hit's the haints! Hit's the haints!" Jedidiah yelled. "Hit's a'comin' outta that old holler tree. Hit's a woman and I can see hits ghost hair comin' out o' that tree. Look, Cletus! Look over yonder on the side o' that holler tree!"

"Let's get on outta this here place!" Cletus yelled. "Let's get on our way ta Californy!"

"Sounds mighty fine ta me, Cletus. Ya comin along, P Joe?"

"Yep, I'm a'comin' with ya," P Joe replied as he scrambled after Cletus and Jedidiah. "I'm a'comin' too."

All three men turned and took off running up and over the levee as fast as their legs could carry them.

"Ophelia! Ophelia, wake up!" Lily whispered loudly as she shook Ophelia's shoulders and tried to pull her to her feet.

"Oooohhh," Ophelia moaned, struggling to get to her feet. "I told you I would faint, didn't I?"

"Yes you did, and I'm sorry if I didn't believe you. Come on, let's get going. We need to get Tillie's body into the barn. The men who were following us are gone; they have no idea we took the body. They think Tillie and Duck's ghosts came along and snatched the bodies into the spirit world." Lily giggled as she continued. "When they heard you snoring and moaning while you were coming to, they thought it was the haints calling out their names, so they took off running for California."

Ophelia sat silently staring at Lily in confusion for a moment as she tried getting her bearings.

"What?"

"I'll tell ya later, let's get out of this smelly tree."

Lily pushed Tillie's body out through the opening in the hollow tree and then rolled out beside it. Ophelia gave another groan and rolled out onto the ground. Both girls were drenched in sweat and Ophelia was still rather pale.

"What happened?" Ophelia asked again.

"Well," Lily replied, laughing. "After you fainted, I stood there and watched as two men came out of the path complaining about not being able to find Tillie's body. It seems they were going to steal Lily's locket and take off for California. Come to find out, they weren't the ones who killed Tillie and Duck after all. Seems as if they did know who the killers were, but they never mentioned their names. After a while, when you started waking up and moaning, they thought you were a haint – with a little help from me – so off they went, up and over the levee on their way to California.

"Anyway, let's cart Tillie and Duck to the barn and then we can go see if we can help Mr. Bushy get away from those men who have him tied up."

"Lily, I think we should tell Sheriff Beaumont and let him take care of that problem."

"If we do that, André won't let us go along. He'll wake Benny up and let him help rescue Mr. Bushy, and we'll be stuck in my bedroom for the rest of the night."

Ophelia stood there staring at Tillie's body and scratching her head.

"Okay," Ophelia slid her hands down her face and sighed. "Let's go and get this over with."

"Okay," Lily said. "You grab her legs again and I'll grab her arms."

Both girls stood and lifted Tillie's body as they started up the side of the levee. By the time they got to the top, they were both huffing and puffing. Tillie and Duck's ghost were nowhere to be seen.

"This is one heavy woman," Lily gasped, as she let Tillie's head drop to the ground.

"Yes...she...is..." Ophelia replied, dropping Tillie's legs to the ground. "I sure didn't think she would be this heavy since she's such a little person."

After a few seconds, the girls lifted Tillie and Duck again and started struggling toward Lily's house. The going was a little easier now that they were walking down the levee. Once they got the bodies into the barn, they laid them on a bale of hay and covered them with an old horse blanket to keep the cats away from them.

"Okay," Lily said, sitting down on a bale of hay. "Let's go see if we can help Mr. Bushy."

"Let's just go wake the sheriff and let him do it, Lily. I don't want to go back out into that river bottom."

"We don't have time, Ophelia. Mr. Bushy may be dying!" Lily whispered.

"We may be dead too if we go over there snooping around that bunch of thieves! I'm not going!"

"Okay, I guess I'm going alone," Lily whispered, getting up to leave.

Ophelia rubbed her hands down the sides of her face again, this time leaving big, dark lines of river muck from her eyes to the top of her neck. She must have picked up some dirt as they carried Tillie's body. She sighed deeply and paused, deciding what to do.

"Okay, okay... I'll go with you."

# 2

## MR. BUSHY

Bushy slowly lifted his eyelids and gazed through hazy, throbbing eyes, seeing nothing but a blur. "Where in a hound-dogs-hind-leg am I?" he muttered to himself. He was sitting down with his hands pulled back and tied behind a tree and his ankles were tied together.

It was nightime and the river fog was swirling around him. The moon was bright but the fog blocked his vision.

Then it all came back to him in a rush of memory; the fight with the three thieves after they ambushed him, thinking he was going to get away after swinging them into each other, then thinking "he's gonna get me" seconds before feeling the searing pain of the jagged knife slicing through his calf.

All in all, the thieves had ambushed him, took his pack mule loaded with hides, and cut up his leg. Remembering the events which happened in the dusky hours before dark awoke the terrible pain in his leg. It radiated through his leg like red-hot coals from Hades shooting into the air. Looking down at his throbbing leg, Bushy saw where someone had wrapped a dirty rag tightly around the wound.

"Here I was watchin' fer that ol' Tillie Brown's sticky fingers and completely missed them thievin' buzzards," he mumbled. He grimaced as he tried moving his leg to ease the agony. "For some reason the murdering thieves want to keep me alive."

Groaning and looking at his wound, he whispered low, "Lord have mercy on my old wicked soul. I swear on Barnaby's britches, if this here pain don't ease up I'm gonna drag myself into that river and hold my head under till I'm ah goner."

Looking up toward the bushwackers, Bushy squinted as he peered through the dense fog. All three of them were snoring with their mouths wide open, their snorts echoing across to the other side of the wide river. Half empty bottles of home brew lay cradled in their arms, and judging by the broken bottles behind them, they must have simply pitched each bottle behind themselves after finishing it off.

The remnants of an old, floppy, felt hat lay smoldering at the edge of the fire; evidently the owner lost it during the scuffle. All three men were facing the fire with their heads resting on dirty, rolled up bedrolls, their feet stretched toward the smoldering embers to keep the pesky insects away from them. The bottom of the smallest man's shoe was beginning to steam as hot embers slowly crept closer to his wet shoe. From Bushy's line of vision, the man resembled a pencil with the face of a weasel. As a gentle breeze blew some of the river fog away, Bushy could distinguish the man's pointy nose. His upper lip came close to touching the end of his nose each time he exhaled from his mouth. The lower part of his mouth and chin blended right into his neck. Large patches of hair were missing from his head and beard as if he had caught the mange from an old cur dog. His two front teeth were oversized, and all of his bottom teeth seemed to be missing, enabling his bottom lip to be sucked into his mouth as he inhaled. When he exhaled, his lower lip would shoot out of his mouth and flap in the breeze.

He was dressed just as the other two men – in bib overalls and whitish shirts. Their shoes were full of holes, but their clothes looked fairly new. Being the thieves they were, Bushy was quite sure their newer clothes had probably been snatched off a farmer's clothes line.

The fella sleeping closest to Bushy was the one who used the skinning knife. He was cradling his whiskey bottle in one arm and the big, glistening knife in the other. He was a big fella with big, rounded facial features. He had his big floppy hat pulled low over the top of his eyes; his only visible features were his large, bulbous nose and his fat, flapping lips. He was totally toothless with flapping lips just like the first guy. His hair was long, dirty, and black as coal; it hung down his back almost reaching to the ground.

Furthest away from the fire lay the third fella. If Bushy remembered correctly, this one was a lot younger than the other two and had been the easiest to latch on to — his long, dirty blond hair was tied at the nape of his neck with a strong leather strap, making a perfect clasp to latch on to.

Every so often, the young fella's right leg would jerk up and down like a dog scratching fleas, and he would wave his pistol around in the air as if he was dreaming of chasing something or someone. He was wearing a dirty straw hat with two dried-up chicken claws stuck into the top, looking like antlers.

While trying to get a better look at the three, Bushy caught a slight movement out of the corner of his eye. Darting his eyes in that direction, he spotted two large Copperhead snakes slowly slithering their way toward the campfire. One snake looked to be maybe five feet long, the other a tad shorter. Their bodies were as thick as Bushy's wrist, and they were darting their tongues in and out as they slithered closer to the hot embers. The bigger snake was headed straight for the big fella. The other snake stopped, looked in Bushy's direction and headed for Bushy's boot. Bushy gave his tied ankles a big thud on the ground, shooting pain up his leg. With a sigh of relief, Bushy watched as the snake twist its body back toward the fire. It quickly slithered up to the leg-jerking fella; every time the man's leg jerked, the snake raised its head and hissed loudly.

Bushy realized he had only a matter of minutes before the snakes awakened the three thieves, taking away any chance of escaping.

The embers close to Weasel-man's shoe were now flames; at any moment the shoe itself was going to catch fire. A snake was about to crawl up the big fella's pant leg. Bushy only had a couple fleeting moments.

"Get a move on, Bushy," he muttered to himself, straining at the ropes holding his hands and ankles. "... or you're a dead man."

From behind the tree where he was tied came the sound of branches rustling and soft, hesitant footsteps.

"Psst!"

"Mr. Bushy," a voice quietly whispered. "It's me Lily! Me and Ophelia are here to help you get away."

"Are you awake?" said a different soft voice.

"Mr. Bushy, can you hear us? Can you walk at all? I'm going to untie the ropes back here but I don't think we can untie the ones on your ankles without getting caught. Can you manage to do that yourself?"

"Ahh. Bless ya hearts, me lasses," Mr. Bushy whispered. "What'cha doin' out here in the middle of the night, me lovelies?"

Mr. Bushy spoke with a terrible Irish accent when he spoke to the Quinn children.

"We're here to help get you away," Lily replied.

"We better hurry," Ophelia bent down and whispered as she looked at the men beside the fire. "Any minute now that snake is going up that one fella's pant leg and I reckon it will cause a powerful ruckus."

"Hound-dogs and handkerchiefs," Mr. Bushy muttered frantically as he watched the snake slither closer and closer to the big fella's pant leg. "Let's hurry it up."

Bushy felt the ropes around his wrists slacken.

"Okay, your hands are free. Can you feel them enough to untie your ankles?"

"Nope, I can't lass, cuz my fingers are sound asleep. You're gonna have ta come on around and untie 'em for me."

Lily scurried around and quickly started working at the ankle ropes as Mr. Bushy let out a soft whistle. Up from the woods trotted his horse Digger.

Digger was a good horse and at times, it seemed he could almost Mr. Bushy's mind. He was a black and white paint pony. Mr. Bushy had traded some bear hides to a Blackfoot Indian for Digger and Mr. Bushy had gotten the best end of the trade.

"Ophelia," Lily whispered after untying the ropes, "I think we are gonna have to help him up. Can you get up at all, Mr. Bushy?"

"Of course I can, me girl!" Mr. Bushy replied, rolling over and getting up on his hands and knees.

"Over here, Digger, come on over here, boy" Bushy whispered, motioning to his horse.

Digger ambled over and lowered his head so Mr. Bushy could hold onto his halter straps. Once he was up on his one foot, with Lily and Ophelia's help, Mr. Bushy was able to put his good foot in the stirrup and swing his bad leg up and over Digger.

"Come on you young'uns," Mr. Bushy whispered. "Get on up here with me."

He reached down and swung Lily up behind him and helped Ophelia get in front of him. Ophelia grabbed Diggers' mane as Mr. Bushy turned his horse to take one last look at the three thieves sleeping by their fire.

The biggest snake's head was already into the man's leg when the skinny fella's shoe and the bottom of his pant leg finally caught on fire.

Within seconds, chaos broke; the skinny fella awoke and began a stomping dance as he tried putting out the fire on his clothes. In one swift motion, the big fella jumped up, dropped his skinning knife and empty whiskey bottle, and started jumping around to get the Copperhead out of his pant leg. After quite a while, he reached down, took a hold of the snake's tail and jerked it out, flinging it into the trees. In a matter of seconds, the skinny fella's whole pant leg was on fire and the big fella was down on the ground moaning in pain – the snake must have bitten him. The second snake had quickly slithered away, but the youngest fella was still snoring and jerking his leg. Then the skinny fella took off running toward the river with his pant leg blazing in the moonlight.

"Let's get outta here," Mr. Bushy murmured weakly as he gave Digger a kick with his good heel. When they passed the other horses, Mr. Bushy slowed Digger down and told Lily to reach down and grab a hold of his pack mule's lead rope and pull him along behind them. She did so, and off they went down the path through the river bottom toward the levee.

When they got to the levee, Mr. Bushy was weak as water; he was leaning heavily against Ophelia with Lily trying to hold him up so he wouldn't squash Ophelia or fall off his horse.

Mr. Bushy looked exactly like his name implied: a big, bushy man. Lily wasn't quite sure if Bushman was his real name or if folks just called him Bushman because of the way he looked. He stood almost six and a half feet tal, l and was as broad as the side of a barn. His hair and beard reached almost to his waist, and both were red and curly. He had a big, toothy smile and a loud, booming laugh. His clothes were made of bear hides. In the winter he wore a long brown grizzly bear-fur coat that reached all the way to the top of his boots; it had a spacious, furry hood to cover his head and part of his face from the sharp winter winds of the Ozark Mountains.

When the days were sunny, he wore his "eyeball covers" – that's what he called them. He made them from thin pieces of wood, cut to fit each eye socket. He cut openings – oblong slits – across the middle of each eye cover, and covered it with pieces of black fabric. They were held to his head with a long strip of thin leather woven into a strap which wove through the wood pieces and wrapped around his head. He said they kept the sun out of his eyes and made it possible for him to see things in the brightness of the summer sun or the glare of the sun off the winter snow which other men could not see. He claimed his eyeball-covers had saved his life many a time, and refused to leave his cabin without them. At times, he wore them pushed back onto the top of his head, making his fiery-red hair stand up around his head in a feathery poof, kind of like the brim of a woman's bonnet. Mr. Bushy must have lost his eyeball-covers in the scuffle, because they were not on his head, and his hair looked like a massive, tangled, red bush.

Ophelia carefully took Digger's reins from Mr. Bushy and urged the horse up and over the levee. Once they got to the other side, it was easier to kept Mr. Bushy from falling off the horse.

When they reached Lily's house, the girls slid down from Digger as Mr. Bushy lay his head on Digger's mane. Lily ran up to the house, all the while calling for André to come outside and help get Mr. Bushy off the horse and into the house.

*SLAM!*

The door to the back porch flew open, and André came running out. He was bare-footed and in his long night-shirt.

"Help us get Mr. Bushy off his horse!" Lily called out. "He's been hurt bad and I don't think he can sit on his horse much longer."

"What in ta'nation happened he'ah, Lily-Beth?"

"I'll tell you all about it when we get him down."

"Ah'right, but ya bet'duh not be getting inta somethin ya shouldn't be gettin' inta. It's the middle of the night!" André angrily replied. "What are ya'll doin' out he'ah ina'ways? Ophelia, does yor'ah mama know yor'ah out he'ah snoopin' around with this he'ah wild Lily-Beth?"

Ophelia looked sheepishly at André and spoke softly, "No, sir, she ain't knowin I'm here."

"Well, ya best be getting' on home 'fore yor'ah mama wakes up and see's ya gone and then she's gonna wake up yor'ah Pa and *he's* gonna come chargin' ov'ah he'ah like the calv'ree and I'm gonna have ta try and explain ta him what ya two got yor'ah selves inta durin' the middle of the night."

André gave Ophelia a very stern frown and turned to Lily to say, "And you, Lily-Beth, you go home with Ophelia and be sur'ah ta tell her mama and pa just what kind o' trouble ya got yor'ah friend inta."

The girls didn't move a muscle; they were thinking about what they should be telling André and what they should be keeping to themselves when the back door slammed open again. Here came Caitlin and Benny, still dressed in their nightclothes.

"What's going on, André?" Caitlin asked in a loud whisper.

"Whoa! Is that Mr. Bushy on that horse? Is he dead?" Benny yelled.

"Keep your voice down, you clodhopper!" Lily yelled back to Benny, "You're going to wake the dead." Lily was afraid an unwelcome listener might be eavesdropping.

Just as André got to the horse, Mr. Bushy started slipping off his horse, headed for the ground.

*Oaf!* André caught Mr. Bushy under the arms and staggered back a bit. Benny ran to help André, and together they carried Mr. Bushy into the kitchen and sat him on a chair so he could lean onto the kitchen table, where he came to a little bit and moaned loudly.

"André, me boy… I never thought I'd see yor ugly face again! Right now you're lookin' mighty purty ta me! I've been beat on, cut on and banged up like a piece of tough ol' bull afore it goes in the fry pan. These here young'uns rescued me like the Knights in Her Majesty's Royal Army I tell ya! These two lass's dragged me up onta ol' Digger, grabbed my pack mule and off we went, lickity-split. They were purt near as fast as that thur Tillie Brown is in pinchin' my hides."

Lily and Ophelia turned and stared at each other in wide-eyed panic. They had completely forgotten about Tillie and Duck. Great dread captured them; they knew they would have to tell about Tillie and Duck being dead. And Lily knew quite well André was going to be mad as a hornet at them for going into the river-bottom in the middle of the night.

"Ah, André…" Lily said in a low, quiet voice, nervously twisting a lock of her hair and scratching her elbow. "Ahh… Tillie Brown and her parrot are dead, and their bodies are in our barn. Ophelia and I found them when we went down to the river-bottom a few hours ago."

André, Caitlin, and Benny – even Mr. Bushy – slowly turned to look at Lily and Ophelia with disbelief.

"What did ya just say, Lily-Beth?" André said quietly.

Dread plummeted Lily's heart into her stomach. She was quite familiar with the tone of voice coming out of his mouth. When André spoke calmly and quietly in regard to a situation, it usually meant he was highly upset.

André Beaumont was part Louisiana Cajun from his pa's side, and part American Indian from his ma. His ma and pa had migrated to Caruthersville from the Louisiana bayou when André was just a small child. He had black, curly hair and dark, black eyes. He was over six feet tall, broad shouldered and always ready with a smile for everyone, except for Lily that is, whom he said was his "burden to bear in this life".

All the ladies of Caruthersville considered André a very handsome man and a great catch for Caitlin; to Lily, André was a big, fat thorn in her side. He was forever watching her and making sure she didn't have too much fun in life. Sometimes he spoke with a slight Cajun accent which, in Lily's opinion, was extremely irritating. But he loved Caitlin and Caitlin loved him, so Lily continued to show him respect as her brother-in-law and head of their home. But he was quite annoying.

"Well," Lily stammered a bit as she answered, "to make a long story short, we found their dead bodies down beside the path in the river bottom, then some men came along looking for them, but real quick-like we carted the bodies and hid them in the hollow tree by the mouth of the path along with ourselves. We waited there until the three men finally left before we carted them on into our barn so you could take care of them in the morning."

With that said, Lily and Ophelia stood there looking at the rest of the folks, and the rest of the folks stood there staring back at them, carrying a stunned look seeming to say, "Are you out of your mind?"

Slowly, in a low whisper, André replied, "One mor'ah time please, Lily-Beth. Ya bet'duh tell us one mor'ah time and give us the long story instead of the short one."

"Okay," Lily sighed. Then she proceeded to tell the four of them the whole complicated story from start to finish.

When she finished her story, she swallowed and said, "And that's it!"

Before André had a chance to say anything, Caitlin jumped right in. She had her hands on her hips, her face was beet-red, and the look on her face was a little frightening.

"Lily Elizabeth Quinn, don't you ever go into that river-bottom again. Do you have any idea what goes on down there? That is NOT a place for young ladies to be running around in during the dark of night. And you, Ophelia Knudson!" Caitlin's eyes crackled with sparks as they darted over to Ophelia. "You are to go right home and tell your Mama and Papa about this whole shenanigan; I am quite sure they will tell you the same thing. Now you two take André and Benny out to the barn and show them where you put that poor Tillie Brown's body while I take care of Mr. Bushy's leg. After you show them where you hid that body, both of you high-tail it to Ophelia's house and stay there. Don't you be coming back here all alone, Lily Elizabeth. I am very sure Mama Corina will let you stay there. Maybe she will even take you both out to the woodshed for a whoopin'; if she does, you tell her I said 'good enough for you'. Now get on out of here so I can take care of Mr. Bushy's leg! And don't be making any loud noises. I don't want Tessa waking up and coming down here. She will be very upset if she sees what happened to Mr. Bushy. Do you understand?"

"Yes, ma'am," Lily replied.

It was silent when Caitlin stopped her rant. It was alarming to hear soft-spoken Caitlin go on a rant.

Right before Lily moved out of earshot, she heard Mr. Bushy say in a low whisper, "Tillie Brown was no poor ol' woman; she was a mean ol' buzzardette is what she was."

"Buzzardette? Hmm, what's a buzzardette?" Lily thought to herself.

As Lily opened the door to the porch, she overheard Caitlin's stern response. "Mr. Bushy, Ms. Tillie Brown was a wonderful, re-sourceful woman who had to eke out a living all alone in this world. Now I don't want to hear another bad word out of you about a woman I think was quite admirable. And, please don't call her a buzzardette. I do believe you just now made that word up."

Lily hesitated on the other side of the door, holding it slightly open to keep listening. When Caitlin turned around to put some water on the stove to boil, Mr. Bushy muttered, "Humph. Admirable? My hinny."

Ophelia was lagging back, waiting for Lily to catch up with her.

"I think we are in some deep chicken poo," she whispered to Lily. "Ma and Pa are going to be really, really mad. I'm thinkin' Ma won't let me come over here ever again."

"It will all blow over in a few days, and she will be okay with it. I'll tell her it was mostly my fault and you really shouldn't be in trouble for what I did."

"Well, that's mighty righteous of ya seeing that. It was ALL your fault! I didn't want to go back out there, remember? I wanted to wake up Sheriff Beaumont and let him take care of it all," Ophelia hissed. "Now, look what's happened. We may not be able to see each other ever again. This is terrible!"

Lily stopped, put her hands on her hips and faced Ophelia.

"Oh stop it, Ophelia. It's going to be all right," Lily said, putting her arm around her friend and giving her a hug. "Let's go show Tillie and Duck to André and Benny."

The barn door was standing open when the two of them turned around, and out through the door walked Benny.

"Where did ya put the bodies, Lily?"

"Move out of the way and I'll show you," Lily answered grumpingly. "They are right on the first hay bale, covered up with a horse blanket."

"No," Benny said sharply. "They aren't."

Lily and Ophelia walked past Benny and stopped at the first hay bale. The horse blanket lay in a pile on the ground, and the bodies were gone.

Turning back to Benny, Lily frowned and said, "What happened? They were right here!"

"Well, you said they were here, but they aren't here now. Did you leave the barn door open? Maybe some animal came in and carried them off."

"No, we didn't leave the door open. Where is André?"

"Ah'm right behind ya." Lily jumped, startled. She spun around to face André.

"They were right here, André. Really. Ophelia, tell him they were right here."

Ophelia was staring at the hay bale. She looked up at André with frightened eyes, shaking her head in agreement with what Lily had said.

"Yes sir, Sheriff Beaumont, they really were right here. We carted them all the way up and over the levee and into this barn. What happened to them?"

"Well, ah don't rightly know Ophelia. But, whatever'ah happened to 'em, they'ah gone now. Ah do believe an animal got in he'ah and carried 'em off. You two cannot go ov'ah ta Ophelia's tonight. Ther'ah must be ah black cou'gah out ther'ah wanderin' 'round this area. Benny and I will ride on ov'ah and let yor'ah pa and ma know ya'll be he'ah safe at our house all night. Go own in the house, Lily-Beth, and let Caitlin know about this he'ah problem, and don't be riling her up with any mor'ah talk of what ya'all seen down ther'ah in the riv'ah bottom, ya hear'ah? I do believe she's riled up enough ta badger me fur the rest of my life."

"Yes, André, she is, and I won't," Lily replied.

"Ah'right, now get on inta the house and don't leave, ya he'ah?"

With that said, André and Benny turned away and started saddling up their horses while Lily and Ophelia slowly shuffled back toward the house.

"Well," Ophelia said with a smile, "I'm glad they're going to my house and not us. This way Mama and Papa will have a chance to cool off before I see 'em."

"That's true, but it would have been more fun to go ourselves and look for Tillie and Duck's ghosts along the way."

"What do you think happened to them, Lily? No animal dragged them off. When animals drag a body or another animal off, if the thing is dead, they eat it right where they find it. And whoever did this didn't take one single chomp out of 'em or there would have been blood on the floor of the barn."

The girls stopped, sat on the top step of the porch, and stared at the barn.

"You're right, Ophelia; it wasn't an animal dragging them off. I bolted the barn door from the outside. It must have been the true killers. Maybe they followed us here and snatched the bodies when we went to help Mr. Bushy! No, they wouldn't do that... they had the chance to keep Tillie's body after they hit her on the head. There is no reason why they would come looking for her again – they already took all her gold." She paused. "I'm just plum out of answers. How about you?"

Ophelia raised her arms palms up. "Me too, Lily. I have no ideas."

"Lily! Is that you out there?" Caitlin's loud whisper came through the screen door. "Why aren't you two on your way to Ophelia's house?"

"Yes Caitlin, it's me and Ophelia." She and Ophelia stood up and walked to the door.

"Tillie and her parrot are missing from the barn, and André thinks an animal got in and dragged them off. He told us to stay here until morning, and he and Benny took off for Ophelia's house to tell Mr. and Mrs Knudson that Ophelia is safe here with us."

"Come on, Ophelia," Lily whispered. "Let's go see how Mr. Bushy is doing."

# 3

## THE WATCHER

S oft moonlight flowed gently into Lily's bedroom, softening the dark shadows lurking in the corners, but Lily and Ophelia did not notice the bright moonlight or the watcher at the window. They were exhausted from their adventures in the river bottom and had fallen sound asleep as soon as their heads touched their pillows.

Neither the horse nor the rider made the slightest movement as they stood watching. Other than a blink, the horse would stay completely still whenever its master held pressure to its sides; only moving when the pressure was released. It was a magnificent animal standing seventeen hands high and black as midnight. Its mane would have swept the ground if not for the rider keeping it trimmed. His coat glistened and shimmered in the moonlight as he involuntarily flexed his massive muscles. When the eastern horizon finally began pushing a sliver of smoky morning color into the sky, the horse and rider slowly moved on.

As dawn gently eased in, the smells of a fresh day filled the horse and its rider with tranquility. Serenity returned to the fertile Missouri earth like a warm blanket emitting the lingering fragrances of yesterday's wild flowers.

Night creatures were slipping into their dens, and day creatures had not yet began their rustle. It was the "Void of Silence" – the few fleeting moments when it is neither night nor day. Wildflowers had not yet lifted their eyes to the skies and bumblebees were still slumbering, waiting for the warm rays of the sun to dry their wings and send them on their daily search for nectar. The grass was still wet from the early morning dew; spiders were waiting lazily for the sun to dry their webs so they too could go about their never-ending labor of trapping food. Nothing moved or cried out to the world. Nothing, except the horse's hoof beats against the hardened earth echoing deeply across the countryside, through the river bottom all the way to the mighty Mississippi River. A sense of restful harmony permeated everything.

As the rider walked the horse slowly along the top of the levee, the sun slowly revealed itself, stretching its slender fingers up and over the horizon, silently moving across the rolling hills of Tennessee, across the Mississippi, up the levee and into the Missouri delta. Its golden tendrils slipped slowly into the trees with a sense of power, melting the last remaining bits of fog and scattering the dark shadows of the night.

"Ahh," the rider sighed, lifting her face to the early morning sky. Soaking up the warm tenderness of the Missouri dawn was like holding a newborn child in your arms and feeling the excitement of promise for that new life. As with a new life, no evidence of evil arose from the river-bottom during these early dawn hours.

"This is the time of day we live for, my boy. It cools the troubled soul and sets one's mind at ease with this world. It is a new day with new promises and the future is mine to form in any fashion I see fit," the rider whispered to the horse.

Slowly walking along the top of the levee, she watched as daybreak burst into full bloom like a flower opening its petals in the warm summertime. Butterflies began to rotate their wings to dry them in the warm tendrils of sunlight and waited with anticipation to begin their search for the wildflowers growing along the levee. Gradually, small land creatures began rustling in the underbrush as they stretched their legs and peeked up through the foliage to smell the new day and see what wonderful things the world had in store for them. In the distance, roosters began their morning wake-up calls, Mourning Doves cooed their mournful songs, and Chickadee's sang in the golden light of daybreak.

As the horse and rider approached an opening in the woods, the horse stopped and turned so the rider could look across the river bottom to the river. Sitting atop the horse, the view for the rider was pure splendor. Huge paddlewheel steam boats were lined up, waiting to pull into the Caruthersville docks to unload and reload their cargo before heading back down to New Orleans, or upriver all the way to Dubuque, Iowa. Loud reverberations of firing-up steam engines mixed with the clanging of boat horns and resonated off the deep waters of the river and echoed far. It made one's soul long for journeys to faraway places.

# 4

## FINDING TILLIE AND DUCK

Lily's eyes popped open as dawn broke the eastern sky, but she continued lying in bed listening to the soothing sounds of the new day, gathering her thoughts and wondering what could have happened to Tillie Brown and Duck.

Giving Ophelia a nudge, she whispered loudly, "Ophelia, wake up! We have get on over to your house. The sooner we get there the quicker we'll get this over with. Come on, I can smell the coffee brewing and bacon frying. Caitlin must be up and about.  Let's get going."

Ophelia mumbled something then rolled over onto her side as she tried ignoring Lily's nagging.

"Come on, come on. Get up.  Let's go eat and get going."

"Okay, okay," Ophelia answered crossly. "I'm coming. I don't see why you're so all-fired up about getting a whoopin' in the woodshed." With that said, Ophelia rolled out of bed and got dressed.

Creeping down the stairs to not wake anyone who was still sleeping, they walked into the kitchen and found Caitlin, André and Mr. Bushy already at the table.

"Howdy-do, lass's?" Mr. Bushy's voice boomed out. "And a top-o-the-morning to ya both! Sleepin' in, are ya? Benny boy's already out in the barn doin' his chores."

"Howdy, Mr. Bushy," both girls replied. "And a top-o-the-morning to ya."

"Good morning Caitlin, André," Lily said.

"Good morning, Mr. and Mrs. Beaumont," Ophelia said.

"Mornin'," André mumbled, peering over the top of his coffee cup.

"Good morning, you two beautiful girls. How was your short night's sleep?" Caitlin smiled happily at both of them. Gone was the anger from the night before.

Lily looked at her older sister and thought of what a kind person Caitlin was. Not only had she taken over the raising of her three younger siblings since their parents death, but she had also gone through a heart-wrenching period when her childhood sweetheart was lost to the ugly jaws of the Civil War.

. When the war ended and Michael did not return, the military notified his family that they had looked diligently but could not find his body or any of his personal belongings. Everyone in Caruthersville thought he had either lost his memory which caused him to wander away in search of something familiar, or he had been killed in action and buried in some unmarked grave deep in the mountain forest.

After many months of searching, The War Department of the United States contacted Michael's family and told them they believed, Michael had died during the battle of Chickamauga, Tennessee; not too far from the place where his was born and raised as a small child.

The battle of Chickamauga was a fierce battle; under the command of Generals William Rosecrans for the Union and General Braxton Bragg leading the Confederacy. Approximately 4,400 Union soldiers were killed or missing and 3,700 Confederate soldiers were killed or missing.. The south had hastily gathered up their dead and buried them in marked and unmarked graves wherever they could find a spot. Many of the dead Union soldiers were left in the battlefields from early September until the later part of December; when the Union military finally retrieved their remains and buried them in head-to-toe in trenches, or any spot available on the battlefield. Those buried by the military were not given markers of any kind;

since identification had been stolen off the bodies along with most of their clothing or, the bodies were so decomposed their remains were not identifiable so the bodies were rolled into trenches for burial. Evidently, or so the Department of War told his family, Michael had mistakenly been buried with the Union soldiers in one of the trenches and there was no way his family could go and find his body. So…they were pretty much forced to leave Michael's body there in the battlefield and continue on with their lives. At that time, Caitlin told her immediate family she already knew Michael had passed on. It seems as if Michael's spirit had come to her one night as she was escaping from her kidnappers and Maude Burbank, and Michael had told her he loved her but he could not return to the living.

"Our night was wonderful, Caitlin," Lily said with a big smile. "I didn't wake up one time during the whole night. Did you, Ophelia?"

"No, I didn't either, Mrs. Beaumont. I slept like a lazy dog full of food." Ophelia grinned and gave a chuckle.

Caitlin smiled at the two of them and turned back to the cooking stove.

"Well, that's great. Take up a plate and have some breakfast before you go on over to Ophelia's house. Now, Lily, you behave yourself while you're at Ophelia's and don't be getting into any mischief. Okay?"

"Okay, I won't."

"Humph…" André grunted as he gave Lily a big grin. "Now'ah… that's gonna call up some powerful magic on yor'ah part ah do believe," he drawled.

Mr. Bushy let out a deep laugh and André chuckled.

"Okay," Caitlin spoke up gently. "You two men can stop it right now. Lily cannot help it if mischief follows her around."

"Ah know, ah know," André chuckled. "Ah do love ya, Lily-Beth. But ya have ta admit, dilemmas jump on ya like fleas on a dog. Ain't that right?"

"Well, I reckon so," Lily laughed sheepishly. "Yeah, I don't just reckon it's true, I know it's true. Wonder why that is?"

"Well, lass," Mr. Bushy spoke up with a big smile. "You are what is called a problem solver. Problems may jump on ya like fleas-on-a-dog, but ya always seem ta solve them problems."

"Thank you, Mr. Bushy," Lily said. "I will hold onto that thought."

By this time, both girls had gobbled up their breakfast and were ready to take off for Ophelia's house. Giving both girls a kiss and a hug, Caitlin shooed them out the door.

"Maybe you should go along with those two, André, and make sure they get there in one piece and don't go off on an adventure. Ya think?"

"No, Caitlin love, ah'm sur'ah they'll be ah'right, if anyone takes on that Lily-Beth they'll let her go real quick-like once'st they hear'ah a bit o' that ther'ah chatterin' mouth."

"Come on Lily, let's get on over ta my house and get this over with," Ophelia sighed as she ran down the porch steps.

"Okay. Let's race to the bottom of the levee," Lily replied.

So off they went, and of course Ophelia won by a ten-foot lead. Laughing, they stopped, caught their breath, then set off in a slow walk. Once they got to the narrow trail running along the top of the levee, they stood looking down at the river bottom.

Ophelia grabbed Lily's arm as she said, "Don't even think about it, Lily. You promised your sister and Sheriff Beaumont you wouldn't even take one step into that river bottom. Come on, let's go."

"Okay," Lily sighed. "You're right. I did make that promise."

Turning in the direction of Ophelia's house, they began walking along the path and talking. After a few minutes, they spotted a rider on a big, black horse ambling toward them.

Lily grabbed Ophelia's arm as she said, "I've seen that horse before, Ophelia. That's the horse Caitlin rode into town when she escaped from Maude Burbank out at Yoder's farm! Wow! Isn't that a beautiful horse!"

The big, midnight-black horse was prancing its way along the top of the levee with its extremely long mane gracefully moving with the slight breeze. With each prancing step the horse took, his mane swayed and gently flipped into the air before floating down to cover the entire left leg of the rider. Long, feathery hair covered each of his fetlocks and its coat glistened in the early morning sun.

Sitting atop the horse was none other than Tillie Brown and Duck, in the flesh! Lily and Ophelia stood paralyzed in open-mouthed shock as the big horse trotted up to them.

"Hey! Close ya mouths before ya citch a fly and choke on hit, ya empty-headed gals," Tillie said with a laugh.

"*Aawk! Aawk!* Close ya yappers! *Aawk! Aawk!* Close ya yappers!" Duck squawked.

"Tillie," Lily stammered. "Wha—what is going on? How—?"

"Well, I don't rightly know that thur myself," Tillie said with a grin. "But I'm as happy as a flea on a dog. I was whippin' 'round inside that thur barn of yor'n when all of a sudden-like, God himself – or so I guess – slapped me on the back real hard-like, and WHOOSH! I was back in my body! I started in hackin' up a fur ball from that dang cat of yor'n sittin' on my chest and chokin' and a'gaspin' fur air and then my eyes popped right on open and I was back with the livin'! Strangest durn thin' I ever did know of. And by the way, the back o' my head gots a big ol' goose egg from whur ya was a'bangin' hit on the ground, thanky kindly. I tol' ya ta stop bangin' my head on the ground, now din't I?" Tillie chuckled.

"Anyway, ol' Duck here still weren't breathin'," Tillie continued, "so's I picks 'em up and starts in smackin' 'em on the back, figgurin' I might could do the same fur Duck as the good Lord done fur me, and all of a sudden, POP! Goes his eyeballs, and here we are! Yep, strangest durn thin' I ever did see. Well, we got on out o' that thur barn after some serious strugglin' with that dang door since ya locked us in from the outside. Then I give a big ol' whistle fur Tally-Ho here, who was jest a'waitin fur me in the woods, and off we go. I don't rightly understand hit and I never will, but that's jest the way hit is and I give the good Lord on high a big 'thanky' fur doin' hit!"

Lily and Ophelia were just standing and staring at Tillie and her horse. Duck was flying around Tillie's head and Tally-Ho was staring off across the river bottom. Duck looked a little worse for wear: his feathers were all ruffled and cock-eyed on the top of his head. He had lost his crawfish catch-net hat, and a big glob of mud was hanging along one side of his head. Every time he took a fly around Tillie's head, he jerked his head to one side as if he was having a hard time seeing through all the mud on his face.

"Duck," Lily called out. "Sit down and I'll clean that mud off of you so you can see a little better."

"*Aawk*! Got no time fur that!"

"Let the buzzard be," Tillie said. "He's a stupid ol' bird and I'm tard of keepin' 'em cleaned up. Let 'em be a mud-ball. Hit's what he likes."

"Well, gals, I got ta be goin' on me a hunt. I'm gonna find them thur fellers who tried ta do me in, even iff'en hit kills me a second time around! Lily Quinn, you jest keep ah tight holt on that thur locket o' mine and iff'en ya ever find my Pa – or a soul who has my blood – give hit to 'em and tell 'em my story, ya hear?"

Lily nodded her head yes and continued staring at Tillie with amazement, eyes wide. Ophelia had started sweating and was looking a little pale.

"Tally-Ho!" Tillie yelled out at the top of her voice as she gave her horse a kick in his sides.

Tally-Ho reared up on his hind legs, slammed back down and flew past Lily and Ophelia, creating a breeze as he went.

"*Aawk*! Tally-Ho, and away we go! *Aawk*! Away we go! *Aawk*!"

With open-mouthed bewilderment, Lily and Ophelia turned around and watched them ride away.

Ophelia looked at Lily and said, "I was getting a little light headed there for a minute, Lily. That was the strangest durn thing I *ever* did see."

"Yep," Lily replied in a whisper as she kept her eyes trained on Tillie, Duck and Tally-Ho. "Yes it was."

They was already a quarter mile away, but the girls continued standing and staring after them. Tillie stopped, turned back and lifted her hand as if to wave good bye, then suddenly stood up in the stirrups then sat back down and whipped Tally-Ho around as she started yelling and kicked her horse into a full run right back towards them.

Tillie Brown's arm came up, pointing her pistol directly at Lily and Ophelia. *BOOM!* A gunshot rang out, and Lily's vision went black, exploding into a million stars.

# 5

## THE RIVER RATS

When she came to, Lily found herself hanging upside down, with her head flopping against the back of a stranger. Glancing over to the right she could see Ophelia's head bouncing against the back of someone else.

Keeping her head down and her eyes barely open, Lily could only see two men walking; the man carrying Ophelia was much taller than the man carrying her.

The men trudged on along the pathway for another half-hour or so, and all the while, Lily lay flopped over the man's shoulder like a rag doll. She didn't move; she didn't moan or whisper a single word. There was no way she wanted these men, whoever they were, to know she was awake.

Then both men began huffing and puffing from the strain of carrying them so far, until she and Ophelia were finally plopped onto the sandy riverbank. Keeping her eyes almost completely shut, Lily watched as the two men waded into the river and pulled a large raft up onto shore. Without saying a word to each other, the men once again slung the girls over their shoulders, walked to the raft and hoisted them aboard.

It was a usual river raft – a tent attached to one end, supplies and firewood stacked on the other. Lily and Ophelia were taken into the tent and dumped, not too gently, on a pile of dirty, smelly blankets, which must have been the men's beds.

Once outside the tent, the two men began to talk loudly. One of them began playing a fiddle as the other man sang a song Lily recognized from the Louisiana bayou:

> On my way to Big Mamou;
> I don't need no woman
> tell me what to do!
> I don't need no woman
> tell me what to do!
> Going back to Big Mamou.

Lily took a good look around the tent. Bare necessities – a few pans, a coffee pot, and bags of coffee were the only things inside the tent.

"Psst!"

It came from the pile of blankets piled next to Ophelia.

Jerking her head around, Lily peered into the pile; covered from head to toe with the dirty blankets sat little Gertie P. Wilkes. She was rolled into such a small ball Lily had to look twice to see her.

This was Granny Wilkes' granddaughter. Granny Wilkes was a preaching woman married to a non-churchgoing man, and most of the folks who knew Granny would rather cut their tongues out than say anything the least bit disrespectful to Granny Wilkes or about her to anyone else. Every Sunday she rode her wagon for miles around the area picking up children and taking them to Sunday school, and after Sunday school, she make sure every last one of the children had a belly full of food before she took them back to their farms.

Well, Gertie P. was Granny Wilkes favorite granddaughter, and Granny Wilkes made sure everyone knew about it. Granny was just as stern with Gertie P. as she was with all the other children, but everyone knew Gertie P. was the apple of Granny Wilkes' eye.

Gertie P. was only five years old, but she had the mouth of an adult. She was a thin little girl with the prettiest red hair Lily had ever seen – it was quite long, and it curled around her pale face and shoulders in ringlets. Although, right now, her hair looked more like a wild, red bush growing out of the top of her head then it soft hair. Despite the fact that Gertie P. was a sassy little thing, Lily couldn't help but like her. She had big, blue eyes set against her pale skin and angular features. On the end of her generously freckled, turned-up nose sat a pair of spectacles with a pink ribbon tied into a bow on one of the earpieces. Gertie P. was usually the first one to smile and laugh.

Lily's little sister Tessa was best of friends with this gal, so they spent most of their free time togther. Gertie P. was the only child of Preacher Wilkes, Granny Wilkes' son, over in Hayti, but she spent her summers with her Granny in Caruthersville so she could be close to Tessa. From the first day of meeting her, Gertie P. had insisted everyone call her "Gertie P." and refused to acknowledge anyone who did not address her as such. She was a pistol, as Granny Wilkes called her, but Tessa loved her dearly, so the rest of the family put up with her bossiness.

"Gertie P.," Lily spoke in a soft whisper. "They got you too?"

"Well, of course they did, Lily Quinn," Gertie P snapped. "Do ya think I swam out here and crawled into this here tent all by myself just for fun? I was outside on Granny's front porch waiting for the sun to come up a bit more because Granny said I could go over to your house and play with Tessa just as soon as the sun came full up and I had a bite of breakfast! Well, just as soon as my Granny went out to the privy, shut the door and probably had her drawers down, those polecats snatched me right off Granny's porch. Now my day is ruined! I'm hungry, and Tessa's day is ruined too! But I'm sure she ain't hungry like I am."

"Ok," Lily replied. "But keep your voice down; we don't want them to know we are awake. And no, I didn't think you came out here on your own, it was just a question. I'm shocked to find you here."

"Well, it was a stupid question. Who's that with ya?" she asked as she looked around Lily. "It's that Ophelia gal, isn't it? I'd know her anywhere with all that white hair. Is she dead? Please don't say she's dead, Lily. Wake her up, wake her up. I don't want her to be dead!"

"No, she isn't dead; she's just knocked out a bit from the knock on the noggin they gave us. She'll come-to in a minute."

"Oh, good. That's good. They didn't even knock me on the noggin; they just snatched me right up and put their stinkin' dirty paws over my mouth. Yuck, that was nasty!"

The fiddle player stopped playing as he and the other man called out loudly, "Hey, ov'ah he'ah! Come on, get on quick. We gotta get out of he'ah 'fore somebody comes long."

Lily recognized that accent. He was from the bayou.

"Hey, we got us some gals ta take on ta Nor'lins an sell. But we gotta be getting' out o' he'ah quick."

"Who are they?" yelled a man on shore.

"I don' be knowin' who dey are! Come take a look see if ya wont ta."

"Okay, I'll jest do that."

Lily felt the raft wobble angrily as more men climbed aboard.

"Come on Willie, get ya'self on up he'ah on dis he'ah raft and let's shove off," the first men said.

"I'm a'comin'." This man seemed to be struggling to get on the raft.

"We be wastin' goot time, yes?"

The raft moved and jerked as the men got themselves settled. As soon as they were a ways out onto the river, the raft settled down and the ride became smoother.

Lily watched through half closed eyes as one of the men entered the tent and snatched up the coffee pot and a bag of what Lily thought must be coffee. He stood there for a few seconds looking at the girls. Lily and Gertie P. didn't say a word – they held their breath and pretended to be out cold. The man turned and walked out, and in walked one of the two men who had just climbed aboard. Looking through slitted eyes, Lily recognized him.

It was Corn-Shuckin' John!

Corn-Shuckin' John was born and raised in Caruthersville and had gotten his nickname way back when he was a kid when every year he won the corn-shucking contest during the summer harvest fair. He was tall, lanky, and had long, skinny arms and hands with long, boney fingers. He wore an old straw hat and his hair was pulled back with a leather string at the nape of his neck. His bib overalls were dirty and his shirt was hanging out the sides of them. He had on a pair of raggedy boots and his pant legs looked as if he had not rolled them up when he walked through a mud hole. Folks said he was faster than lightening when it came to shucking corn and no one else had even a chance to win. Some said his record would never, in the history of mankind, be broken. He could shuck thirty-five ears of corn in one minute. Now some folks said he left too much silk on the ears, but they had to admit, all the husks were gone.

Corn-Shuckin' John's eyes almost popped right out of his face when he spotted Lily, Ophelia and Gertie P. He bent his long, lanky body over so he was no more than six inches from Lily's face and said in a low whisper: "Lordy, Lordy, what have them bayou fellers gone and done. Thur fixin' ta get us all strung up by the Neck-in-a-Noose Gang, is what thur fixin' ta do! Whur in the world did they snatch-up all three o' ya? We ain't takin' ya down the river! Iff'en we do, Sheriff Beaumont and Mr. Knudson will skin us 'live. Gertie P., whur did they come across you, ya little rascal?"

Gertie P.'s face turned into a distorted mask of anger as she heat-edly whispered back at Corn-Shuckin' John. "Now, don't ya be callin' me a rascal, and where do ya think they found me, Corn-Shuckin' John? They nipped me right off my Granny's front porch while she was in the privy and I'm gonna tell you something else. If ya don't take me back to Granny's, my Pa's gonna burn the bottom of your feet off your legs with hot coals of fire before he sends you down to the *lake-o-fire*, I can promise you that right here and now! You do know my Pa is the preacher-man in Hayti, don't ya?"

Gertie P was shaking her finger right up against Corn-Shuckin' John's nose as she continued. "And... and... my Granny is Granny Wilkes and she is gonna whoop your behind till it falls right off and bounces down the road like a ball and *then* she's gonna open up her Bible and read it to you until you're so tired of hearing it you'll become a good, decent person the way God made you to be! You best not be fooling with my Granny! She's a preachin' woman, and she don't take no lip from nobody, especially when it comes ta someone snatching up her Gertie P.! You may not know it, but I'm Granny's favorite, and she will whoop ya good and proper if ya hurt me! And she'll put a Christian curse on ya, so... put that in yer pipe and smoke it, Corn-Shuckin' John!"

"Now Gertie P," Lily whispered softly. "Granny Wilkes always forgives folks if they ask her kindly. Corn-Shuckin' John, Granny Wilkes will forgive you and give you her blessing if you return us safely. Gertie P. is just worked up about being nipped away from her Granny's porch."

If the three other men outside the tent had not been talking and carrying on so loudly, they would have heard every word Gertie P. was saying.

Lily gave Gertie P. a poke in the side and whispered, "Keep your voice down a bit, Gertie P.!"

"Stop poking me, Lily Quinn," Gertie P angrily whispered back, a little softer.

"I know'd hit Gertie P., I know'd hit!" Corn-Shuckin' John replied. "Oh Lord, have mercy on my soul. This here cain't be happenin'. This here thing wasn't 'spose to end up like this here. You gals stay right cheer and don't make nary a sound, cuz them thur fellers from the bayou is some mean'uns. They'd jest as soon dump ya in the river and hold ya down until ya fill plum up with water, iff'en ya know'd what I mean. Iff'en they find out what they done did, all three o' ya be goners. So don't utter a peep now. Not one single whisper of ah peep. And when ya get back ta Caruthersville, ya better be puttin' in a good word fur me an Willie with everbody, includin' that Granny of yor'n, Gertie P., fur getting' ya out of this here problem we're in. Is hit a done deal?

Lily and Gertie P shook their heads vigorously in agreement.

"Okay. I reckon I gotta get Willie in here fur some reason so we can figger out how ta get ya off'en this here raft. I gots ta think on hit fur a bit."

Lily and Gertie P. looked at Corn-Shuckin' John with eyes wide and once again nodded their heads in agreement.

"Hit might take a bit," Corn-Shuckin' John whispered. "But I *will* be back and get ya off'en this here raft."

He backed out through the tent flap, and Lily looked over at Gertie P. Lily put her finger up to her lips in a signal not to say a word; Gertie P. nodded in agreement. When Lily gently put her hand over Ophelia's mouth in case she woke startled and cried out, her eyes popped open and she looked at Lily with wide eyes and nodded her head, letting Lily know she had heard everything.

Quietly, the three girls sat and listened to the activity going on outside the tent.

"Well, I reckon with dem tree gals we can take a break from all dis goin' up an down dis riv'ah an start goin' inta da bayou for a bit. Et's closer to Nor'lins and we kin make more runs. What about dat, yes?"

"Dats okay wit me, LaFitte, cuz I don't like dis riv'ah runnin'. Too much work fo me."

"Everting's too much work ta you, Girard. Yor'ah too lazy ta knock da dead flies off yor own face, yes?"

"Ah reckon so…" Lily heard quite a bit of laughing.

"Well," Corn-Shuckin' John spoke up. "Hit look likes hit's fixin' ta buck up a storm. Say, Willie; let's take some of them thur logs back behind the tent fur balance. This here water is gonna start getting' a bit rough, I kin feel hit in my bones."

"Go right on ahead," Girard said to Corn-Shuckin' John. "Me and LaFitte done be plum tucker'd out afta lugging dem gals all da way from dat levee. We had ta out-run dat ol' Tillie Brown. We kill't her yesterday! Her and dat crazy perroquet o' hers was dead I tell ya!

"We took da poke o' gold, den to-day we see her sittin' on dat big ol' back horse o' hers an dey come chargin' down dat levee and she be yellin' at da top o' her voice, 'Tally-Ho, Tally-Ho!', and ever time she yells, dat big ol' horse start runnin' faster. She be trying ta get dem gals away from us. I swear dat was a haint. Hit had ta be a haint! She was dead, I tell ya. She was dead! So we had ta take off runnin' tru' dat mud ho' of a riv'ah bottom, carryin' two bodies. Why in da world would anyone wont ta be livin' in dat riv'ah bottom? Et's noting but a big o' hole ah quicksand, an et's a good ting dat horse o' hers be too big ta get round dem trees, or she woulda caught us fur sur'ah. Ain't dat right, LaFitte?"

"Dat's true. I tink it was a haint too. I hear tell dem haints be looking like anyting dey wont to be lookin' like, yes?" LaFitte replied in his deep, gravely voice.

"That thur is true!"

Lily recognized Watermelon Willie's voice; he was about the same age as Corn-Shuckin' John, and folks said they were distant cousins since their families were always hanging with each other at all the town gatherings. Watermelon Willie had gotten his nickname a long time ago. As the story goes, it was when young Willie Puckett ate three big watermelons at the watermelon eating contest during the summer harvest fair.

Watermelon Willie was a short, stocky man with extremely short legs for a man. The upper part of his body was longer than his legs. His whole body looked as if someone had put a stopper around his legs when he was young so only the upper half of his body grew. His arms were stocky, as were his legs, hands, fingers, and even his feet. He never wore shoes, even on the few times he went to Sunday church, a wedding, or a funeral – Granny Tomason said it was because he could not find shoes wide enough to fit his feet. Watermelon Willie's voice interrupted Lily's thoughts as he continued his story.

"One time, me and John here be down around that big o' lake in the Oh-zark Mountains, way down deep in them hills and we wandered upon this here ol' empty farm house back in them thur woods and we decided ta stay a while, seeing that it was getting dark an all, an we was running from some strange fellers. Well, we closed up that old house best we could, went up the stairs to the only room with a door on hit and et us some supper. Then we fell sound asleep in front o' that ol', cold farplace. Well, long about midnight—or there abouts—we hear the big o' roar of a mama bar', and jumped right up to take a peep out the broke winder and what do we see in that bright moonlight, but these two lil' black bar's all huddled ta'gether by the old broke-down barn. Thur was this big ol' black cat jest a'creepin' right up on 'em. All of a sudden-like, outta them thur woods and inta the moonlight charged this here big mama bar. She was prolly ten feet tall and jest as white as my shirt used ta be, and her far-red eyes were a'glowin'. She came chargin' after that cat and runned right on through them two little bars, jest like they was never even sittin' thur, and then she headed straight for that cat. Well, that big o' cat turned tail and took off a'runnin' as fast as his legs could carry 'em. After ah few minutes that big mama bar comes walkin' back on all fours ta them little young'uns and 'fore she got very close, she started in fadin' away! Them little 'uns was runin' right up ta thur mama jest a'bawlin' and a'cryin', but afore they got thur, she vanished into thin air. Ain't that true, John?"

"Yep, that's right. And me and Willie didn't sleep nary another wink that thur whole night. We was scare't o' that big ol' mama bar haint but we was more scare't of that thur big ol' black cat wonderin 'round in them woods huntin' fur someone ta eat. Cuz I hear'd once them big black cats can jump thirty feet or more and that winder weren't even twenty feet up from the ground."

"Ya ain't seen haints a'tall till ya see dem evil bayou haints," LaFitte spoke up with his deep gravelly Cajun accent. His voice was gruff and raspy as he started telling his tale. "Dey be black as coal and scary as ol' Lucifer himself. Won time, down deep in da bayou, me and mon père, we go fishin' in da swamp an a big storm come blowin' inta dat bayou. We find us a itty-bitty shack high up in da Spanish mossy trees an we sit fur a long time, listening to dat storm howlin' and whippin' da trees round. Da sky be black as midnight and da black water was churnin' and boilin' as et tried ta get up inta da trees. We was still sittin' when da time fo suppa come and go and dat storm still nev'ah give up. Round 'bout midnight or so, et finally let up, so we look out 'tween dem boards and we see some dark shadows slippin' an slidin' among dem big trees.  Mon père, he whisper, real quiet in my ear, and say: 'dat's fantôme noir. Soyez très calme, he be tellin' me dat black haints was in da bayou and I should be real quiet. Well, I cain't see dem fantômes too good, but I *could* see dem dark shadows slippin' round dem trees; dey go in an out, to an fro in dem spanish mossy trees, like dey be hunting fo someting. Dat Spanish moss be barely movin' a 'lil bit as dem fantômes slipped in an out. We was real quiet and din't hardly take in air an da fantômes kept slippin' round dem trees fur a good while, but den dey start in gathering, real slow, round da bottom of our tree like dey know we was up dere and was wantin' ta git to us. I was shakin' in my boots, but mon père, he sits waitin' and leans ov'ah and again whispers real quiet in my ear an says; 'pas encore mon fils, he be tellin' me to wait a lil' bit longer. Well, I din't fancy waitin' no more minutes when I cain't be seeing none too good in dat co black bayou, but mon père, now he can see like da big bayou cat at night, so I know he know what was happenin, so I sit still.  All of a sudden, I hear da scream of da black swamp cat and I looked down at dem black fantômes and dat black cat was right amongst dem. I could see da eyes o' dat black cat an dey was glowin' in da dark. Dat big o' cat was screamin' and swippin' at dem black fantômes and dem fantômes was takin' off inta da darkness o' da night. Mon père laughs deep down in his chest an gives a soft whistle and up inta dat shack jumpes dat big black cat.  It stood dere starin' at me for a long time 'til mon père says some soft words to et and et set down and started purrin' like a chaton. Next morning when we wake up, da big cat is gone and so is da storm and dem fantômes."

"Let's go on down da riv'ah," Girard said rather shakily. "Dis talk o' fantômes noir got me spooked, yes?"

LaFitte gave a deep, gravelly chuckle, but he and the other three men sat there quietly for a few minutes contemplating LaFitte's story – or so Lily thought.

"Good idee," Corn Shuckin' John spoke up. "Willie, let's get them thur logs moved 'round the back end of this here raft afore that thur storm blows in on us. Whatcha think? Think hit's fixin' ta come on in? I'm a'thinkin' hit could be a big 'un."

"Yeah, I reckon so, John. I kindly feel hit in my bone, like hit's comin' on in."

"Maybe we otta be pullin' up an findin' us a hidey-hole fo a while. Ya think, yes?" Girard asked.

"Naw," Corn-Shuckin John jumped in and answered. "Hit ain't gonna be that bad. We jest need ta get a bit of balance on this here ol' raft."

"Fine wit me," Girard replied. "I'm gonna play us some music on my fiddle while ya do et."

Girard started playing his banjo, and LaFitte started singing some Louisiana Bayou song about losing his lovely "Cher", but Lily couldn't understand most of it.

The three girls heard Watermelon Willie and Corn-Shuckin' John drag some logs around the back of the tent and start in whispering while they were stacking them against each other.

"Oh Lordy, Lordy," they heard Watermelon Willie gasp. "What'd they go and do that fur? We be goners, I tell ya, we be some dead ducks hanged by the neck iff'en the Neck-in-the-Noose Gang finds us, I tell ya! They done cooked our goose."

The "Neck-in-the-Noose Gang" was a group of marshals and judges who traveled the circuit from the top of Illinois down to the bottom of Louisiana. They were notorious for putting criminals on the hanging tree, and these two knew that kidnapping children was one of the most heinous crimes committed in the eyes of the marshals and judges. Kidnappers did not stand a chance of going free; in fact, they would be hung immediately after their trial and nary a soul would shed a tear.

"Shh! Keep yur voice down. Now this here is what we gonna do. I'm gonna let them gals know that thur be some floatin' logs out here and fur them to—real quiet-like—slip one off the back o' this tent and take off a'swimmin' fur shore. I'm gonna pass em' one o' my little skinnin' knives so they can cut a hole in the back o' this here tent."

"Psst," Corn-Shuckin' John whispered softly. "Psst!"

"Hey! You gals, ya hear'd that? Iff'en ya do, poke on the back o' this tent. Now don't slip out 'til them two others be full o'whiskey, and when ya do slip inta the river don't start in a'kickin' til ya be away from this here raft. Ya jest gonna have ta take a chance with the snakes and such, but ya'll make hit. Take off yor shoes so ya won't sink ta the bottom and hang 'em 'round yor neck so's ya can put 'em on once'st ya git on shore. Ya hear me? Might be best iff'en ya wait til hit gets kindly dark so's LaFitte and Girard cain't see ya."

Lily, Ophelia and Gertie P. poked on the back of the tent and Corn-Shuckin' John slipped a small knife under the edge of the tent. Then he and Watermelon Willie went back around to the front of the raft, where they joined in the singing. Watermelon Willie picked up a guitar and joined Girard in playing some music.

The day dragged on and on, and soon the girls could tell it was getting to be late afternoon. The tent was getting hot and humid, and all three girls felt parched from the humidity. The men had not brought them anything to eat or drink all day, and Gertie P.'s stomach was growling loudly; she kept whispering "I'm hungry," until she fell asleep. It seemed like it had been days since Lily and Ophelia had gotten up and set out for Ophelia's house, but Lily's stomach told her it had been about eight hours.

Finally, Corn-Shuckin John slipped into the tent and quietly sat a jug of water and some jerked meat down in front of the girls.

"Not too much longer now, gals," he whispered "And when ya take off, take off swimmin' that-a-ways," he said, pointing to his left. "I'm gonna be guidin' this here raft closer to that shore jest as soon as hit starts in gettin' dusky-like."

He turned around and kind of staggered as he picked up another jug of whiskey and left. Lily felt the cooling, late-afternoon air come in as Corn-Shuckin John slid in and out of the tent flap. She quietly lifted the back of the tent a few inches and let some of the air flow inside.

"Ahhh…" Ophelia sighed. "That feels so nice. Why didn't we think of doing that a long time ago?"

"I don't know, but it sure is helping now. Let's let Gertie P. sleep a while longer. We can save her some of this water and jerked meat, and maybe her little belly will stop growling."

Quickly, dusk settled over the river and Lily decided it was time for them to slip out the back and swim for shore – they could hear the men starting to slur their words from too much corn-mash whiskey. Soon, one of the men started snoring; a second one soon joined him.

"I'll take the first watch," Corn-Shuckin John announced.

"Dat's fine wit me," LaFitte answered. "I'm gonna check own dem gals and see if dey be sleepin', yes?"

Lily and Ophelia hurriedly shoved the jug of water and the jerked meat under an old blanket, rolled over onto their sides and shut their eyes. Ophelia started softly snoring and Lily left her own mouth hanging open. LaFitte entered the tent, stood there a minute and then turned around and left.

"Dey all be sleepin'. Dem gals don't make much noise all day. I hope day be good 'nuff ta sell."

"What a buzzard," Lily thought. "He didn't even bother thinking about us being hungry or thirsty!"

After what seemed like forever, a third man started snoring, and Corn-Shuckin John stuck his pole into the flap of the tent and gave it a shake.

Quickly Lily started cutting the back of the tent, and Ophelia gently put her hand over Gertie P.'s mouth as she slowly shook her awake. Gertie P. came awake with a start and whispered, "I'm hungry."

"Here," Ophelia whispered back, handing Gertie P. some jerked meat. "Eat this and here's some water to wash it down with. It's time to leave."

"Yummy," Gertie P. mumbled as she gobbled down the jerked meat like a feast fit for a king.

"Okay, that's done," Lily whispered. "Shall we get out of here while Corn-Shuckin John still has a soft spot for saving his neck?"

"I think so," Ophelia replied in a low whisper.

"Me too, Lily," Gertie P. said.

The wind was picking up; the raft was starting to move choppily on the water as Lily stuck her head out the back of the tent.

All three girls could feel the boat being poled towards the shore until Corn-Shuckin' John quietly said, "This here be a mighty fine spot in this river," as if talking to himself.

The raft slowed somewhat and through the river mist, Lily could make out the river bank about twenty-five feet away from the raft. Corn-Shuckin' John pulled back on the poles in the shallow waters, almost slowing the raft to a complete stop. Not a cloud was in the sky and the moon was bright enough to light up the way to the edge of the shoreline.

"This is what we have to do," Lily whispered. "We have to slide this log off and quietly slip it into the river while one of us holds it still for two of us to slip in and get a good hold on it. I'll hold the log up against the raft and you two slip into the water. Keep your bodies below the log and try to put your hands on the sides where they won't see them. After you two are in, I'll slip into the water and give the log a push away from the raft. Gertie P, you hang on up there at the furthest end of the log where there is three little stubs to hold on to. Ophelia, there's a stub right in the middle of the log you can clamp onto and I'll hang onto that there little branch still attached to this end."

As they slipped the log into the river, Gertie P. give a little gasp and pointed into the dark river water. All three girls stared wide-eyed as a big water moccasin slithered up to their log. If Gertie P.

had not spotted it, the snake would have been easy to miss in the dark of the night. It leisurely eased itself over the log and, thankfully, kept right on swimming past them. Its body was dark brown, almost black, with some lighter gray around its head. Water rolled off its head and sloshed down its back as it slithered up and over the log, the moonlight creating sparkles and colorful rivets of water while it glided over the log and swam away. Following right behind it was another one; this one stopped, slithered up onto the log and looked at Ophelia for a moment before it too slipped back into the black water and slithered away into the darkness. Right behind the second snake came three smaller ones, slithering around the log; not bothering to crawl over it.

"Come on," Lily hesitantly whispered after they watched the snakes slink off into the darkness. "We have two choices: either we get into this river and go home, or we can be taken down the river and the good Lord knows what will happen there. I really don't like the idea of becoming someone's slave on some island."

"Well," Gertie P whispered confidently, "I'm going home and ain't no snake gonna stop me. Come on you two, let's go."

Once again, they heard Corn-Shuckin' John say in a quiet voice, "This here be a fine night fur a swim right cheer in this shaller spot."

With that said Gertie P slipped into the water and pulled herself to the front of the log and motioned for Ophelia to join her.

"Oh mercy me, and God love a duck," Ophelia whispered hesitantly as she slipped into the water.

Once both Gertie P. and Ophelia were holding on tight to the log, Lily let go of the log, slipped into the water, grabbed a hold of the branch, and using her foot, she gave the log a slight shove – pushing them away from the raft. Frantically kicking their legs under water, so as to not draw attention, they began pulling away from the raft.

Once they put a bit of a distance between the raft and themselves, they popped their heads all the way up above the log and looked back. They watched as the three men continued sleeping on the front of the raft, with Corn-Shuckin' John poling the raft back out into the center of the river so as to catch the current which would carry them further down the river.

He turned and looked their way and lifted his pole as a signal to them that they were in safe territory.

"Okay," Lily whispered so her voice wouldn't carry across the water, "let's kick harder so we can reach shore before we run into any more of those snakes!"

"Sounds like a plan to me!" Gertie P whispered loudly.

Pulling themselves up onto the top of the log, they frantically kicked their legs and used their hands to push the water away from the log.

When they were almost to the edge of the river bank, they heard some yelling and turned to see what was going on with the men on the raft. By this time, they were close enough to shore to give one big push so as to reach out and pull the log into a clump of tree branches which had fallen into the edge of the river. Turning their small log around, they strained their eyes, hoping to see the raft, but it was too far down the river and the river fog was closing in and blocking their view.

"Dem gals dun cut a hole in da back o' dis tent! Wur'd dey get da knife, I wonder? Et must o' been one o' der pere's knives cuz et was sharp, dat's fur sur'ah. Ya din't even he'ah 'em atall, no?" LaFitte's yelling shouts echoed up the river.

A lot of yelling and shouting echoed up the river as the men evidently began looking for the girls.

"I hope they all fall into the river and the snakes get them!" Gertie P. whispered, "They deserve it!"

"Ah, looky here," Waterman Willie yelled out. "They done took one o' our balancin' logs. They must o' slipped off'en this here raft way back yonder! Well, we don't have ta worry none 'bout 'em. Them snakes be getting' 'em in no time a'tall. This here river be chuck full o' them water moc's. Iff'en they be in this part of the river, they best be getting' on outta here cuz them water moc's be on the hunt."

Watermelon Willie was yelling so loud his voice was echoing up and down the river onto the riverbanks.

Hearing Watermelon Willie's warning made all three girls look up into the branches of the fallen tree as they checked out the water swirling around their legs. The tree limbs were hanging in their faces and the wet leaves were sticking to their necks. The water was muddy and dark, and the tree branches smelled of dead animals. Their clothes were already muddy from the river water and their hair was matted tight to their heads.

"Let's get out of here, " Ophelia said as she splashed up onto the riverbank.

"Not so loud Gertie P!" Lily whispered. "Our voices will carry down river just as theirs did coming up the river."

Slowly and quietly, the girls clawed their way up the steep dirt bank of the river, all the while keeping one ear tuned to the river for any voices floating up to them. Corn-shuckin' John had pushed the raft back out into the current and it had quickly drifted further downriver and was rapidly getting too far away for the men to spot them on the riverbank.

Reaching the top of the riverbank, Lily picked up a stick and started beating at the tall grass growing along the river.

"We don't want to sit down on a snake while we put our shoes on, do we?" she whispered.

"Nope!" Ophelia and Gertie P said in unison.

Bending down, the girls put on their shoes and stood up looking around the river bank.

"Well," Lily said. "It looks like we're on the Tennessee side of the river."

"That's a fine kettle of fish now, isn't it?" Gertie P. stated in a squeaky little voice. "How are you gonna get us back home, Lily Quinn? And how far downriver are we? Tell me that!" Gertie P. was standing in a defensive pose with her hands on her hips.

"To tell you the truth, Gertie P, I don't know if we're in Tennessee or Mississippi."

"We were on that raft an awful long time," Ophelia said. "I have a notion we're all the way down into Mississippi."

Lily looked at Gertie P. and started laughing. She was covered in river mud from her head to her toes. Even her face and hair were covered in mud. She must have rolled around in the muddy riverbank as she struggled in her attempt to get to the top, because even the back of her dress was plastered with mud.

"What in tarnation are you laughing at, Lily Quinn? Don't you be laughing at me, you should see yourself! You look like you just swam out of a mudcat hole!" she shouted, and then she started laughing so hard she fell on the ground and rolled around some more.

Lily and Ophelia looked at each other and began laughing. All three of them looked like they had been swimming in a mud hole.

"Well," Lily laughed as she tried wiping mud off of her face. "Let's get going and maybe we can find a path leading up the river. If we don't find a path, we'll have to walk through these woods. Grab a big stick, both of you, so we can beat the bushes as we go and maybe scare off the critters."

The further they walked in the woods, the thicker the trees grew; wild ferns covered the ground. Repeatedly they heard the rustle of leaves as squirrels, chipmunks, or whatever scurried away from the noise they were making with their sticks.

After a bit of walking through tall grass and tangled vines, the girls came upon a narrow path leading through the shadowed trees not too far away from the bank of the river. Following the narrow path north, it widened a bit as they got a little further up the river. Every once in a while other narrow paths led off into the forest, but they decided to stay as close to the river as possible. They knew for certain they would eventually make it home, or across the river from home, if they kept walking close to the river.

Gertie P. began complaining about being too tired to take one more step; soon she was almost thirty feet behind Lily and Ophelia.

So Lily, with help from Ophelia, lifted her onto her back for a piggy-back ride.

The narrow path soon merged with a larger wagon path; tall Elm and Sweetgum trees stretched their branches across the wagon trail and created a tunnel, which blocked out the dwindling light and would soon make it too difficult for the girls to continue their journey.

"Look over there," Gertie P. whispered in Lily's ear as she pointed into the dark woods, "It's a light. Maybe it's a cabin and someone living there will help us."

The girls stopped and stood there for a few minutes looking at the light far off in the distance.

"What do you think, Ophelia?" Lily said.

"Well," Ophelia answered uncertainly, "It looks a bit of a long walk to reach it, but I reckon we should go see; or do ya think it might be unsafe? Could be whoever lives there is harmless, but it could be someone scary. I'm not like the idea of staying all night out here in this wilderness with all the night critters either, how about you?"

"Put me down, put me down!" Gertie P. demanded, "I can walk now. But... thanks for letting me take a ride, Lily."

"It's about time," Lily replied with a sigh. "You're one heavy little, skinny girl. Your legs are boney and your arms are choking me!"

"Sorry."

Standing in the middle of the dirt path, peering apprehensively into the forest, all three of their minds were buzzing with which choice to make. Should they stay on the path and maybe make it into a small town, but take the chance of meeting up with some night animals along the way? Or should they risk it and venture into the forest with hopes of finding a cabin and shelter for the night?

Looking up through the tree branches above them, Lily saw the sky turning darker by the minute and she knew the dusky moonlight would quickly disappear, along with any hope of seeing the wagon trail. Her gut told her the night creatures had already started their forage in the forest, so she made a decision for all of them.

"I think we should go see what it is. We won't go too close; just close enough to take a look-see. What do you two think?"

"I reckon we should."

"Me too."

# 6

## THE CABIN

"Okay," Lily quietly whispered. "But this is what we have to do. Gertie P., you have to be very quiet so we can sneak soundlessly up to whatever it is. Are you ready?"

"Let's go," the other two softly whispered together.

Cautiously, the three girls crept into the woods with Lily going first, then Gertie P., then Ophelia. The night sky was growing darker and darker by the second. It wasn't but a few seconds when Gertie P asked if Lily could see what it was.

"Are we there yet?" Gertie P asked.

"Not yet, Gertie P." Lily said.

Not even two minutes later, she asked again.

"Not yet, Gertie P."

Two minutes later, she asked again.

Stopping and turning around, Lily murmured softly, "Gertie P., you have to be very quiet. Don't even whisper a word! Just in case it's some bad folks and all, we can't let anyone hear us, you understand?"

The five-year-old was looking up at Lily with her big blue eyes wide open and her lips trembling a bit. She whispered very quietly, "Okay, Lily, I'll try. But, I don't know if I can keep that promise. Sometimes my mouth just opens up and words start jumping right out and I can't stop them. I promise you, they just jump right out. It's kindly scary sometimes I tell ya, kindly scary. What should I do about that?"

"For starters," Lily whispered, "If you don't keep those words inside your head, we are all going back to the road and then Ophelia and I will leave you there by yourself until we find out what is going on out here. And remember, the night critters will be out roaming around any minute now. You have to stop those words from jumping out before something hears you and we get ourselves into a big, scary mess."

Gertie P. nodded and made motions of locking her lips shut and throwing away the key, and nervously started wringing her little hands.

When they were approximately 30 feet from the light, they stopped, stood behind a large Sweetgum tree, and leaned around it to stare at a little cabin built into the side of the hill.

The burning orange light of the lantern threw an orange hue on everthing in sight. It looked as if the back half of cabin was built into the small hill nd most of the roof was covered in dirt with grass and vines growing wildly in evry directions looking like a man's head that was in dire need of a haircut. The wooden walls were weather-worn and grey, with vines dangling down from the roof on each side, draping the windows and door with their swaying shadows. A gentle breeze was causing the vines to rock gently back and forth across the glowing windows. From a distance the only thing they could see was the bright orange glow of the lantern...making the cabin look even more sinister than it already was. Clementine vines meandered up the walls and adorned the edges of the roof. The flower blooms were closed for the night, but Lily was sure blossoms would cover the roof and walls in the morning. The cabin sat in the middle of an overgrown clearing full of weeds, grass and wild flowers; the cabin looked quite sad – the window frames were sagging and the door was crooked. Tall grass and prickly thicket bushes had grown up around the house and were hiding any type of porch that may be attached to the door. Most of the big Sweetgum trees had long ago been cut back from the little cabin, but the remaining ones formed a canopy over the edges of the clearing and created shade for the top of the cabin roof during hot summer days.

There was no path leading up to the cabin door, so Lily was sure it had not been used recently, but the light from the lantern was illuminating its brilliant orange glow.

Lily took Gertie P's right hand gently, and motioned for Ophelia to take her left hand. Silently, on their tip-toes, the three of them crept towards the cabin until they were next to one of the windows. Dropping Gertie P.'s hand, Lily stood on her toes and peeked through the window. Dusty cobwebs were hanging in clumps from the rafters, glistening in the light of the lantern; silvery dust motes floated in and out of the light beams. The cabin was just one large room. She couldn't see anyone inside, but in the middle there sat a small, wooden table with one rickety, wooden chair, and in the middle of the small table sat the lighted lantern.

Butted up against one wall was a good-sized cot with several blankets neatly folded on one end on the other end of the cot was a neatly folded was a thin feather mattress. On the back wall was a fireplace made of large river rock and in the hearth hung a cast-iron cooking pot. Sitting on the fireplace mantle were eating utensils and personal items. Firewood was neatly stacked half way up the wall next to the fireplace, and a rifle hung above the firewood. A long wooden table, stained with black walnut juice, stood along that back wall that Lily assumed was built into the hill. She had seen a table just like this in Frake's Butcher Shop in Caruthersville. Mr. Frakes' table was used to cut up hogs and chickens. Between the fireplace and the long table was an empty space with hooks and a nail sticking out of each wall board and that was about all Lily could see from her vantage point.

"No one is inside," Lily whispered. She turned back to Ophelia and Gertie P. "There is lots of cabin stuff, so someone must live here, but there are cobwebs hanging from the rafters, so it's probably been a while since anyone stayed here. I didn't see any clothes or hats or anything sitting around. It's kinda like they went on a journey but tidied up their house so it would be ready for them when they returned. Should we go in? I don't think anyone has been here recently, since the tall grass is not bent down and the cobwebs inside the cabin are almost sweeping the floor. What do you two think? It is strange that the lantern is still burning. I can't figure that out, that's for sure."

As the three girls stood there contemplating their circumstances, the distant howling of wolves came to them, carried from the surrounding hills. The howls sounded far off, but Lily knew that was a misconception. She knew wolves had the ability to echo their howls so a human could not distinguish where they actually were. All three girls immediately turned and backed up against the outside wall and stared into the now dark, murky forest.

Lily's mind raced back to the stories her pa had told her about the wolves in Europe and the warnings passed down from one generation to the next. He had told of how wolves can smell fear from miles away and will start running to their victim as soon as the smell of panic reaches their nostrils. He had told Lily and her siblings' stories of wolves in the Black Forest of Germany, howling, calling to the folks living deep in the woods, begging them to come out of their cabins and bring them food.

It was said the forest folk were able to understand what the wolves were saying, and often times they were captivated by it. There were ghastly tales about the fate of the folks who opened their doors to the wolves. The men who had done so had been savagely ripped from their doorways to vanish forever, leaving their families alone in the deep woods to fend for themselves, or worse yet, left to make an attempt to get out of the forest before the next nightfall when the wolves would again come calling.

"We're going inside right now!" Lily quickly said, grabbing one of Gertie P's hands. Ophelia grabbed the other hand and the two of them ran to the front of the cabin, dragging Gertie P. along with them. Just a few steps before reaching the tiny front porch stoop, they heard guttural growls coming from the edge of the forest. Glancing back, chests tightening with the weight of fear, they saw fiery orbs – red eyes – spark in the darkness as the pack of hungry wolves sprang through the trees and charged across the clearing.

Gertie P. let out a high-pitched shriek. Not hesitating for a second, all three of them flew onto the stoop. Lily pushed the door open, thanking God that the door was not locked, and she and Ophelia shot inside the cabin, pulling Gertie P. stumbling along behind them. Lily and Ophelia slammed the door shut and slid the latch; with shaking legs, they slumped against the closed door.

With only two inches of wooden door between them and the children, the wolves snarled and growled as they started scratching and clawing at the wooden door. One of the wolves jumped up and tore at one of the windows. Lily and Ophelia ran to different windows, slammed the shutters closed and slid the latches across each shutter. Gertie P. backed away from the door, screaming loudly.

Suddenly the wolves began running away from the cabin in a flurry of loud yelps and howls. They sounded afraid.

Lily and Ophelia looked at each other with relief in their eyes.

"That was a close call!"

"You can say that again."

"I think I'm kind of bleeding down my stocking," Gertie P said in a quavering, squeaky little voice.

"Ophelia," Lily continued speaking, not even noticing what Gertie P. had said. "Did you feel the movement of, maybe, like a *person* brushing past us when we jumped through the door?"

"Yes I did! In fact, I felt more than one – whatever it was – brush past us."

Lily and Ophelia had completely forgotten about Gertie P., who was still standing in front of the door with tears streaming down her dirty face.

"Gertie P," Lily said as she walked across the floor, "are you okay?"

"No," Gertie P blubbered. "One of those devil-wolves scratched my leg. He got a good hold on my dress with his teeth, but you and

Ophelia jerked me away from him in the nick of time. I had my head turned around watching him. He was a mean one! He had blue eyes, and the whites of his eyes were red!"

Gertie P. stood still, continuing to stare at the door with tears running down her face, her sobs breaking the silence.

"Lily," Gertie P. finally said, looking up to her. "You know what he did just as you and Ophelia slammed that door? He winked at me! I saw it! It was like he was grinning and then he winked at me! I do believe he was ol' Beelzebub himself!"

Lily pulled Gertie P. close and held her, trying to comforting the little rascal.

"Well, whatever he was, you're safe now. Let's see what we can find to clean up that scratch on your leg."

Gertie P. turned so Lily could check out her stocking where blood was seeping through. The back of her dress hem had a large hole torn in it.

As Lily fixed Gertie P.'s dress and the scratch on her leg, Ophelia picked up a broom and began sweeping the cobwebs from the rafters. When Lily was finished with Gertie P., she picked up a shorter broom and pushed the fallen cobwebs into a pile next to the outside door.

Looking around the room, Lily noticed a long, wooden table pushed up against the wall under the window she had been peeking into while they were still outside the cabin. It had thick, sturdy legs and a bulky, solid top. The table was clean as a whistle and whoever lived here had rubbed oil into the top, making it shiny and smelling clean. Sitting on top of the table were a couple tin pie plates, some tin cups, rags, an old, tin coffee pot, what looked like a tin of coffee, two books, and a stack of old papers. Hanging on the wall next to the table were three ropes of dried apples and a rope of dried onions.

Sitting on the table, leaning against the wall, was a large wind-up clock with various trinkets and personal keepsakes lined up on either side of it – a few hand-carved animals and a young woman. Lily picked the female figure up and studied the fine details. It was like looking at a miniature person. The only color on the figure was the eyes, which had been painted blue with extreme detailing.

Sitting the figure back in its place, she turned to Gertie P. and said, "You are one lucky young lady. That wolf almost got you, didn't he?"

"Yes he did, Lily, yes indeed! I thank the Good Lord on high, as my Granny would say, for having you and Ophelia snatch me through that door in the nick of time!" She shuddered. "It was scary! It truly was mighty scary. I'm beholden that my best friend Tessa wasn't here! I don't think she could bear this. No," She stared into space for a few seconds then shook her head sharply. "No, I don't think she could bear it at all. I will definitely have to tell her this whole tale. Don't you be telling her first, Lily Quinn. She's my best friend in this whole world, so I should be the one to tell her. Okay?"

Gertie P. was standing with her hands on her hips and a scowl on her face as she stared at Lily.

"Okay, Gertie P. You can tell Tessa."

Ophelia had unrolled the feather tick onto the cot and was already lying down. She looked so comfortable. Lily and Gertie P walked over and sat down beside her.

Opening her eyes, Ophelia said, "Let's grab some of those dried apples before we fall asleep. I'm still hungry. Those berries sure didn't fell up my belly – how about you all?"

"Sounds good to me," Gertie P. replied, jumping up and grabbing a rope.

Sitting the rope of apples on the cot, all three of them ate as many as their stomachs could hold before lying back and trying to get comfortable.

"Let's all lay sideways on this cot, that way we can all fit a mite better."

"No, no, no. I can't sleep that way," Gertie P. stated firmly.

"Okay then, scootch on over and make some room, or we will never fit on this little bed."

After scooting and scootching around a bit, they finally got comfortable. It was still a hot night, but Lily knew the night air might bring in a chill, so she pulled a patchwork quilt onto their feet. Soon all three girls were sound asleep.

# 7

## THE HAINTS AND JOHN "LIVER-EATING" JOHNSON

Lily awoke to someone tapping her leg over and over.

"Stop it," she mumbled.

*Tap, tap, tap.*

Lily frowned before she opened her eyes and looked at Gertie P. and Ophelia. Without even looking at her, Gertie P. continued poking Lily's leg. Glancing over to where Gertie P. and Ophelia were staring, Lily saw what they were gawking at.

The window shutters, which Lily and Ophelia had tightly closed and locked, were now wide open, flooding the little cabin with flickering, feathery moonlight. A slight, chilly breeze blew gently through the open windows, making the flimsy curtains flutter softly in its wake. In front of the dark, wooden table sitting against the far wall, a young woman stood dressed in a delicate, white dress, which was floating and swirling around her with the slightest movement of her body. The dress was translucent and glistening in the iridescent light of the moon; it seemed to mov around the woman on its own power. She was humming a slow version of the tune "Yankee Doodle". The rhythmic movement of her body was slow and graceful; her silvery-blonde hair swayed with the music, cascading down her back and reaching almost to her knees, swirling around her dress. It was hauntingly mesmerizing. Wispy tendrils of hair floated above her head as she turned one way and then another. Sitting on the top of her head was a little small white cap with ruffles around the edges. It was not big enough to serve a purpose of any kind.

Lily could see the table right through the woman. She appeared to be a glistening figment of imagination. Every detail about the woman could clearly be seen, but she definitely was not a flesh-and-blood person. Then, with a faster tempo, the fascinating apparition began singing the merry tune with a beautiful, haunting voice as she mixed what looked like bread dough in a large wooden bowl. After each chorus, flour would go flying about the room in clouds of white puffy dust as she raised her hands above her head, gave a few snappy claps and called out "America!"

Abruptly, she stopped singing and danced a little jig, clogging her thick-soled shoes against the wooden floor.  She spun around in a circle, clapping her hands above her head, still stomping the wooden floor with her shoes. On the third spin-around, she came to a startled halt right in from of Lily, Ophelia and Gertie P.

Lowering her hands to her sides, the woman gave the girls a little curtsy and spoke with a lovely smile and a British lilt.

"Welcome to our humble dwelling, my ladies. What an honor it is to have you as guests. Our usual guest, a rather grumpy old curmudgeon, has not visited in quite some time now. All he endeavors to do is shoot at us with his strange-looking musket and give a yell-out whenever he catches a glimpse of Polly Susannah. He does frighten her so.

I do hope you delight in your holiday here. Haggis and porridge will be ready precisely at nine-o'-clock, my ladies. Polly Susannah, Agatha and I were on the *Mary Rose*, sailing splendidly across the ocean for the Americas when she went down off the coast of South Carolina. What a terrifying, ghastly experience that was. Agatha would not accept the fact that we were lost to the violent sea – she kept holding onto that wooden beam and screaming for someone to help us. Well, there was absolutely not one living soul lingering about to help, since they too had all sank to the bottom of the raging sea.

So I hugged my Polly Susannah to my bosom, and we too sank to the bottom of the wretched sea, with Agatha holding onto my bustle. I remember seeing dolphins and beautiful fish leaping and swimming in circles around us then all went black. But here we are now in this beautiful cabin in this wonderful American wilderness, and Percival came to join us as quickly as he could. Isn't that a splendid thing? Were you also on the *Mary Rose*? She was a beautiful ship, was she not? Percival's ship, the *Angustieas*, went down off the coast of Florida with all that treasure aboard; none of which matters now, for – as you can see – we finally made it here, exactly where we are supposed to be. A splendid jolly turn out, tis it not?"

Not knowing what to say to an apparition, the girls lay there staring at the young woman. The woman looked to be about Caitlin's age, with striking blue eyes and freckles across the bridge of her nose. Somewhat startled, Lily realized the wooden figure on the mantle was a carving of this young woman.

The woman stood there for a moment, smiling at them, then tilted her head to one side and said with her lilting British accent, "Polly Susannah, are you hiding under the feather coverlet again? I can see you, my silly daughter, so you may as well come out and greet our beautiful, young visitors before you frighten them. If you hurry, we shall take tea and scones out and have our tea with Pa-pa."

The woman gave a soft, tinkling laugh, dusted off her hands, gave the girls another little curtsy and vanished in a swirl of glittering sparkles that scattered across the cabin like snowflakes.

Lily, Ophelia and Gertie P. watched in bafflement as the coverlet at the end of the bed began to move, as if someone was wrestling around trying to get out. Then there at the foot of the bed stood a little girl about Gertie P.'s age. She was dressed just as the woman had been; her hair was also silvery-blonde. But instead of being in long beautiful curls flowing down her back, Polly Susanna's hair looked as if she had taken the scissors to it. One side was whacked off within two inches of her scalp and the other side was frizzed around her face and shoulders. On her nose sat a pair of spectacles exactly like

Gertie P.'s. Her eyes were twinkling with mischief, and she had a big grin on her face. She looked at them with intense curiosity. Lifting her pointer finger, she leaned across the bed and touched each one of their noses as she counted.

"Number one girl, number two girl, and number three girl! And you ALL look beef-witted! I must have jargogled your heads! And look at you!" she said with gusto as she gave Gertie P.'s toe a good tweaking. "Your hair looks like elf-locks!"

She leaned further across the foot of the bed, squeezed her eyes shut, threw back her head, and opened her mouth wide as she laughed loudly, all the while pointing at them.

She twirled around a few times, making her dress flow into a milky-white cloud of sparkles as it floated around her body; with a giggle she reached over and gave Gertie P.'s big toe another good, hard tweaking and stuck her tongue out, showering all of them with sparkly spit. She skipped out through the closed door, calling out, "Come Periwinkle, let us go see Pa-pa!"

Immediately, the bed began to bounce wildly up and down with scratching and scrambling sounds coming out from underneath. Out scurried a big, shimmering, transparent dog!

"Must be Periwinkle," Lily thought.

Periwinkle had transparent drool dripping off his big, transparent tongue, and his scruffy fur glistened brightly in the moonlight. It looked as if Polly Susannah had given him the same haircut she had given herself. On one side of his body his fur was so short it stuck straight up, and the other side was long and shaggy, reaching almost to the floor. Stopping at the end of the bed, the big hound looked at the girls and gave a big, whole-body shake, sending sparkles of fireflies shooting into the air. He bounced around the room in a happy frolic before taking off after Polly Susannah. Just before he got to the door, he came to a skidding stop, sprinted back towards the dark, wooden table where the woman had been mixing bread and put his big paws up on the edge of the table. With his mouth he grabbed the bread dough out of the wooden bowl. Whirling around, he stopped, hung his big head down and looked sheepishly at them out of the corner of his eyes as he hunkered down close to the floor and skulked a few feet towards the door. Then he gave the bread dough a big shake and raced out the door; all the while showering flour all over the floor. Out through the closed door he raced, just as Polly Susannah had done. As his last leg was about to go through the door, he stuck his head back in, looked sheepishly at them one more time, then gave his left leg a little jerk and slipped through the door.

Lily, Ophelia and Gertie P. looked at each other for a minute and then started laughing.

"That was scary…and funny!" Gertie P. finally gasped.

"Yes, it was," Lily and Ophelia nodded.

"Do you think there's anyone else in here?"

Ophelia and Gertie P. looked at Lily with wide eyes.

Quietly Lily whispered, "I don't know, but I hope not. That was a dream, right?"

"It's no dream!" Gertie P stated matter-of-factly. "That Polly Susannah gal took my spectacles! How do you like that! She ain't a very nice haint if you ask me, and I don't like her!"

No sooner were the words out of Gertie P.'s mouth when the door burst open and into the room flew her spectacles, landing with a big bounce on her lap. She gave a little squeal and jumped. Then the door slammed shut.

"Do not be pinching our guest's belongings, Polly Susannah," The sound of the woman's scolding voice came floating through the door. "It is not proper and I shan't be having it. I shall tell Pa-pa straightaway if you do it again."

"But I lost mine in the waves of the sea, Mother," Polly Susannah replied in a sad little voice. "Okay… it shan't happen again."

After staying right where they were, with the coverlet drawn up to their chins for a while, the girls finally worked up enough courage to venture off the bed.

Flour was everywhere. It covered the long tables, the floor and the bed. Even the rafters were showering white, sparkly bits of flour onto the floor. Polly and Periwinkle's foot and paw prints could be followed across the floor and up to the door where they vanished.

"What's Haggis?" Gertie P. asked

"I have no idea, but it doesn't sound very tasty to me!" Lily replied.

On the small pot-bellied stove sat a pot full of hot tea, with a pie-tin full of biscuits next to it. Grabbing up some biscuits, the girls gobbled them down as they took big drinks of tea between bites of biscuits.

"Pretty good for being ghost biscuits, huh?" Gertie P. said with a laugh.

"Let's clean this floor for whoever lives here and then maybe we can get out of here," Lily said.

Lily and Ophelia gathered up the brooms and started sweeping as Gertie P. wiped off the long tables with one of the rags. Together they cleaned and set everything back into its correct spot. Afterwards, the girls stuffed their pockets with the rest of the biscuits and looked around the cabin with satisfaction. They closed the windows and latched the shutters, poured the left over tea onto the bottom of the pot-bellied stove and restacked the wood logs, which had fallen off the neatly arranged pile.

Looking at Gertie P. and Ophelia, Lily motioned them over to the outside door and slowly, just a bit, eased the door open. The night sky was still dark. They saw nothing out of the ordinary; night critters were still calling out to the dark sky and the Great-Horned Owl was still calling its mate.

Looking up into the sky, the girls could see millions of stars twinkling like diamonds on a black velvet cloth in the west. Misty river fog was still hugging the tall grass in the clearing.

Lily took one step out the door, and immediately the creatures of the night became silent; the atmosphere took on an eerie sensation of disturbance. Out of the corner of her eye, Lily caught a hint of dark shadows darting through the fog, moving from tree to tree as if trying to advance on the little cabin without being seen.

Hearing a rustle by the side of the cabin, Lily turned her head and caught a glimpse of a shadow moving near the corner of the cabin. The shadow was too tall to be a wolf, and Lily was sure she saw an arm reaching around the corner as if it were getting ready to move closer. Just as she jumped back inside the cabin and slammed the door shut, she felt a resistance on the door coming from the outside; as if someone had just started to give the door a push to open it. The howl of a coyote came from the roof of the cabin and echoed throughout the forest.

Quick as a wink, Lily threw the bolt across the door and suppressed a shiver as she spoke in a hushed whisper, "It's still too dark," she gasped. "Let's make ourselves a good luck charm to carry through the woods when we decide to leave."

"Good idea," Ophelia whispered back.

"How about a cross?" Gertie P. whispered unsteadily. "Granny always carries one with her and she says it has saved her life many a time."

"That sounds like a good idea to me," Lily stated nervously.

Not bothering to light the lantern, all three girls sat down in a circle under one of the windows. The bright light of the moon streamed through the slits in the shuttered window and illuminated the small area on the floor where they sat. They began to rip one of the rags from the table into ribbons and braided themselves each a cross to carry in their pockets. Once they finished, they each had a little raggedy-looking cross. They agreed on the idea to leave two strings hanging from the top them so they could be tied to their wrists; that way, evil spirits who may be lurking in the woods would see the crosses and be frightened away. They were mighty sure it would work, because Gertie P. insisted Granny Wilkes would agree.

"Also," Ophelia said in a hushed whisper, "as we run through the forest we have to keep our arms swinging high in the air so the evil spirits will see our crosses and dare not come close to us."

Ophelia barely got the words out of her mouth they heard someone whistling. All three girls stopped whispering and froze right where they sat as they tried to hear whoever was approaching. Lily saw a shadow move across the window pane through the shutters.

Grabbing onto Ophelia's arm, Lily stared at the other window. They all stared in silence. The shadow moved to the door and turned the latch.

*Rattle.*

*Rattle.*

With every movement, the door shoved inward a bit. After trying the door, the shadow walked to one of the windows.

*Click. Click. Rattle.*

Frozen to the floor, the girls barely breathed as they watched the windows for any shattering glass.

"I think we have a peeper," Ophelia whispered.

*Click. Click!*

The shadow tried to get in through the door again. Gertie P. gave a little whine of fear.

Lily took Gertie P.'s hand and held on to it while silently putting her finger to her lips, motioning to Gertie P. to be very quiet.

"They can't get through the bolt," Lily mouthed to the girls. "The latches on the shutters and the bolt on the door are too strong, even for a grown man."

Abruptly, the door started shaking violently as the shadow tried to get inside.

"Zebadiah Monroe, you in there? Let me in!" A man's deep voice yelled through the closed door. Then muttering, as if to himself, he said, "You dang Monroe's be the most pesterin' fellers on God's green earth."

Yelling louder than before he yelled out, "Let me in, you crazy old man, or I'm a'gonna bust this here door down and then get you and all your eleven brothers and tie all of ya up to a tree and pour honey on ya for the bars!"

Immediately Lily jumped up and snatched up all their things as Ophelia softly ran over and grabbed the rifle off the wall. Ophelia

knew she probably couldn't shoot it, but at least it might scare whoever it was off and saw a rifle pointed at them.

*Bang! Bang! BANG!* The pounding persisted.

"Dad-blame it, Zebadiah!" the man bellowed.

An animal's guttural growl came from outside the door as the
girls quietly backed against the far wall of the cabin.

With her heart pounding and her chest heaving from fear, Lily
put her head against the wall; instantly the wall opened behind her.

Grabbing Gertie P. and Ophelia's arms, Lily pulled both of them
into the little room she had backed into. The room was barely big
enough for the three of them to squeeze into. The little room was
black as pitch, and Lily was sure it was full of spiders, and probably
snakes too, but it was a great hiding place for right now. It must have
been carved out of the hill behind the cabin as a hiding place. Lily
and Ophelia felt around to find something to bolt the door shut, but
there was nothing around that they could feel.

Gertie P. once again began whimpering so Lily and Ophelia
wrapped their arms around her until she calmed down.

"Find a crack, if you can," Lily whispered. "Let's see if we can
watch the outside door."

"Right here's one," Gertie P. said in a shaky little whisper. "Right
here by my face."

She was able to peek out the long, narrow crack in the hidden
door, and Lily found another good-sized crack right under the fireplace mantle. This one looked as if it had intentionally been created
for peeking out. Ophelia found another crack in the door a few inches from the one Gertie P was peeking through.

"The bolt is lifting on the outside door," Ophelia quietly whispered, amazed.

Peering out, Lily watched as gradually, bit-by-bit, the bolt on the
outside door edged up. Whoever was trying to get in had pushed
a long, thin skinning knife between two of the thick door boards
and was slowly pushing it up to raise the bolt. Suddenly the bolt fell

with a loud *THUD* and a man's hand slipped around the edge of the door.

Gertie P. gave a little groan and Lily felt Ophelia put her hand over Gertie P.'s mouth as she whispered in her ear to please be quiet. Gertie P. was holding onto Ophelia for dear life, and Ophelia was hugging her tightly, trying to keep her calm.

Holding her breath, Lily watched the tall, muscular man slowly slip into the cabin and looked guardedly around the room. Stepping through the door, he banged his head against the framework.

"Dad-blame it!" he muttered. "It gets me evertime! Zebadiah, I'm gonna get ya, you ornry old cur dog!"

He was almost as tall as Mr. Bushy, but not quite as big around.

"That old saw-bones cousin of your'n done ruin't my arm, Zebadiah!" The man yelled as he stretched out his right arm and moved his shoulder about; as if trying to get a kink out of his arm.

"Zebadiah Monroe, come on out here!"

The man was dressed in the everyday apparel of a mountain man. He had a fur hat sitting on top of his head with earflaps which could be pulled down over his ears during the bitter cold winters, but right now the earflaps were turned up. His clothes and knee-high boots were made of animal skins. His beard hung almost to his waist; his mustache grew down each side of his mouth and blended with his beard. Sticking out from the bottom of his hat hung a lot of dark brown, wavy hair. His skin was weathered and tanned (as were all mountain men) and his face was full of wrinkles. Lily guessed him to be about the same age as Mr. Bushy, but it was hard to tell with all the facial hair.

Then Lily recognized him. It was John "Liver-Eating" Johnson! Staring in disbelief, Lily recognized him from pictures she had seen. She remembered the tales and rumors about him. He was once married to a beautiful Flathead Indian woman who was killed by a group of young, renegade Crow Indians. That began John's long hunt for revenge. Folks who knew him back when the incident happened said he went on a mad rampage, seeking revenge for his wife, and his rage continued to this day. As each report filtered into the small river towns, parents spoke in hushed whispers about his capers. Women-folk called him a hero and said, "Good for him; no man should lose his wife to a murdering bunch of renegades". The men folk had great respect for Johnson and his courage. Rumor had it that he got his nickname by eating the liver of his victims. Hopefully that was just rumor. Silently standing behind the peephole, Lily kept that thought in mind and did not move a muscle!

In through the door walked the biggest black dog Lily had ever seen. Its head seemed to be as big as a barrel and its body was large enough for Gertie P. to ride him like a horse. Its eyes were gleaming, bright, and yellow-green, and they were staring straight at Lily.

"Stay!" John commanded.

The big, black dog walked further into the cabin and sat down on his haunches in front of the open door, all the while keeping his evil-looking yellow eyes focused directly at Lily and the fire-place. It was as if he knew she and the girls were hiding behind the fireplace.

Another low drawn-out guttural growl rose from deep within the dog's chest. It wasn't loud, but Lily could hear it.

"Oh, Lordy," Lily thought.

John stood in the doorway of the cabin for a few seconds before stepping in and closing the door behind himself and the dog.

He stood there looking around for a minute, pulled out his pistol and kept it in his hand as he walked over to the long, wooden table which stood along the side of the cabin and looked around as if hunting for someone lurking in the shadows. Slowly, he put his hand under the table and gave a jerk. Out fell a big skinning knife and a rifle. Again he put his hand under the table and jerked out a smaller pocket knife.

In a low, gravelly voice John spoke quietly, without even looking at the fireplace.

"Pake McEnnis, if that's you, and not Zebadiah Monroe behind my farplace, you cowardly pile of dog's dung, ya better come out right now." Slowly he raised his pistol and pointed it right at Lily without lifting his eyes to see where he was aiming.

Lily could not believe her ears!

"Oh horse-feathers," Lily thought. "This must be "Liver-Eating" John's cabin! Maybe we should have taken our chances with the wolves. God love a duck, we are goners for sure."

She quietly pulled Ophelia close and whispered quietly who the person was. Gertie P was shaking pretty badly, but was doing a great job of not letting out a peep.

Turning back to the peep hole, Lily watched as "Liver-Eating" Johnson whipped his head toward the back of the cabin and cocked it to one side as if listening for something. Slowly he turned his whole body and stared at the fireplace for what seemed like forever. Then he turned his head and stared at the bed.

The bed had been fixed exactly the way the girls had found it, but there on the bed frame hung Gertie P.'s spectacles, with her long, pink hair ribbon tied in a bow and hanging off one earpiece!

In two steps he was at the side of the bed picking up the spectacles. Turning them around in his hands, he kept looking back at the fireplace and then back at the spectacles. Slowly he raised the spectacles to his face and tried to put them on.

Bending the ear wires out, "Liver-Eating" John stretched the spectacles across his face and tried to make them reach his ears.

He held the spectacles up to his face and looked around the cabin. The ear wires were hooked into the hair on the side of his face and the round glasses were perched on the top of his nose.

"Whoa", he said in a soft voice. "This little gal is blind as a bat!"

Looking over at the fireplace and giving a deep-chested chuckle, he laid the spectacles down on the bed, picked up his knives, rifle, and the pistol, and turned towards the door.

Just before he shut the door behind himself, he yelled out, "Y'all can come on out from my farplace hidey-hole and get these here spectacles back on that little gal's face. She's as blind as a bat! I'm leavin' and won't be back fur a long time since it's getting' a mite crowded in these here woods. Take the old rifle with ya when ya leave, since ya already have it with ya and ya might need it against them there haints that be forever and a day pesterin' me. Jest give 'em a big ol' scream and shoot off that thur rifle at 'em and they'll take off fur a bit!"

He slammed the door shut, walked off the front stoop and was gone, whistling as he went.

All three girls stood silently for a bit as they continued staring out the peep holes in the wall, then Lily pushed the hidden door panel open and wordlessly they all filed out and stood inside the cabin's main room.

"Who was that?" Gertie P asked.

"Just some mountain man I guess," Lily said as she and Ophelia looked at each other knowingly. There was no way they were going to tell Gertie P. the story of John "Liver-Eating" Johnson.

"He was plenty scary. And so was his dog," Gertie P. whispered, wide-eyed.

"Okay," Lily said as she walked over and placed the bolt back across the outside door. "It's not light enough for us to leave just yet, so let's lay down a bit longer until daylight comes on." Lily acted as if nothing strange had just happened. "I'm still a bit tired, how about you?"

"So am I," Ophelia said with a yawn.

"Me too," Gertie P. piped up in her little squeaky voice.

They unrolled the feather tic and each of them grabbed a blanket and climbed back onto the bed.

Not too far from the cabin, they could hear gunshots, yelling, and yelping wolves. But, soon they were sound asleep, sleeping too soundly to hear the scratching and whining at the door and windows as the hungry wolves returned to the cabin in hopes of finding their prey.

Gertie P. was the only one awakened when the shimmering shadows – the same woman and child, along with a much older woman – returned to the cabin and softly floated around the room, doing what seemed to be daily chores that women from that era in time would be performing early in the morning. The younger woman's body once again took shape next to the wooden table and once more began kneading bread dough in the large wooden bowl.

At first glance, the older woman appeared to be kneading bread dough just as the younger woman, but then the older woman walked to the fireplace and began stirring something in the cast-iron pot hanging inside the fireplace. Actually, there was no fire blazing in the fireplace, but the old woman didn't seem to notice. With great effort the old woman stirred the empty contents of the big iron pot. Every few seconds, hot embers would spark up the chimney as though a real fire was burning.

Gertie P. was mesmerized by the stir of activity going on in the little cabin.

The old woman was dressed in a long, black, mourning dress and her entire head was hidden under a hood attached to the dress. Many times in the past she had seen older women wearing the same type of mourning dress when their husbands passed on.

Hunch-backed and shuffling slowly, the old woman moved about the cabin in a somber mood. Once or twice, Polly Susannah walked over to the old woman, hugged her and kindly took the wooden ladle from her gnarled, bent hands and stirred the contents of the kettle for her.

Only once did Polly Susannah walk over to where Gertie P's spectacles lay and pick them up, looking at Gertie P and grinning widely. As she continued standing beside the bed, her grin slowly disappeared; a solemn gaze and slight frown materialized on her transparent face. Slowly tilting her head to one side, she spoke in a soft solemn voice.

"My Pa-pa drowned in the sea just like Granny, Mama and me. For a long time he was with us here in the wilderness, but now he said he has to go on to someplace else. Now I am a part-orphan just as you are. Me, Mama and Granny fell off the ship when it was on its side and now we don't know if we should go find Pa-pa or stay here. Mama wants to stay in this beautiful cabin if Pa-pa is with us, but now he is gone and we don't know what to do or where to go or even how to get there. Do you know where we should go or how to get there? Who are you and where did you come from? Can you help us find my Pa-pa? You are all street waifs, is that not right? There are many street waifs in England, huh? You sure do look like street waifs with your strange tattered clothes, elf-locks and bloody stockings. And your friends are wearing men's britches. Did the lot of you come from a faraway country like the South Pacific Islands? No… you have red hair, so you must be from Ireland?"

Polly Susannah grinned broadly and stated matter-of-factly, "Well, Ireland is a fine place to hail from, my wee friend! So we can be friends, can we not?"

The younger woman turned and spoke solemnly to Polly Susannah and immediately Polly Susannah carefully sat the spectacles down.

"She needs some glasses," Gertie P. thought to herself. Periwinkle was asleep on the foot of the bed with his big head resting on Gertie P.'s feet, but she could not feel the heaviness of his head. Every so often, his tail would start wagging and he would let out a soft "woof".

The older woman stood up, turned to the younger woman and spoke with a tender tone.

"Victoria."

Then, just as silently as they had appeared, the four apparitions slowly began wavering and small fragments of their images slowly floated away in a sparkling array of tiny, twinkling orbs of light as they faded into nothingness.

Gertie P. jumped out of bed, grabbed her glasses and shoved them into Polly Susannah's transparent hand. The little girl-ghost put them on her face and grinned at Gertie P.

Just before they were completely gone, Polly Susannah turned, looked at Gertie P. with a big smile, lifted her hand and gave a little wave with her pointer finger. Then they vanished completely. The only thing left behind was the aromatic smell of stew cooking and the glittering of surreal sparkles.

Right before the last bit of sparkling dust left the cabin; the glasses sailed back into the room from thin air and once again landed in Gertie P's lap. The sound of tinkling laughter echoed throughout the little cabin. Attached to the wire rim of her glasses was another pink ribbon.

"Fine! I didn't want to give them to you anyway. Besides, I need them more than you do!" Gertie P muttered. "And thank you kindly for the pink ribbon! Pink is my favorite color."

Gertie P rolled over as much as she could, and fell back to sleep.

# 8

## AUNT DOLLIE AND "BOB" THE INDIAN

The moment she opened her eyes, Lily knew morning had come to the little cabin in the woods. Wispy tendrils of warm sunshine slipped between the cracks in the shutters and filled the room with warm smells of morning as the hot, humid heat of southern Missouri started staking its claim on the day.

Puffs of dust motes playfully floated in and out of the velvety rays of sunshine. White, fluffy dandelion seeds had slipped through the windowsills and were now dancing and twirling alongside the dust motes like miniature fairy skirts, twisting and turning with each puff of air. The chirping of a multitude of birds and the early morning call of a hawk released the tension built up in Lily's shoulders. She relaxed a little. She stretched and yawned.

"I smell stew cooking," Lily said to no one in particular.

"Hmmm…yeah, I reckon so," Ophelia muttered, half asleep.

Sitting up, Lily realized there was too much room in the bed. Gertie P.'s spot was empty!

Instantly awake, she glanced over at the door. It was still bolted shut, as were all the windows. Ophelia was still sound asleep.

"Gertie P.?" Lily yelled.

"Gertie P.! Where are you?"

Ophelia bolted up with a dazed look on her face.

"Where is she?" Ophelia asked frantically.

"Gertie P.!" Lily and Ophelia yelled at the same time.

"What?" A muffled voice yelled out. "I'm back here in this little room. I found some stuff we may be able to use."

The back wall swung open and out walked Gertie P.

"What is that?" Lily asked.

"It's a storage room, and it leads right into the little space we hid in last night."

"What?"

"Its a room with a lot of old junk stuffed into it. I found some old cooking pans and some moth-eaten blankets. There is a window at the very top of the room so the sunshine can light it up."

"Where is that smell of stew coming from?" Lily asked Gertie P.

"The haints came back last night and they had Granny Agatha with them and she was cooking stew over the empty fireplace, even though the fire really wasn't burning. But unlike the biscuits, there is no stew for us to eat this morning. And that little gal haint put another pink ribbon on my spectacles and threw them at me again. She thinks we are all orphans."

"Why didn't you wake us up?"

"Because I didn't want to, is why."

"Oh… Okay," Ophelia said as she rolled her eyes. "I guess that's a good enough reason for you."

Gertie P. spoke again in a whisper.

"It was different than before; the granny called Polly Susannah's mother Victoria and the granny was dressed in black. Polly Susannah and her mother were not singing or laughing and Polly Susannah stood beside me and told me about her Pa and how he died in that ship and now he left them because he had to go someplace else and Polly Susannah and her Mama don't know where they are supposed to go.

She also thinks we are all street waifs from Ireland or England. When they finally left, they broke into a thousand sparkly pieces and drifted up through the roof along with that big old hound, Periwinkle."

All three girls sat staring at the ceiling as if maybe the apparitions were sitting on the rafters.

"Well," Lily said, "It looks like they are gone again. Let's eat something."

All of them took the biscuits and dried apples from their pockets, and gobbled them down.

Cautiously Lily walked over and eased the front door open. Nothing seemed to be amiss about the early morning. Sunlight was winding its fingers through the thick forest as it flicked away the last remaining bits of fog and eased itself into the little clearing. The mournful cry of a Lake Loon echoed across the river and was carried up to the cabin with the morning breeze. An answering call resonated from further away.

Soothing coos from Mourning Doves filled the air, and wild flowers opened their eyes as they lifted their heads to the early morning warmth of the sun. Day critters were singing their songs and calling out to the world. Nothing was awry in the forest as daybreak slid its fingers into the forest, flicking the shadows away from the hidden places and coaxed the trees and ferns awake. Squirrels and chipmunks bustled around trying to find food for their morning meal.

Standing on the little front stoop, the girls quietly looked around for a few minutes as they took in the calming comforts of the Missouri morning. There were no signs of the wolf pack from the night before and no evidence of the ghost-like apparitions they had encountered during the dark hours of the night.

"Well, are we ready to go?" Lily asked as she pulled the door shut behind them.

"I think so, Lily. Let's go," Ophelia answered.

"Come on you two," Gertie P. yelled as she jumped off the stoop and took off running, "I want to go see my best friend and have a grand chat about my adventure."

Off they ran with Gertie P. leading the way, all of them holding their handmade crosses high above their heads so as to scare away haints or spirits who may be lingering in the semi-dark shadows of the forest.  When they reached the edge of the path, they stopped, took a good look down both ways and stepped out onto the path.

"I'm taking off my shoes so I can feel the warm dirt," Lily said as she bent down and removed her shoes.

"Ahhh, this feels so good," Gertie P. said; she too stepped out of her shoes.

Lily shuffled her feet in the powdery dust, enjoying the feel of the sun-warmed earth.

"Come on," Lily said. "Let's keep running for a while and maybe we can reach a town – or maybe even Caruthersville – before the day gets too far along. I have no idea where we are or how far down we floated on that raft."

"Sounds good to me," Ophelia said as she and Gertie P slung their shoes around their necks. "And while we're at it, let's see if we can find us some wild berries again. I'm still hungry."

After walking a while, they slowed down and began looking at the sides of the path for wild berries. Finding a large patch of blue-berries, they all reached into the bushes and began picking them as fast as they could eat them. The berries were small but tastied mighty fine after eating such a little bit of food for so long.

*Clomp, clomp, clomp.*

The sound of a horse slowly plodding along the hard-packed earth echoed over the hills.

All three girls stopped, turned around and looked back down the pathway from where they had come. There, in the distance, was a lone horse pulling a wagon as it leisurely trudged toward them. It was too far away to make out who was driving the wagon, but Lily didn't feel any alarms going off in her head, so the three of them stood along the edge of the wagon path waiting for the wagon to catch up with them, hoping they could hitch a ride.

When the wagon drew a little closer, Lily realized the horse was an old, worn-out nag. His back was swayed so low a rider's feet would drag the ground if they were to get on the poor fella's back. To keep the sun out of the old horse's eyes, on his head sat an old, straw hat with holes cut out for his ears to keep the hat on his head; the brim of the hat was wide and floppy and hung down along the sides of his throatlatch, its hide was dirty brown, and its mane and tail were almost white. He looked like an old Palomino whose days of beauty were long gone. The old fella had his head down and was taking his time, nodding his head and plodding along the wagon path.

The driver was tall, but Lily couldn't yet make out if it was a man or a woman. As the wagon drew a bit closer, Lily could see they were wearing overalls and a short-sleeved shirt, so it could be a man, but on the person's head sat another straw hat just like the old horse's hat and this one had a great big sunflower stuck into the brim. Lily determined it was a woman. There was also a dog sitting beside the woman, and on its head was a hat just like the old horse's hat. It was the ugliest dog Lily had ever seen. Its head was huge and even from the distance, Lily could see drool hanging from its mouth like strings. The dog was covered in copper-colored fur. It looked a little shaggy. Its jowls hung down to the middle of its neck, pulling its face down with it. As the wagon drew even closer, Lily noticed the bottoms of the dog's eyes were also pulled downward, exposing the underside of his eyeballs. It was one sad looking hound dog.

"Good grief and gopher holes!" Gertie P. blurted out. "What in the name of tarnation is she doing here?"

Lily looked over at Gertie P. who was standing in the middle of the wagon path with her hands on her hips and a defiant look on her face.

As the wagon drew closer, Lily could hear the driver singing a catchy little tune. As soon as the driver noticed the girls standing beside the road, she started pulling back on the old horse as if the poor old horse was flying along the pathway like a streak of lightning.

"Whooaa, Ebenezer. Whooaa," the driver called out loudly. "Ease up there boy; take it eeeeeasy."

"The only way Ebenezer is going to 'ease up' any," Lily thought to herself, "is to fall over dead right on the spot."

As soon as the old horse came to a complete stop, the driver stood up, put her hands on her hips and stared at Gertie P. By now the woman was close enough for Lily to see her hair – a long, blonde braid wrapped around her head. Her face was distorted into an awful scowl. She was a big-boned woman, quite tall, with arm muscles that looked like a man's. Her eyes were as blue as a pleasant summer sky, but the angry look on her face was a bit frightening.

The big hound stood up on all-fours and started barking with its ears standing straight up and its tail wagging furiously. He launched himself off the bench and hit the ground running, racing toward the girls. His jowls were flapping back, revealing all of his huge teeth, and globs of drool were flying everywhere. Lily and Ophelia froze right where they were, but Gertie P. bent down, held out both her hands and yelled, "STOP!"

The big hound skidded to a stop and plopped down on his haunches within inches of Gertie P.'s face. She put her hands on the big hound's head and vigorously rubbed his ears as she looked straight into his eyes.

"Good boy, Barnabas, good boy!" Gertie P. said.

The dog gave her a big, slobbery lick right on her face.

Slowly, Lily eased her way over and stood beside Gertie P., so as to shield her from the woman's wrath, but Gertie P. shoved her out of the way, stood up and gave the woman another one of her famous face-distorting frowns. Gertie P.'s mouth was in a downward grimace and her eyebrows were forced down so far, Lily could barely see her eyes. Her nose wrinkled up like a little prune stuck on her face.

The woman's face was just as distorted as Gertie P.'s was! In fact, except for their hair color, they looked like mother and daughter!

Both the woman and Gertie P. stood there frowning and staring at each other for a few minutes until finally the woman spoke up and yelled out, "Stop starin' and frownin' at me, ya little sassy-pants, and get your sorry self into this here wagon. Gertrude Primrose Patterson Wilkes, what do you think you're doing way down here in Mississippi? Do your mama and papa know where you are? And what do you think

Granny Wilkes is going to say about this, huh? She's gonna tan yor hide good is what she is going to do! And who, by the way, are these sorry-looking gals you have with you? What did ya'll do, fall into a mud hole and waller around? Are you three running away from home or something?"

The woman looked angrily over at Lily and Ophelia. "Gertie P. is way too young to be hanging out with the two of you. What's the matter with your heads, huh?"

By now, Lily could see and hear the resemblance between the two of them. "Good grief," Lily thought. "Lord have mercy on this world, here's another Gertie P. But this one's all grown up into a grown woman. This could be danger for the whole country."

Gertie P. also had her hands on her hips.

"Ain't none of your business so get out of here and mind your own bees-wax, Aunt "Nosy-Rosy sittin' on a Posy"! Go on now! Git!"

"The only gettin' I'm gettin', young lady," the woman shouted loudly as she made a move to get down from the wagon, "is I'm gettin' down from here and I'm gonna snatch you up and whoop your bottom for havin' such a sassy mouth."

Then she climbed down from the wagon and started walking toward Gertie P. That was when Lily realized Aunt "Nosy-Rosy sittin on a Posy" had a baby riding in a pouch attached to her back. The baby was peeking over the aunt's shoulder and gave Lily a big, toothless smile. He had a head full of blond, curly hair and big blue eyes.

Lily stepped forward and started waving her hands in the air.

"Hold on, hold on, both of you. Gertie P, we are not going to chase off anyone who may be able to help us, and I do believe you should talk a little nicer to your Aunt.

"Aunt Nose – er, Ma'am – I think you have the wrong idea of what we are doing here. We didn't run away and drag Gertie P with us. We were nabbed by some menfolk who planned on taking us down to New Orleans to sell to the island slave traders and we managed to get away and then we had to spend the night in an old, haunted cabin way out in the woods. We are tired and hungry."

"Ya don't say. Well, I'm Gertie P's Aunt Dollie, and I'm gonna whoop her just cuz she has such a sassy mouth. Come here, you little Irish wildcat!" Aunt Dollie yelled.

"I don't think so, Aunt-Nosey-Rosey sittin'-on-a-Posey." Gertie P. shouted at her aunt. "You can try, but you can't catch me with that butter-ball little Sammy P. on your back!" She took off running down the wagon trail.

"Sammy P.?" Lily thought, "What's with the 'P' business?"

"Citch me if ya kin, citch me if ya kin, Aunt "Nosey-Rosey-sittin'-on-a-Posey!" Gertie P shouted back, mocking Mrs. Dolly's accent. She turned the curve in the trail and disappeared from sight.

Quick as a flash, Mrs. Dollie whipped Sammy P. off her back and thrust him into Lily's arms.

"Hold this here young'un and don't let him down come hell or high water!" she hollered as she took off after Gertie P.

"Get her, Barnabas!" Mrs. Dollie called out to the dog, who, in a mad dash, took off after Gertie P. In just a few flying leap, s Barnabas was ahead of Mrs. Dollie and out of sight as he too turned the curve in the road.

Lily and Ophelia stood there looking after Mrs. Dollie and Barnabas, then down at Sammy P. He was staring right back at them for a few seconds until his little face crumpled into an awful grimace and he started screaming with an ear-piercing howl at the top of his lungs.

Then the old horse, Ebenezer, started stomping his left foot and braying like a mule.

Nervously Lily began patting the baby's back as Ophelia walked over and started rubbing his head. All of a sudden he stopped bellowing, looked at both of them and broke into a big smile which transformed his face into the face of a little blue-eyed angel.

Wiggling and pushing away from Lily, Sammy P. obviously wanted to get down.

"Down. Down peeze," he said with a happy little baby giggle.

"DOWN PEEZE!" he bellowed.

Ebenezer was still braying loudly and stomping the hard packed ground.

"Okay, okay," Lily gently replied.

"You better not!" Ophelia spoke up. "Mrs. Dollie said not to let him down for any reason. She said 'come you-know-what, or high water', so you better not do it."

By this time, Sammy P. was wiggling and squirming so much is was getting difficult to keep a tight hold on him.

"How about," Lily panted, "I'll let him down and we can both hold onto his hands so he can't get away."

"Okay, let's give it a try."

Carefully Lily let Sammy P slide down to the ground, and just as the tip of his toes touched the ground, he was off and running. Faster than Lily or Ophelia could react, he scampered over to Ebenezer and wrapped his arms and legs around Ebenezer's front leg. The old horse stopped braying and returned to quietly munching on the grass growing along the middle of the road.

Both girls walked over to Ebenezer and reached down, thinking to pry Sammy P away from the old horse's leg. Immediately the horse swung out his hind leg, gave a loud snort and tried to give Lily a kick.

"Whoa!" Lily shouted as she jumped away.

Ebenezer laid his ears back and began bellowing again. Then he stomped and kicked at Lily again.

Sammy P. started laughing and Ebenezer kept right on hee-awing, as if he knew he was making Sammy P laugh.

"I think he is a little weasel," Ophelia snickered. "Look at the wicked look on that little face! He knows what he is doing, the little monster."

"Well, horse manure!" Lily muttered.

"Same here," Ophelia laughed.

"What are we going to do now?"

"I don't know, she told you not to let him down."

"I know, I know, but I already did. So, now what should we do?"

"I'll take a dried apple out of my pocket and hold it out to Sammy P. Maybe he's hungry and will come and get it."

"Okay. It's worth a try," Lily said.

"Look what I have, Sam!" Ophelia squatted down and spoke softly, so she wouldn't scare the little guy.

"Shammy!" he frowned and bellowed out his name.

*Stomp. Stomp.* Ebenezer seemed to be agreeing with the baby.

"Okay, look what I have, Sammy."

"Yum… Yum… " Ophelia acted like she was taking a bite out of the apple.

Without hesitating, Sammy P. let go of old Ebenezer's leg and scurried over to Ophelia. Quick as a wink, she snatched him up and backed away from the horse. Ebenezer gave one last bray and went back to chomping on weeds.

"Where are Gertie P., Mrs. Dollie and Barnabas, I wonder?" Lily said to Ophelia.

"I'm sure they caught up with Gertie P. by now, don't you think?"

"I would think so. Let's get in the wagon and go on up the roadway and see if we can find them. What do ya say?"

"Sounds good to me, if you think you can get old Ebenezer to move."

"No problem," Lily replied. "I'll climb up there and you hand Sammy P. to me so I can hold him while you climb up, then we'll move on."

Lily walked over to the wagon, climbed up and reached down and took Sammy P. from Ophelia so she could climb up.

Once they were both seated and Sammy P. was being held tight in Ophelia's arms, Lily took up Ebenezer's reins and gave him a gentle slap on his hind quarters. Slowly Ebenezer came alive and once again began plodding along the pathway.

Lily and Ophelia sat for quite a while in silence, each of them in their own thoughts as the wagon slowly meandered along the road.

"Do you think he could move a little faster?" Ophelia whispered, as she leaned closer to Lily's ear.

"Well, I don't think it would hurt to try." She gave Ebenezer a sharp snap on his hindquarters and sharply urged him on. Old Ebenezer picked up his gait and progressed into a trot.

So, off they went with old Ebenezer bouncing them back and forth with his crazy trot. Eventually they must have gone what seemed like a mile when Ebenezer slowed way down as if he were too winded to go any faster.

Lily looked at Ophelia, and Ophelia looked at Lily.

"Well, where do you think they are?" Lily finally said.

"Beats me."

They both looked around the forest trying to spot the tall Mrs Dollie.

By this time Sammy P had fallen asleep – a good thing, Lily thought.

Off to the right of the wagon, the girls heard the barking of a dog and turned to watch as Barnabas came charging through the trees heading for the wagon. Not far behind him came Mrs. Dollie carrying Gertie P. on her shoulder like a sack of potatoes. She was running fast, and Gertie P. was flopping around like a wet rag.

"Get in the back of the wagon!" Mrs. Dollie yelled as she ran towards them. "Quick! Get in the back of the wagon and take Sammy P. with you."

Immediately, Lily and Ophelia scrambled over the buckboard seat and pulled Sammy P. along with them. Sammy P. never opened his eyes. He kept right on sleeping as if nothing was going on around him. Barnabas jumped up onto the seat as Mrs. Dollie dumped Gertie P.'s body next to them on the wagon bed, jumped up onto the seat and gave Ebenezer a sharp slap with the rains and yelled "Hee-yaa! Get going boy. Get us out of here!"

Surprisingly, Ebenezer took off with a burst of energy as he jerked the wagon along the bumpy trail. Every few minutes, Mrs. Dollie V gave the old horse another smack on the hind-quarters to keep him moving along quickly.

Lily was holding Sammy P. tight to keep him from bouncing around the bed of the wagon, and Ophelia had Gertie P.'s head resting on her lap. It wasn't easy holding onto Sammy P. with one hand and the side of the wagon with the other, but Lily managed it.

Finally, Mrs. Dollie pulled back on Ebenezer's reins and called out, "Hold up there boy, let's slow-down a bit and give your poor old bones a rest."

With that said, Ebenezer eased down to his usual slow plod.

"Lily, put Sammy in my back sling and you two gals get on up here beside me. Barnabas, get in the back and keep an eye on Gertie P. If she wakes up, you let me know. Come on up here you two, and I'll be tellin' ya what happened."

After putting Sammy P. in Mrs. Dollie's sling and climbing over the buckboard seat, Lily asked her what in the world had happened.

"Well, to start with," Mrs. Dollie said, "Please don't call me Mrs. Dollie or Mrs. Dollie Violet. That's what my granny was called and it drives me crazy when people call me that. You can call me Aunt Dollie. Drop that P business too. You can call Sammy just plain old Sammy. That P stands for Patterson. All our middle names are either Violet or Patterson and that is irritating. I don't know why Mama and Papa gave us all the same middle names, but I don't like it. The only reason I gave it to Sammy is because Mama was there when I birthed him.

"Well," Aunt Dollie said as she looked back down the road, "when me and Barnabas finally caught up with that there wild young'un, low-and-behold, so had two of those men who snatched you gals from Caruthersville. One of them already had Gertie P. slung over his shoulder and was tramping off through the woods with her. Luckily, Barnabas saw them before I did and he stopped right in the middle of the road—giving me the sign of trouble brewing—so I stopped, squatted down so's no one could see me and took me a good look-round. When I finally spotted them I discovered I wasn't too far behind, so I was able to sneak up on those two. Me and Barnabas followed them fellers for a bit and we could hear them talking. They were talking just as if they were the only ones around for miles, too stupid to realize Gertie wouldn't be out there all by herself I guess. And it seems as if, after you gals got away from them, they shoved those two other fella's into the river and beat them with the rafter's poles every time they tried to get back on board. And then these two fellas were on their way back to Caruthersville ta nab you three gals and do away with ya! They were going to stash Gertie somewhere and go back down this here road and find the two of ya. Listening to the way they talked, both of them fellas are from the Louisiana bayous.

"Well, after listening for a bit, I quietly reached down and picked me up a big ol' solid tree branch and started running at them. Well, I caught 'em by surprise but they heard me coming a few seconds before I took a powerful swing with that tree branch and smacked that skinny Cajun fella right in the jaw making a couple of his teeth fly right out of his mouth. I was aimin' for his head but I was a bit off. The other fella dropped Gertie, and then Barnabas took a flying leap at 'em, knockin' 'em to the ground. If I hadn't snatched up Gertie and started running back to the road, Barnabas would have chewed that fella up. Well, that skinny fella was on the ground rollin' round moaning and groaning and the other feller was cussin' and swearin' at Barnabas. I heard them stumbling up as they started coming after me. I couldn't turn around or I would have lost my hold on Gertie, but I could hear them coming and I think we lost them sometime before we even got close to the wagon trail. I don't think they had horses or they would have caught up with me real quick-like. I am mighty glad you gals got old Ebenezer moving and up here close when you did. I might not have been able to go much further with that little whipper-snapper flopping around on my shoulder. So thank you for helping out."

"No problem at all, Aunt Dollie," Lily said solemnly. "Do you think Gertie will be okay when she wakes up?

Aunt Dollie looked over at Lily with a big grin as she said, "Gertie is too mean of a young'un to be bothered by a little thing like a knock on the noggin'."

"Well, I sure hope not," Lily replied, "because if she's hurt, my little sister Tessa is going to attack me like a wild cat for hurting her best friend and I just might as well take off for unknown places."

"Ah-ha… So you're THAT Lily. Lily Quinn, I believe it is, right?" Aunt Dollie laughed as she turned and gazed at Lily. "Gertie's Ma and Pa have told me all about that little Tessa and how Gertie loves her dearly. Gertie thinks she is Tessa's guardian angel, even though Tessa is bigger than she is. Now, tell me. How did you three get into this fine-kettle-of-fish?"

"Yes, I'm Lily Quinn," Lily said with a smile. "And this is my friend Ophelia Knudson. As far as how we got ourselves into this mess, yesterday morning, bright and early, me and Ophelia were walking along the top of the levee going to her house when we met up with Tillie Brown and her horse Tally-Ho."

"Did you say tin-can Tillie?" Aunt Dollie interrupted Lily. "Why, that rowdy woman knows everyone from here to the Garden of Eden. What was she doing along the levee near Caruthersville?" Aunt Dollie laughed robustly as she continued, "Was she 'pinching' something she *urgently* needed, or was she pestering that Mr. Bushy for one of his hides? Tin-can Tillie is known far and wide for following that poor mountain man around and sneaking up on him to pinch one of his hides. Every once in a while she snatches a few hides off his pack mule and takes off running like a wild woman just laughing at the top of her voice. She aggravates that poor fella so much he finally declared he just plain ol' can't stand the woman. Personally I think she does it because it's a fun challenge for her."

"How did she get that name? I've never heard her called tin-can Tillie before."

"I have," Ophelia laughed. "My papa always calls her tin-can Tillie. For a long time, I thought her first name was tin-can and her last name was Tillie"

Aunt Dollie gave another deep hardy laugh and continued with her story.

"Well, the way she got that there particular name was because down south of Natchez just before you get to Baton Rouge, there's a big island called Prophet Island. There was a time when the only person on that island was Tin-can Tillie and she claimed it as her own island. She named it Dennison Island, after her pa I guess, and even went so far as to go into both Natchez, Mississippi and Baton Rouge, Louisiana trying to get them to officially change the name. The reason she wanted it, or so she said, was because it was filled with the spirits of dead Creek Indians who perished in the grisly collision between the steamboat *The Monmouth* and the steamboat *The Warren*; which was towing a sailboat called *The Trenton*. Well, on that fateful dark, foggy, rain drizzling night of October 31, folks who witnessed it said the air was filled with so many souls it looked like a white sheet raising up from that rive. Reporters and newspapers wrote the story of how 360 Creek Indians perished and it is locally believed that their ghosts, to this day, still linger on Prophet Island. It's said that, except for tin-can Tillie, not one person will step a single foot onto that island because the few who attempted it right after the collision vanished and have never been found and its believed their bodies were carried off by all those spirits living on that island.

Now, here's where the tin-can comes in. I don't know why she was on the island when the accident happened, but I reckon she had her reasons. After the accident, Tillie built herself a camp right in the middle of the island and constructed herself a fence all the way around her camp and the fence was strung up with tin cans so close together that if any animal or person came within yelling distance and happened to step on a certain spot, those tin cans would start in ringing like church bells going off on a Sunday morning. And it's said the ringing was that of a funeral song, not just the clanking of tin cans.

Tillie swore the only thing those dead Creek Indian haints wanted was a place of peace from the torment they suffered in that horrible wreck, and they knew her island was the perfect peaceful place.

She knew most of those Creek Indians personally, so she stayed on Prophet Island for a while and paid her respects by burying the dead bodies as they floated up to the islands shoreline. I reckon it took quite a while for all those bodies to be found. After a few years, she figured she had done all she could for her friends, so she moved on. That's when she moved up closer to Caruthersville, I do believe. Before she moved onto Prophet Island she was living down Natchez way in a little cabin close to the river with her six horses and a half dozen or so cats. Now…I don't mean barn cats, I mean mountain cats. She had this one particular big old cat named Puddin' and it was as tame as old Ebenezer here."

"Tame?" Lily thought to herself.

Ophelia poked Lily in the side as she silently mouthed, "Tame?"

Lily giggled, and Aunt Dollie kept right on talking. "Now, I know you gals don't think old Eb is very tame. I heard him braying like a mule while I was running after Gertie P, so you must have done something he didn't like to our little Sammy. Like… maybe you let Sammy's feet touch the ground and off he went, quick as a lightening bug and latched onto old Eb's leg? Old Ebenezer here has some mule blood in him, but the only thing he got from that mule was the braying."

Aunt Dollie laughed loudly and looked over at Lily and Ophelia.

Sheepishly, Lily and Ophelia both looked over at Aunt Dollie and shook their heads yes.

"Well," Aunt Dollie snickered, "I told you not to let him down. He's a fast one, that's for sure. I wasn't fearin' for little Sammy, I was fearin' for you gals. Old Ebenezer doesn't take kindly to anyone pulling Sammy off his front leg. And—

"Well, Lord-love-a-duck." Aunt Dollie stopped talking about old Ebenezer, "Looky-looky at who we have a'coming upon us. Land o' Goshen. I'm not in the mood for this fella today, that's for sure," she said with a deep sigh.

Walking single-file toward them was a large group of Indians. Each and every one, including every woman, was leading a pony.

"They're Kickapoo," Aunt Dollie said in a quiet whisper. "They're mighty friendly folk, so give them a nod and a smile and be respectful."

Lily watched in silence as the wagon and the Indians drew closer. The Indians were dressed just as all the other folks along the river except for the feathers in the men's hair and the pretty beads twined into the women's hair.

Lily had seen many Kickapoo in her life; the women were beautiful and the men were handsome in Lily's eyes.

One Indian in particular stood out from the rest. He was leading the line of his fellow Indians and he was extremely tall. His hair was black as a raven, and his eyes were piercing black as well. His skin had a beautiful red hue to it and he walked with the proud stride of a leader. His hair flowed down his back, almost to his waist; and attached to one side was a cluster of eagle feathers.

Prancing along behind the handsome leader was a Paint horse, and it was just as stunningly handsome as its owner. Its black markings began below its ears and flowed down his back like a cloak as it covered its hindquarters; the rest of its body was white. Its stride was as noble as the man's leading it. With each prancing step, the horse flipped its mane in the breeze.

The Kickapoo women were not in a single line; they were clustered together behind all the men in a large group chattering and laughing among themselves as they led their ponies behind them. The women sounded like a flock of squawking Magpies, but all talk and laughter come to an abrupt stop as Aunt Dollie drew the wagon closer to them.

When the leader of the Indians came close to Aunt Dollie, he and Aunt Dollie both stopped. All the men kept staring straight ahead. The leader stood staring at Aunt Dollie and Aunt Dollie sat glaring right back at him. They continued staring at each other for what Lily thought must have been an uncomfortable five minutes.

Finally Aunt Dollie gave a big chest-raising sigh and said in a slow drawn-out manner, "Howwwdy Bob. How ya'all doin?"

"Bob?" Lily thought as a grin spread across her face, "Bob?" Lily had to suppress a laugh as she looked at the magnificent looking Indian and thought of his name being Bob. He looked more like a "Chief Roaring Lion" or maybe "Chief Leaping Leopard". Certainly not Bob.

"We are doing well, my beautiful Violet Song Bird. Have you come to accept my hand in marriage?" The handsome Indian spoke with a voice as smooth as warm honey going down ones throat, and he had a special twinkle of merriment in his dark eyes.

Aunt Dollie gave another big sigh, rolled her eyes to the sky and replied with a cold sharp tone of voice, "Land-o-Goshen, Bob. Not in this lifetime or the next! My Audie Lee is still alive and kicking and I am still in love with that big, old grizzly bear. But thank you anyway for askin' and I am always honored that you are still interested in me even though I am carrying this young'un of Audie Lee's on my back. I'll love Audie Lee forever, so I'm thinking you should ask one of those pretty little gals back yonder to be your wife. And, by the way," Aunt Dollie said with an exhausting sigh, "My name is Dollie Fletcher to you. So please stop calling me "Violet Song Bird". Any way you look at it, I certainly cannot claim to be any type of a song-bird. Unless you're talking about the horrible squawk of a peacock, I don't think I qualify."

"Pffft," frowned the big Indian as he spit on the ground. "No brains in the heads of the young, and they are lazy to go along with it. They carry no beauty compared to you, my Song-Bird. Marry me and I will give you many handsome sons and beautiful daughters." When Aunt Dollie's only answer was another scathing glare, Bob smiled and heaved a big sigh.

"I will wait patiently," he said as he looked at Aunt Dollie with a heart-melting, beautiful smile.

"Well, you'll be waiting until Judgment day comes a'callin'," Aunt Dollie stated, matter-of-factly.

He grinned. "I will be waiting."

"I'll be seeing ya, Bob. And don't forget, my name is Dollie Fletcher to you. But I'm thinkin' you should be callin' me Mrs. Fletcher. It's more proper-like."

Before Aunt Dollie turned her head away, Bob gave her a big wink and another wide handsome smile and said softly, "I will wait".

Two of the other male Indians muttered a low "humpf" slightly shaking their heads, as if they thought Bob was a little off in the head but didn't want to come right out and tell him.

With a mumble, Aunt Dollie's face turned beet-red as she turned toward Lily and Ophelia and muttered, "Don't know where he got that silly 'Violet Song-Bird' name but it ain't my name, and it maddens me! I sound like a caterwauling calf when I sing, as you all know by now."

She gave the group of Indians a nod.

"Well, we gotta be movin' on. Good-bye, adios, toodle-oo and cheerio to all of you," she announced loudly, giving old Eb a sharp slap with the reins. The old horse was so caught off guard, he took off with a jump and a jerk, knocking Lily and Ophelia clean off the wagon bench.

Hitting the ground with a loud *thud*, both Lily and Ophelia rolled a few times before scrambling up in a frightened frenzy and taking off after the wagon. There was no way in heaven or earth they were going to be left behind with a man who was in love with Aunt Dollie and was now feeling the scorn of rejection.

The whole group of Indians began laughing loudly and clapping their hands with mirth at Lily and Ophelia.

Aunt Dollie slowed the wagon down just a mite as she called out to Lily and Ophelia.

"Sorry girls. I didn't mean ta startle old Eb and make him jump like that. Climb on up here real quick-like so we can get on out of here. I'm in no mood for the likes of Bob."

Scurrying as fast as they could, Lily and Ophelia managed to get up onto the wagon bed then scrambled onto the bench next to Aunt

Dollie where they held on tightly because Aunt Dollie was once again smacking old Eb making him move right along in a fast clip.

"Well," Lily said to Ophelia once they were back on the wagon bench. "I guess that was pretty funny. If we hadn't been the ones falling off the wagon, we would have thought it was very funny." Lily and Ophelia both started laughing.

"You're as good as new," Aunt Dollie stated as she looked over at them. "No blood or broken bones; you'll be fine and dandy."

Aunt Dollie raised her hand up behind her head as she waved goodbye to Bob and the rest of the Indians.

"Ya might run into some rowdy characters up the trail a-ways so sleep with your eyes open. See ya'll next time," She yelled back at Bob and his followers. She then whispered for only Lily and Ophelia to hear, "I hope that next time never comes."

"I will not harm Audie Fletcher," Bob called out loudly to Aunt Dollie, "but I will be listening for word of his departure into the spirit world."

Snorting, Aunt Dollie muttered, "Humpf. I'd marry up with a big ol' grizzly bear before marrying up with that big-headed buffoon."

"What was that all about, Aunt Dollie?" Gertie P.'s squeaky little voice came from the back of the wagon. "And how did I get into your wagon? Did you catch me and knock me on the noggin? My head hurts and I have a bump on my head the size of a goose egg! I'm telling Granny on you, and she is going to whoop you something awful!"

Lily turned and looked into the back of the wagon. Gertie P. was rubbing her head and frowning. Her hair was sticking out worse than it had been before, and Barnabas had his head resting on her shoulder, looking up at Lily with his soulful eyes.

"Well, go right on ahead little Miss blabber -mouth, and I'll be telling your Ma and Pa how you ran away from me and got caught by those two river rats and almost got took down the river and sold. Although I would have only pity for the person you ended up with. After one day of listening to that sassy mouth of your'n, they would boot you right out and send you packing. And no, I didn't hit you on your noggin. Those river rats did, and lucky for you, Barnabas spotted them and we were able to snatch you away before they took you too far."

"What about that Indian, Aunt Dollie?" Lily asked, "Where did he get the name 'Bob'? That's a mighty strange name for an Indian, isn't it?"

Aunt Dollie laughed deeply before she answered Lily's question.

"Bob isn't his real name. His real name is Mahkateaa Wiitekoa Mahkwa, or Black Owl Bear in Kickapoo, but everyone called him Bob seeing that Mahkateaa Wiitekoa Mahkwa is too much for a mouth to say."

"Anyway, Audie Lee carried him home one night after rescuing him from a black bear – isn't that a strange twist of fate? Who'd a thought Black Owl Bear would get mauled by a back bear. That bear got ahold of him and ripped his back into shreds of meat. And ever since he healed, which took three months or so of me cleanin', washin' and puttin' salve on his back, he has this crazy notion that I am supposed to be his woman. During the whole ordeal, he was the orneriest cuss I ever did meet up with. He was a big ol' baby is what he was. All he did was demand this and demand that, whimper about one thing and whine 'bout another. Waa, waa, waa. He was a big ol' cry-baby. I pity the woman who marries up with that fella. He may be a handsome devil, but he is as bothersome as a grizzly bear with a toothache!"

"Well," Gertie P. leaned over the wagon bench and grinned into Aunt Dollie's face, giggling. "Mr. grizzly-bear with a toothache is on his horse and they are all following us. I keep waving at him to go away, but he just keep right on ignoring me like I'm invisible or something. Maybe we should go back and explain to him just who I am! I think he is keeping an eye out for you, Aunt Dollie. And I'm thinking Uncle Audie ain't gonna be too happy when he hears about that Indian fella wanting to marry-up with you!"

"Uncle Audie knows Bob's intentions and he just laughs."

"Well, I'm gonna tell Uncle Audie he better be watching out for that Bob fella, he might be looking for a way to get rid of Uncle Audie."

"Okay, Gertie P., you can tell Uncle Audie; he will appreciate it."

Gertie P. gave another giggle and climbed over the back of the bench, squeezing in between Lily and Ophelia.

"Well, I don't care what Bob does," Aunt Dollie stated firmly. "Just as long as he leaves me and Sammy alone. Besides, we need to get a move-on so we can get you three gals home before your papa's come searching for ya. We'll stop up here in Ramitown for a bit and visit with Granny Cora. I know Ramitown's sheriff hangs out at Granny Cora's house, since he's in love with Kizzie Mae and all. We'll have him send a telegram to your folks. He'll let your folks know you gals are safe with me and first chance I get I'll be putting ya'all on the train and sending ya on home. Then I can go on over to Surrey Jay's house and have that nice, long stay I intended to have before I ran into you three critters. How does that sound?"

"Oh, wow! That sounds like fun!" Ophelia exclaimed. "I have never been on a train in my whole life! What do you think, Lily?"

"Sounds like fun to me! Thanks Aunt Dollie, but I don't know if Caitlin and André will let me do that. It might cost them too much money to send me home on the train."

"Don't worry about the money; the train ride is free when kidnapped young'uns are returning home. Why, I hear tell they are even delivering young'uns in the U.S. mail these days. The folks doing the mailing will put the right amount of postage on the young-un's shirt and away they go to wherever their ma and pa want to send them. But they have to be small enough to fit into the mail carriers mail pouch. So I don't think you young'uns will fit the bill for that!"

Aunt Dollie gave a big loud laugh at her own quip and continued on. "That is, unless they're carryin' big mail-bags."

"I ain't gonna be stuffed into no mail pouch, Aunt Dollie," Gertie P. announced firmly. "I want to stay and visit with you and Aunt Surray Jay for a while! Please! Let me stay here and visit. Granny Wilkes won't mind. You can send her a telegram and let her know I'm okay and she won't worry her poor head off and go to an early grave thinking about her Gertie P. being dragged off by wolves or bandits."

Aunt Dollie rolled her eyes as she said, "Only if you promise to behave yourself at Aunt Surray Jay's house and your papa agrees to come down and pick you up. One good thing about that idea is that if you stay with me and Surray Jay, Lily and Ophelia won't have to keep an eye on your sassy self while riding the train home."

"Thank you, thank you, and thank you!"

Gertie P. climbed over and gave her Aunt Dollie a big hug, then climbed back into the bed of the wagon and started jumping up and down, announcing, "I get to play with Lela Mae and Dora Belle! Yippee! Lily, you tell my Tessa that I will be right over to your house as soon as I get home and I will tell her about our adventures. And, mind you, don't you go telling her, ya hear. You just keep it to yourself."

"I'll give it my best try, Gertie P.," Lily said. To herself, Lily was sending up a 'flare-prayer', thanking God that Gertie P. would not be riding the train home with her and Ophelia.

"Okay, enough of this yakking. Let's get ourselves over to Granny Cora's house and have something to eat."

With that said Aunt Dollie gave ol' Eb another slap and the old horse moved faster, almost reaching a run as they bounced and jostled down the narrow wagon path.

In no time at all, Aunt Dollie pulled off the wagon path onto a narrow, well-worn trail leading up the side of a small, grassy hill and into a large cluster of Elm trees surrounding a large white farmhouse.

The farmhouse was a two-story, white-washed structure with a wide wrap-around porch reaching all the way around the house. Large Elm and Oak trees stretched their arms over the top of the house, shading it from the summer heat. As they turned onto the path leading up to the house, a large flock of black and white chickens squawked and scattered, running for cover. Dogs started barking and a small donkey on the front porch began braying loudly. The little donkey was no bigger than one of the dogs. It had a dark brown coat with white ears and a little white nose. Down the porch steps it ran and joined the barking dogs as they ran toward the wagon.

In a few seconds the wagon was surrounded by howling dogs and the braying of the little donkey.

"SHUT UP!" Aunt Dollie yelled in her most commanding voice. All the dogs abruptly stopped barking and sat down on their haunches. But the little donkey kept right on braying until Aunt Dollie jumped down, walked over to him and gave him a scratch on his nose as she softly said, "that's enough now, Bellabean." He stopped braying and rubbed her muzzle against Aunt Dollie's overalls.

Waiting quietly beside the wagon was the troop of hounds, gazing up at Barnabas and whining. One of the smaller dogs bounced up and down as if trying to jump into the wagon bed. Barnabas had his sad eyes focused on Aunt Dollie and seemed to be ignoring the lineup of hound dogs.

"Go on, Barnabas, these hounds won't stay quiet for long if you don't take off with them. Go on now, git."

Eagerly, Barnabas lept down from the wagon and off they all went happily barking at nothing in particular. Within seconds the dogs disappeared, and all that was left was the echoing of their yipping.

The front door of the farmhouse burst open, and a young woman yelled excitedly, running down the porch steps.

"Granny, it's Dollie with little Sammy P!"

Aunt Dollie turned toward the young woman, grabbed her up and swung her around.

"You're looking mighty healthy, Kizzie Mae. You still seein' that handsome sheriff? Or have you found another beau to pass the time with?"

Kizzie Mae was a pretty woman with straight, black hair and eyes the color of amber. Her skin looked like warm caramel. She looked thin and willowy in her daisy-yellow summer dress and spoke with a pleasant soft voice.

"Yes ma'am, I'm still seeing Chester," Kizzie Mae softly said. "I am so glad ya'all are here. Come on in and have a sit-down so you can visit with Granny while I cook up some fried chicken and fixin's."

At the sound of the words "fried chicken", all three girls jumped down from the wagon and followed Aunt Dollie up and into the farmhouse with little Bellabean trotting right into the house behind them. Kizzie Mae turned and shooed Bellabean out onto the porch where the little donkey stood at the door once again braying at the top of her lungs.

"If you three gals will go out on the front porch and be with her, she'll stop that awful squalling. We can bring dinner out there so we can all visit together." Kizzie Mae said with a smile. "Gertie P., go on and get Bellabean some oats out of the barn so she won't be begging food from our plates."

"Okay," Gertie P. piped up happily. "Come on Lily and Ophelia, let's go outside and sit with that squalling baby donkey. She's my most favorite animal in the whole world. I'm gonna talk Granny Cora into letting me take her home with me."

"Don't even waste your time, Gertie P.," Kizzie Mae called out. "I heard you, and she's mine and I won't let her go anywhere. Get your own little donkey, you little pest."

"That Kizzie Mae is a meany," Gertie P muttered to herself when they were out of hearing distance, sticking out her tongue. "I don't think she will ever let me have Bellabean!"

# 9

## THE TRAIN

Early the next morning, Aunt Dollie, Kizzie Mae, Lily and Ophelia took the wagon into the Memphis train depot so the two girls could begin their journey home. The train depot in Memphis was much busier than the depot in Caruthersville. The tain stopped at the Memphis' depot for an hour or more taking on water and coal in which time the passengers were able to disembark, go into the Memphis streets and eat at a diner or shop at the many stores intentionally built close to the depot. But that didn't stop food and whiskey vendors from going onto the depot platform to sell their wares.

Along with food and whiskey, vendors of every craft crammed onto the platform; musicians and magicians were being performing for anyone who had an extra penny or two. Ignoring the law against selling animals to passengers, farmers were selling baby chicks, full grown chickens, baby goats, piglets and even a newborn calf.

The sight on the platform was mayhem and chaos as usual, for in Memphis, not only were there vendors selling their wares, but there were also workers running up and down the platform who, for a penny, would perform simple tasks for anyone who needed help – carry heavy baggage, load animals into the stock car, or even run into the general store and purchase a product for a passenger. All of them were pushing and shoving each other and anyone else who happened to be in their way as they rushed to complete one task and move on to another paying customer. Babies were crying loudly, and vendors were yelling out their fares.

"Sweet Tators, get your sweet tators here!"

"Fresh cut watermelon! Fresh cut watermelon here!"

"Baby chicks' right cheer! Baby chicks for two bits apiece!"

The train itself was letting off steam and bellowing black smoke everywhere. Grannies were kissing grandchildren, and husbands were pulling their wives toward the train in an attempt to get on-board before the Granny's talked the wives into staying for a longer visit. Livestock were bellowing at the top of their lungs, and cattle-men and cowboys were screaming and cracking their whips as they forced animals into the stock cars. Horses were fighting their own-ers and owners where yelling at their horses. A few cowboys had done the smart thing and put blinders over their horse's eyes, mak-ing it a lot simpler to lead the stubborn horses into the stock cars. Passengers and local folks were pushing and jostling each other as they tried getting where they wanted to be. It was total chaos. But it was exciting!

A big, burly man carrying two luggage trunks on his broad shoul-ders bumped into Ophelia and knocked her down onto the platform without saying a word of apology. He kept shoving his way to the bag-gage car and muttering cuss words with each step he took. Behind him, hanging onto his shirt tail, was a little boy about six years old with curly, white-blond hair and sparkling gray eyes. As the man bumped and knocked people onto the platform, the little boy would turn around and yell out, "Pardon my paw, Ma'am," or "Pardon my paw, Sir". As the little boy turned around to Ophelia in his effort to apologize for his father's rudeness, he stopped, let go of the big man's shirt tail and stared at Ophelia with a charming grin on his dirty little face as he blurted out, "Land-o-Goshen. Yor as purdy as my Paw's horse. I do apologize fur my Paw's rudeness. My name is Pauly Jackson, and if ya don't mind me saying, I would like ta marry-up with ya when I get my full-grown on. You look jes' like my maw!"

Off he ran with a happy cheer, yelling, "Wait up fur me, Paw! Wait up…I jes' found me a wife!"

Lily and Ophelia started laughing as they watched the little boy run after his pa. That was when they saw Duck perched on of one of the trunks the big man was carrying toward the train.

"*Aawk! Aawk!*" the parrot squawked. "Goin' fur a ride?" Duck flapped his big wings a few times and took off over the top of the train.

*Whoosh.* Duck was back, buzzing by Lily's head as he squawked.

"Watch out fur killers!" he squawked before vanishing into the forest, all the while clucking like a chicken.

The chaotic, frenzied crowd did not notice Duck or his warning, but Lily and Ophelia certainly did and it gave them a feeling of unease.

"Duck is the strangest parrot I ever did see," Lily said.

"I haven't seen many parrots, but… yes, he is," Ophelia replied.

"Wow," Aunt Dollie said as she walked up behind them. "That was a strange thing for that parrot to say. Was that Tillie Brown's parrot?"

"Yes," Lily answered. "And yes, he is a strange bird."

"Well, anyway," Aunt Dollie continued, "Here are some sandwiches and a jug of water for you gals. Now, don't eat all these sandwiches at once, or you won't have enough to last you. You can always get more water at the train depots along the way, and I would suggest you don't leave the train. Those men may still be looking for you."

Lily, Ophelia, Aunt Dollie and Kizzie Mae walked over to the conductor so Aunt Dollie could explain to him what was going on as she handed him the prepaid tickets the ticket master had given her.

"Welcome aboard my train, me lovely ladies," the conductor said with a smile. "I will guard them with me own life."

After kissing Aunt Dollie and Kizzie Mae, Lily and Ophelia climbed up the short steps, turned to wave goodbye and walked down the aisle of the train car to find a good seat for two by a window. Lily jumped into the first seat she found by a window. Ophelia sat down beside her and let out a big sigh of relief, and turned to talk to Lily.

"I am so glad Gertie P. is out of our hair. Maybe now we can relax and have fun on the ride home and not worry about her jumping off the train or pushing someone else off the train while its going!"

"Me too," Lily replied.

Not two minutes later, with loud grunts and groans, some guys noisily plopped down in the seats behind them and gave Lily a couple sharp pokes on the shoulder.

"Hidey-ho, hidey-ho, how'd you gals get onto this here train? We see'd ya climb aboard and figger'ed we better be getting' on this here train too, so's we can make sure ya get home safe and sound so's no-body blames us fur yur departin' inta the next life, if ya know what I mean!"

Jerking their heads around, Lily and Ophelia looked into the eyes of Corn-Shuckin' John and Watermelon Willie.

"What are you two doing here?" Lily hissed.

Jumping up from their seats, Corn-Shuckin' John and Watermelon Willie scurried around and got into the two seats facing Lily and Ophelia. Leaning way too close to Lily and Ophelia's faces, Watermelon Willie spoke in a quiet whisper.

"We got us some im-po-tant information to tell ya. We was hoping to run across ya afore ya got home."

"Well, here tis," Corn Shuckin' John said real slow-like. "After the three of ya jumped off'en that thur raft an – wait – whur's that little young'un? She didn't get kilt did she? I sure hope not, cuz that Granny o' hers will walk me and Willie right dab down to the gates of hades herself iff'en she's a goner. Whur is she?"

"Gertie P. is safe in Memphis with some of her family," Lily quickly replied. "Now tell us what's so important that you have to jump on this train behind us?"

"Whew. That thur's a big o' relief." Watermelon Willie gave a big sigh.

"Well," Corn-Shuckin' John continued. "After you gals jumped off'en that thur raft, them bayou boys shoved me and Willie into the river. We didn't get our guns, we didn't get our grub, and we didn't get anythin' else belongin' ta us. We had to swim for our lives I'm tellin' ya. Them thur water snakes was a'slippin' an a'sliddin' 'round us the whole time."

His face was just inches from Lily and Ophelia's. His teeth were green with scum and his breath smelled of onions. His and Watermelon Willie's hair was plastered down on their heads. It looked as if their hair had never seen soap or water.

"Hit was a struggle I tell ya. Well, them fellers din't know hit but when they started in a'yellin' at us I, real slow like so's they wouldn't notice, got out my little, sharp skinnin' knife and had it behind me when they jumped us. Well, jest as soon as they pushed us in, I took me in a deep breath and under that thur raft I went, and took me a few swipes at them thur ropes holdin' that thur raft together and then I took off a-swimmin' after Willie, jest dodgin' them thur slitherin'snakes and snappin' turtles."

The whole time he was talking about dogging the snakes, Corn Shuckin' John was jerking his shoulders back and forth demonstrating how he dodged the snakes.

"Well, after we reached the river bank, we turned 'round and watched them two bayou boys going on down the river. After about two minutes, we see'd that raft start in a'shakin' and a'shimmyin' then hit started in fallin' apart. Hit was pretty dang funny too." Corn Shuckin' John snickered before he continued with his story. "Well hit was funny 'til we see'd 'em swim to the same side of the river we was on. We was sure they would swim to the other side, but they din't, so here we was on the same side of the river as them two mean critters. So real quiet-like, we start in a creepin' up the river thinkin' we could get ta Memphis and citch the train back to Caruthersville afore they citched up with us. But, that was the same dang thing they was thinkin', I guess. Cuz when we stopped ta find us a hidey-hole so we could take us a sleep and stay safe from all those night critters roamin' the woods, we see'd a campfar over yonder from the river so me and Willie slither up on hit real quiet-like and low-an-behold, hit was them two bayou fellers! Don't know how they got that big o' far started, but they had them a nice campfar and they was eatin' up some rabbit or somethin'. Heck. We don't even know how they got so fur ahead of us. But, anyway, me and Willie here decide to sleep in the woods not too fur from thur camp, seein' that iff'en any woods critters came sniffin' round, those two bayou critters would chase 'em off since hit looked like they had saved thur guns from that old river. Now here's the good part. We was all settled down when them two fellers starts in a'talkin'. And low-and-behold, they said they was gonna go back on up to Caruthersville and get you three young'uns and they was gonna wring yur necks! They wasn't even gonns both-er sellin' ya, they was jest gonna get rid of ya cuz they was mad as hornets! And they was gonna finish gettin' rid of Tin-can Tillie, cuz she was s'posed to be dead and gone already but she outfoxed 'em and hung onto life. They was really mad. LaFitte started in stompin' round thur campfar cussing up a storm and old Girard kept on sayin' stuff jest to get 'em madder. When LaFitte wasn't looking we could see old Girard, with a grin on his face, watchin' LaFitte get madder and madder."

Watermelon Willie was sitting there, the whole time, nodding his head and agreeing with Corn-Shuckin' John. Gradually, Willie's head started moving slower and lower and before Corn-Shuckin' John got to the part about Tillie Brown, Watermelon Willie's eyes were shut, his chin was down on his chest and he was snoring like a bear.

"They said that ol' Tillie Brown was like a cat. She has nine lives and they was gonna get rid of her nine times if that's what hit takes. Well, when we see'd you two young'uns get on this here train, we know'd fur sure we had to get on too. Old man Jasper Juniper, the ticket master, we used to run together in one of them thur – well, we used ta know him, so he jest up and give'd us tickets ta Caruthersville after I tol' him the sit-chee-a-tion and all the mean thin's them bayou fellers is up to."

Feeling kind of sick to their stomachs, Lily and Ophelia sat quietly staring at Corn-Shunkin' John.

"Are they on this train?" Lily asked quietly.

"Ain't knowin' that yet, but I be thinkin' I'm gonna take me a sneaky walk up and down these here train cars and have a look-see fur them thur bayou fellers onces't we get movin'. How's that idee? You two gals jest sit tight right cheer by Willie and I'll do the snoopin'."

"Okay," Lily replied in a low panicky whisper.

With wide-eyed fear, Lily and Ophelia kept their eyes glued to the passenger door as people continued boarding the train. When the train's final whistle blew and the conductor yelled out, "All aboard! The MOPAC is on its way to Saint Louie, Missouri!" Lily and Ophelia breathed a sigh of relief. But then they realized Girard and LaFitte could have boarded one of the other cars.

The engine started huffing and puffing as black smoke bellowed past the windows and the metal wheels started to grind against the rails. The train was quickly picking up speed.

Lily and Ophelia sat watching trees and farms fly past the windows as the train reached its full speed. Black smoke was still bellowing outside, but it rapidly dissipated into the cool morning air. Leaning back in her seat, Lily spoke to Ophelia in a soft whisper.

"Let's have a sandwich and an apple. Maybe it will calm us down. I'm as nervous as a cat sitting by a rocking chair."

"Sounds good to me."

"You think they're on our train?"

"I have no idea, Lily, but I sure hope not. Maybe we should have gotten off and waited a bit with Aunt Dollie and Kizzie Mae."

"No, I just want to get back home."

"Yeah, me too."

Quietly, so as to not wake Watermelon Willie, Lily and Ophelia opened their sandwiches and devoured them before Corn-Shuckin' John had time to return to his seat.

All of a sudden, Corn-Shuchin' John burst through the door of the car in front of them. He was high-stepping it down the aisle just as fast as his skinny legs could carry him. It looked like his knee, at any moment, would start smacking him in his nose. At the same time, the train wheels started screaming as the whole train started slowing down.

"Them thur bayou boys stopped the train!" Corn-Shuckin' John was yelling out to Lily and Ophelia, "I ain't knowin' how they done hit, but get ready to jump cuz they're comin' aboard!"

"No," Lily said loudly. "We are not getting off this train! The conductor will stop them from doing us any harm. Get back here in your seat and let's watch and see what happens!"

Corn-Shuckin' John leaped over the back of his seat and plopped down beside Watermelon Willie.

"I'm tellin' ya gals, ya better get off'en this here train! They be some mean, ornery hombre's and they won't stop 'til they git ya."

"And how do we know they won't see us jump off and jump off after us?"

"Well iff'en ya put hit that way, they most likely would."

"Yeah, that's what I thought," Lily muttered.

"Okay, okay," he said frantically. "Git yourself back into one of them thur privy rooms and lock them doors!"

Lily and Ophelia jumped up, and just short of running, scrambled to the back of the passenger car and slipped into one of the small privies.

Once inside, they bolted the door shut and pressed their ears firmly against it as they strained to hear what was going on outside the privy.

Everything was silent. The rest of the passengers sat in wide-eyed terror, watching for the 'mean, ornery fellers' Corn-Shuckin' John had loudly announced were on their way. Lily and Ophelia heard the door at the end of the passenger car slam open and a loud voice yell out, "Where is dem two little gals who got own in

Memphis? Y'all bet'duh be tellin', or… or who wants da be da first ta be kicked off dis train?

Lily and Ophelia looked at each other with fright and then looked around for a way to escape. The only way out was through the two holes in the privy bench.

"*Eeeww*," Ophelia said quietly.

"I know, I know but that's our only way out of here, Ophelia. Let's go."

Ophelia was breathing shallow and looking pale.

"Take a deep breath, and please don't faint on me," Lily said.

Ophelia nodded as they peered down the two holes.

The inside of the privy hole was full of flies, but most of the waste had fallen out onto the tracks as the train moved along the rails. No one had used the privy since the train pulled out of Memphis, so it wasn't too bad yet, Lily told herself.

"They're in the privy," a man yelled out.

"Two men were with them but they jumped off the train and took off running," a woman yelled out.

"Come on Ophelia, we have to jump right now!"

"Okay," Ophelia answered in a weak voice.

Pinching their noses shut and closing their eyes, they stepped into the holes and fell onto the ground beneath the train. They landed with a hard "bump" on the rocks between the railroad ties. Dropping onto their bellies, they rolled across the rails and ended up on the river side of the tracks.

"That wasn't so bad. Let's get out of here."

Then they heard the two bayou fellas banging on the privy yelling for them to open up the door, they knew for certain that in no time at all the bayou boys would discover how they had escaped.

Running towards the back of the train, Lily and Ophelia heard the men bust the privy down open and then began stomping and yelling for them through the next train car, but the girls kept right on running. Just as they reached the end of the train, they heard the engine as it started building up steam and saw the big steel wheels slowly began turning as the whistle blew and smoke bellowed from the belly of the engine.

"Grab a hold and climb up here quick-like!" a voice called out.

Looking up, they saw Corn-Shuckin' John and Watermelon Willie leaning down from the caboose steps as they held out their hands to give them a hand-up.

Both Lily and Ophelia grabbed a hand and were pulled onto the caboose steps just as the train picked up speed and would have left them stranded on the tracks in the wilderness.

Sitting on the caboose's small little porch, they caught their breath. Corn-Shuckin' John, along with Watermelon Willie, was breathing heavily as they leaned against the small porch railings.

"Looky yonder," Watermelon Willie wheezed, as he stood up straight and pointed to the side of the tracks. "Hit's the bayou fellers!"

Sure enough, Girard and LaFitte were running with all their might as they tried to catch the train. LaFitte passed Girard and was reaching out his hand to grab the caboose railing when Watermelon Willie lifted up his foot and gave LaFitte's hand a sharp stomp. With a yelp and a cuss, LaFitte let go of the rail, and immediately the train was out of his reach. He and Girard stood in the middle of the tracks, raised their guns and aimed at the caboose. Lily, Ophelia, Corn-Shuckin' John and Watermelon Willie all dove for the door at the same time. Somehow, all four of them managed to squeeze through the tiny door and inside the caboose where Corn-Shuckin' John kicked the door shut with his foot.

*PING! PING! CRACK! WHIZ! PING!*

All four of them stayed on the floor as the shots hit the back of the caboose.

"That were a close'un," Corn-Shuckin' John said.

"Yep, hit sure nuf was," replied Watermelon Willie.

Slowly they eased themselves up and peeked out the window. The bayou boys were too far back for their guns to reach the caboose.

Turning around, they took in the view of the inside of the caboose. A small bunk was nailed into one side of the caboose and on it sat a man dressed in a conductor's uniform. He was looking at them as if they were a figment of his imagination. His hair was mussed from sleep, and an agitated frown sat on his face as he struggled to place his spectacles on the bridge of his nose. On the other side of the narrow room hung four unlit lanterns and a large tin of lantern oil secured in a wooden box – also nailed to a table top built into the wall.

The conductor sat there staring at them for a few seconds before shouting.

"Get off my train! What are you doing in here? No one is allowed in this caboose except railroad personnel!"

He pointed his finger at the door, as if they would just walk out and jump off the train

"Get off my train!"

All four of them stood there in silence, staring at the little man in the conductor's uniform. He was a short little fella with skinny legs and arms, and when he jumped off his cot and boldly faced them, he was shorter than Ophelia.

"Out, I tell you! Get out! Get off my train this very minute!" he bellowed in a deep, resonating voice.

Frozen in their tracks, all four stared at the little man, fascinated with the sound of such a deep, booming voice coming out of such a short, skinny body.

Not even moving a muscle, the four of them continued to stand there at the foot of his bed, impolitely gawking at him. They were all captivated by the fury on the little fella's face. His anger had now turned his face beet-red, and the veins on his neck were sticking out as if they were ready to explode.

He began poking Watermelon Willie's stomach with his skinny, short little finger; it was almost comical to watch. Watermelon Willie didn't move an inch, but looked down with a slight frown at the little conductor. Then he put his shoulder against Willie's stomach and tried pushing him out the door.

Reaching under his thin bed mattress, the little conductor pulled out a pistol and pointed it at Watermelon Willie and screamed.

"I want all of you OFF MY TRAIN! NOW!"

"We cain't!" Watermelon Willie said, still standing there staring.

"And just why not, you barbaric fellow?"

"Well," Watermelon Willie slowly replied, "I reckon we jest cain't."

"Well," Lily spoke up for Watermelon Wille. "The train is moving quite fast and if we jump off we will most likely kill ourselves, and that is not a good idea in our way of thinking."

"Well, I guess that's correct, but what are you doing here?"

"We was getting' way from some pretty da – whoops, pardon me you young'uns fur my cussin' – I mean some ornery fellers," Corn-Shuckin' John said. "They're from down in the bayou country and we think maybe they be huntin' fur Tin-can Tillie so's they kin kill her again."

"Whoa," the little conductor backed away from Watermelon Willie and held his hands out in front of himself. "Well, now that you explained what is going on," he said, spreading his arms wide, "you are all welcome to spend the rest of the ride into Caruthersville in here with me in my little home.

"By the way, let me introduce myself. I am Conductor Jacobus Padayachee and I am the head conductor for this train. I have been on this particular train since the first day she started running these rails. Welcome to my train.

Mr. Padayachee bent down and spoke under the bed, "Come out, my furious little guard cat."

Out from under the small bed crept the biggest cat Lily had ever seen. It was three foot long if it was an inch, and with its tail, Lily was quite sure it had to be five feet long! It had long, bushy hair the color of an over-ripe pumpkin, with longer tufts of white fur growing in clumps all over its back. It was also the funniest looking cat Lily had ever seen. The cat's chubby, short, furry legs looked maybe two inches long.

Slowly the cat crawled out from under the bed and clawed its way onto the top of the bed, turned around a couple times and sat down, staring at all the intruders. It had one blue eye and one green eye, and its long, white whiskers hung down from its face too far for a regular barn cat. Its mouth was in an upside down smile as it gave them an aloof superior glare, Lily was quite sure she heard the cat let out a low *humpf* before it slowly closed its eyes. Then, leisurely it fell onto its back, sprawled out like a drunken sailor and began snoring.

Mr. Padayachee laughed and said, "Meet Mr. Twilight. He spends his days sleeping and his nights prowling. He snores like a walrus and eats like an elephant. Once in a while, Mr. Twilight and I will have a stay-over in a town and I let him out to roam the town streets and forest where he finds his own food, but as soon as he hears my whistle signaling for him to come along and get on the train so we can be on our way, he is back here quick as a flash. If anyone tried hurting me, Mr. Twilight would most certainly attack 'em and give 'em a good clawing."

Looking over at the big heap of snoring fur sprawled out on Mr. Padayachee's bed, Lily doubted that.

"Go ahead and sit down, y'all. I've got something to say," Mr. Padayachee said.

Watermellon Willie and Corn-Shuckin' John sat on the floor, letting the girls sit at the table across from the cot.

"I just heard while we were in Memphis that Tillie Brown was found dead in the river yesterday. Reports said they found her horse floating in the river and her big, old parrot was sitting right on top of that dead horse's body as if going for a jolly ride down the river. And one minute before we left Memphis, a young boy came running from the telegraph office and handed me a telegram stating a woman's body was found floating down around Percy's Bend and at that very moment the body was being carted into Caruthersville. They couldn't make out who it actually was, but they are pretty sure it's Tillie Brown. Ain't no other woman been reported missing, and the body had her type of bloomer on and the hair looked just like old Tillie's hair. I guess whoever killed that poor woman sure messed her up.

"I don't rightly know all the facts, but as soon as we pull into Caruthersville's I'm taking me a stroll into the saloon so I can hear what everybody's saying, seeing as Caruthersville is the end of my run for the week. They done had the funeral and put her in the ground this morning."

"Woah," Lily said.

All four of their faces sank with the news. There was silence for a few minutes.

Turning back to the door of the caboose, all five of them walked out onto the little porch and gazed down the tracks to see if they could spot the bayou boys. Nothing and nobody was in sight as far back as they could see.

Corn-Shuckin' John, Watermelon Willie and Mr. Padayachee walked back into the caboose, but Lily and Ophelia sat down on the floor of the little caboose porch and leaned their heads back against the outside wall.

*Clickity-clack. Clickity-clack.*

The rhythm of the train and the clacking of the wheels sent each girl into her own thoughts as the train flew closer and closer to home.

*Clickity-clack. Clickity-clack.*

Their heads began to nod, and soon they were sound asleep.

"Next stop – Caruthersville, Missouri!" Mr. Padayachee opened the top half of the caboose door and yelled out to Lily and Ophelia. Staggering up, Lily and Ophelia leaned over the railing and watched as the train slowly pulled into Caruthersville.

There stood Caitlin, André, Tessa and Benny. Standing right behind them was Uncle Ezzie, Aunt Effie Mae and their boys Paul, Ott, Tom, Robbie, Frank and a few of their cousins. Next to Lily's family was Ophelia's – her mom Corina, her pa Kip, and all her siblings – Steve,

Sofie, Callie, Ceelee, and Delia. Every one of the boys were pushing, poking and bopping each other on the heads until the train eased into place beside the platform.

"Oh, blister-n-bother," Ophelia sighed. "Not 'the boys', most times they drive me crazy on purpose, I do believe."

As soon as Lily and Ophelia stepped down from the caboose, the boys started whooping, hollering and stomping their feet on the wooden platform. As soon as they saw the girls were both okay, they immediately jumped on each other and once again began wrestling around on the platform; even the little boys joined in. Uncle Ezzie, Kip Knudson and André shooed them off the platform where they continued wrestling around on the ground. All the women and girls ran to Lily and Ophelia and began hugging, crying and kissing them. Ophelia's mother was hugging her daughter so tight it looked as if Ophelia was having a problem taking a breath.

Hugging Lily to her chest, Caitlin blubbered, "I was so worried about you!"

"Okay," André announced over the racket of the depot platform. "Let's all get in the wagons and go on ov'ah ta have a picnic at the house. Come on, ya'll. Let's get movin'; I'm hungry."

Since the boys knew André would be quizzing Lily about what happened, all of them jumped into the same wagon as Lily and Ophelia. As soon as the wagon started moving away from the train depot, André turned to Lily.

"Start in with the tellin'."

Ott and Benny pushed to the front and made sure they were sitting on either side of Lily so they could hear the story clearly.

She told the whole story and didn't leave out any of the important facts. She told them of Girard and LaFitte and how Corn-Shuckin' John and Watermelon Willie helped them escape from the raft and how they too had been pushed off the raft and left to die by the two bayou boys. She told of how Corn-Shuckin' John and Watermelon Willie heard the bayou boys confess to the attempted murder of Tillie and Duck.

Every time she stopped to take a breath, Ott would poke her in the arm, laugh, and say, "And?"

When she got to the part about watching John "Liver-Eating" Johnson, all the boys leaned in close so they wouldn't miss a word.

"And?" Ott poked her.

Lily started telling of meeting Aunt Dollie and the line of Indians following Bob along the wagon path.

"Hey, I know that Indian!" Ott interupped. "I saw him at the shootin' contest last summer. He was the best shot of everybody and he took all the ribbons."

"And?" he poked her again.

"Ott, I'm not saying another word until you stop poking me and saying 'and'."

"Ok, ok…"

The rest of the boys laughed loudly and yelled out in unison, "AND?"

"Something else happened didn't it, Lily?" Benny whispered in her ear so no one else could hear.

"If you stop Ott from poking me in the arm and saying 'and, and, and'," Lily hissed back at Benny, "I'll tell you later."

Leaning back, Benny said something to Ott and then Ott leaned up to Lily. He must be coming to apologize, she thought. He leaned in to her ear, bugged his grey-blue eyes out and whidpered, "Aaannnddd?"

As Lily's eycbrows furrowed, Ott leaned back and all the boys began snickering and punching each other again. Then Ott reached around Lily and smacked Benny on the back of the head and it turned into an all-out laughing slug-fest between the boys.

Lily and Ophelia glared at Ott and Benny, stuck out their tongues and with a loud *pffft* showered the boys with spit.

"Uncle André!" Ott stopped slugging Paul and called out with a laugh. "Lily and Ophelia are spitting on us!"

"Well use it ta wash ya'all's dirty faces," André said with a chuckle. "I can he'ah ya'll pester'in 'em. Now, stop playin' so's Lily can finish her tellin'."

All the boys stopped slugging each other and Ott turned to Lily, bugged his eyes out again and mouthed the word "And?"

Lily couldn't stop laughing at Ott as she finished telling her story about the previous day in detail. She did not mention seeing the apparitions.

André said it couldn't have been Girard and LaFitte who committed the murder last night seeing they had been spotted wandering the saloons in Memphis, but he was still watching for them. He said he could hold them until Judge Snow came through, who would decide if they could be tried for attempting to kill Tillie.

# 10

## THE PICNIC

*B*ANG! The barn's smaller door slammed open and out stomped Uncle Pud with Hayseed Monroe tagging right along behind him. Uncle Pud's face was redder than usual as he stomped toward the picnic table and blankets. He was a distant relative of Uncle Ezzie's – or so they said – and at various times he would come ambling around from wherever he was to help with the farm work. All he asked for was to be fed, a place to sleep in the barn, and a few pennies to spend as he wished. Most of the time, Uncle Pud was rather tipsy and disheveled looking. He was short, stocky and almost bald. What little hair he did have was white-blond, as was his beard, as well as the hair on his arms and back. He had a ruddy complexion and sky-blue eyes, and always, always, always wore bib overalls without a shirt. His shoes were over-sized clodhopper boots which seemed to flop off the back of his feet every time he took a step. He was a pretty jolly fella, until someone messed with his homebrew. Then it was a whole different story.

Hayseed Monroe was one of the many Monroe's from over in the Ozark Mountains. He was a long, tall skinny fella with slicked back greasey dark hair, a big hooked nose and a few front teeth missing from a fight or two he had been involved in. When he walked, his long arms and legs seemed to clink and clank and sort of flop around with each step; as if he had no control over their movements.

"Ezzie, André, Kip!" Uncle Pud bellowed as he came out of the barn. "Ya better be teachin' them boys of yor'n some manners. They done pee'd in my whiskey bottle afta pourin' my good whiskey out onta the ground! I din't know it so's I took me a big o' swig and swallered it afore I know'd it was pee! Ain't that right, Hayseed?"

"That's right!" Hayseed Monroe declared, shaking his head upand down.

Everyone sitting at the table was staring at Uncle Pud and Hayseed Monroe with slight grins on their faces as they tried to keep from laughing. Uncle Pud stomped over to the edge of the pigpen, leaned over the wooden fence and vomited.

"Ya owe me boys! I ain't know'n which of ya did hit, but I'm gonna find out! And when I do, I'm gonna whoop ya *good*. Fact is, I might whoop ya all! Ain't that right, Hayseed?"

"That's right!" Hayseed declared again.

Then Uncle Pud vomited again and kept right on retching.

Every one of the older boys started snickering quietly as Uncle Ezzie turned and gave all of them a good hard glare.

"Boys, I don't reckon I'm fond of Pud drinking so much, but I don't take kindly to destroying other people's property neither. It doesn't matter what it is," Uncle Ezzie said.

As Lily looked over at the boys sitting under the big elm tree, it was obvious whom the cuprits were. One glance at Benny and Ott gobbling up food as fast as they could shovel it into their mouths made it perfectly clear who the cuprits were. Ott peeked up at Ophelia real quick-like and gave her a big wink, making Ophelia's face blush. In return, she stuck her tongue out at Ott.

Before Uncle Ezzie or André had a chance to get a word out, Benny, Ott and all the rest of the older boys jumped up and took off running for the levee, each of them grabbing a biscuit or two as they left. Aunt Effie Mae reached out and grabbed little Frankie and Edward Lloyd by the britches as they ran past her.

"Whoa… You two just stay right here," she said. "No need in losing any more young'uns today."

Both Frankie and Edward Lloyd put up a bawling fit, but Aunt Effie wouldn't let go of their briches. Eventually they stopped crying and went back to playing with each other.

"Steven!" Ophelia's father yelled. But the boys were already out of sight, among the trees and on their way to the levee as their whooping laughter echoed back to the house.

"We'll get 'em when they come home, Pud," André said. "You and Hayseed come on ov'ah he'ah and take a sit-down. Grab some of this good food. We wer'ah startin' in ta talkin' 'bout Tillie Brown and who did her in."

After some red-faced huffing and puffing from Uncle Pud, he and Hayseed took a seat with the rest of the adults, grabbed a plate and began eating with gusto.

"Well, who ya figgerin' did hit, André?" Uncle Pud asked with his mouth full of food, looking at André with curiosity.

"Ah don't rightly know, Pud. No witnesses an no evidence a'tall makes it kinda hard ta figure out."

"I hear tell," Hayseed said in his high, squeaky voice; his mouth overflowing with biscuits and jelly. "I hear tell Tillie Brown had a big o' box o' gold dust hidden somer's down round her cabin. My cousin, Zac'ree T. Monroe, says his cousin, Jawbone Hickey, tol' him Berthie Gibbons said her maw's oldest sister, the widder woman Aunt Josie Waddle and the widder woman Hattie Hatcher, was walking down the street with Minnie Moore and Winnie Calhoun real casual-like one Sunday morin' after church," he paused to take a breath. "... And they saw Tillie Brown on that big ol' black horse of hers and she was carryin' a box and that thur box had ah ity-bity hole in the bottom and hit was leakin' gold dust real slow-like all the way through town. Now, that thur may jest be hot air coming from Zac'ree T. and all, but that's what he said, an he swears hit's the gospel truth. And he don't listen to them gossipin' women much a'tall. Now what I'm a'wanderin' is, whur'd she get her money ta gamble all the time. Hit had ta come from som'ers. And the story is she did ah whole lot o' winnin' on them thur gamblin' boats."

"Yeah," Uncle Pud joined in, biscuit bits also falling out of his mouth. "That thur's what I hear'd too. Skinny-John said the same thin' 'bout her burin' a whole lot of gold 'round her cabin along the river, but that thur might jest be gossip cuz Skinny John's woman, Big Bessie, is kindly like the town gossip over in Hayti. Iff'en hit was true, someone would'ah done dug hit up while'st she was gone."

"It's probably just gossip," Mr. Knudson said. "The way Tillie Brown lived, I doubt she had a lot of money stashed away."

"Well," Caitlin spoke up. "I for one admired the woman. She had to take care of herself since she was a small child. That funeral was one of the saddest I have ever attended; seeing that there was not one living relative to mourn her passing. I, for one, was so happy to see the whole town turn out to pay their respects. It certainly was kind of them. It sure is sad they couldn't make a positive indentifcation on the poor woman.

"Well," André drawled. "The body had been in the riv'ah too long for ah sur'ah identification. It has ta be Tillie Brown. No other woman's been reported missing and she had on the same type of clothing and the same color hair as Tillie Brown."

"What do you think, Lily?" Ophelia whispered in Lily's ear.

"I'm thinking we better stay away from town and not go out off until those sorry-looking bayou boys are caught. That's the only thing I'm thinking."

"Yeah, me too."

"How about you ask if you can spend the night here with me, since André is the sheriff and all, maybe your folks will think that's a good idea."

"I already asked, and Pa said no. Said he has a gun just like the one Sheriff Beaumont has, and he ain't letting anyone take me."

"Well, chicken poo."

"Yeah, that's what I said. Well, I didn't actually say it out loud, I just thought it." She giggled.

"Well, ladies," Aunt Effie Mae announced. "Let's help Caitlin clean this mess up so we can be getting on home. Caitlin darlin', when our wild boys come back, you jest give them a sharp tongue and send them on home. They'll be back in no time a'tall. They know if they don't get those chores done there'll be the devil to pay and no supper for them."

"The same with Steven," Mrs. Knudson said as she stood up from the picnic table. "Tell him to skedaddle himself home as fast as his feet can carry him."

# 11

## THE TALES

While Lily and Tessa helped Caitlin clean up the kitchen by washing and putting away the dishes, André helped Mr. Bushy onto the porch and into the parlor. Then they all went into the parlor and got themselves comfy so they could listen to Mr. Bushy as he told his tales of his Mountain's strange and curious happenings. Mr. Bushy referred to the mountain his cabin was on as if it were a person.

Once the whole family was settled in, Mr. Bushy gently pushed the rocking chair into motion and started in with his telling.

Well," he began his telling with a big grin, "I was down visitin' them Oh-zark hill folk one fine summer day and they gave me an invite ta go ta this here big o' shin-dig they was havin'. It was fur the buryin' up of one of thur younger fellers.

"Hit was fur young Tom Monroe. Hit seems he had taken ta drinkin' pretty heavy one afternoon and way on inta the middle of the night, well after the midnight hour, he started in walking down the trail ta his cabin in the next holler over from town. Well, along the way he comes upon an old mama bar. They said she had her two babies' right along besides her and jest as soon as she see'd Tom she waited a few seconds then took off chargin' him. Thankfully Tom had enough of his brains left ta figger out he best get away from that mama bar. So, he climbed up inta a nearby tree and sat on that branch fur the whole night.

Well along comes morning and he's still up in that thur tree, but, when he wakes up he reckons that old mama bar is done gone out of the area, so he puts his foot down ta step on one of them thur low branches and all of a sudden-like, that branch broke and down he goes. Now, this here information is all second-hand; hits what them other fellers was a'tellin' me, ya understand? Well, when that thur tree branch broke, there happened to be another feller drivin' a wagon by who was jest moseyin' 'long the road, an he witnessed the while thing, or so he says. Now, that wagon feller says Tom fell right out of that thur tree as pretty as ya please and kindly floated down almost to the ground. He said hit looked like Tom had sprouted wings and was soarin' like an eagle, kindly swayin' back and forth-like, but then all of a sudden he stopped soaring and slammed right down hard onta that thur ground. Well, the wagon feller said the tree feller just laid thur a few minutes while the wagon feller ran over and knelt down beside him. Then Tom told the wagon feller, 'I kilt that mama bar's maw way back yonder years ago and now she took revenge on me.' And then Tom took his last breath, and he was a goner."

Mr. Bushy gave a deep sigh and continued.

"Well I went on ahead and gave 'em my sorries and accepted thur invite to participate in that thur mourning shin-dig, since I know'd Tom Monroe and all. The other reason being I wanted ta meet this here wagon feller and give him 'the eye' and get him ta tell the truth about the whole thin'. I jest had me a feelin' about that thur tall-tale he was claimin' ta be true. Hit jest didn't have the right smell ta hit, if ya know what I mean.

"Well, I walked on over ta the church house with the other menfolk, and standing right out in front of the church house was the widder woman, Azalea Rose Monroe. Now I'd met Azalea Rose onces't or twice afore and she is one fine lookin' woman. She looked purdy as a picture in that there black dress and a little black hat with a veil like thing-a-ma-jig hangin' down in front of her eyes. And what-do-ya-know, but right next ta her stood old Clay Bloomers, one o' my old neighbor's from way back yonder when we weren't no bigger'n tadpoles, an he was all hugged up on Azalea Rose like he was comfortin' her and all."

Mr. Bushy gave a low snickering laugh.

"Well, right off I know'd if Clay Bloomers was the wagon-feller, the whole dang tale was a big ol' whopper of a lie. But I kept my mouth shut, paid my respects to the widder woman and walked on inta the church house where I took me a stand at the very back of the room. And ya know…I don't think old Clay Bloomers membered who I was.

"Well, with Tom Monroe being from such a big family and all, people was packin' inta that church house like pickles in a barrel; Tom's kin has lived in the Oh-zarks for over a hun'ert years or more. His Pappy comes from a family of twenty nine brothers, all with the same pappy but five different mamas. After one wife had a few younguns, she would up and die on him and then he'd find himself another woman and she'd do the same thing.

"Well pretty soon, in walks Clay Bloomers and he's holdin' Azalea Rose's arm real tender-like and he gently leads her to the front row of the church-house and helps her have a sit-down. Then, he plops his sorry self right down beside her in the very place her Pa should have been sittin' in. He was kindly struttin', if ya know what I mean, right down in front of Tom's pine box, which in my eyes weren't even showin' a wood tick's worth of respect fur Tom. And then, low-and-behold, he puts his arms round Azalea Rose's shoulders, leans over real cozy like an starts in whisperin' in her ear, kindly like he was doin' some comfort talkin'. Which, by the way, shoulda been done by Azalea Rose's Ma or Pa.

Well, right behind Azalea Rose and Clay Bloomers comes all the rest of Tom's close kin. His Ma, Pa and all his brothers and sisters and the church house filled right up until ever space was full and the late-comers had ta stand outside the open winders so's they could hear Reverend Coy tellin' bout Tom's good deeds – some of which were kindly made-up, so be could be put in the ground with tales of goodness.

Well, Tom's wife starts in wailing and old Clay keeps his arm around her shoulders as he gives her a little squeeze. Hit was mighty disrespectful in the Lord's house iff'en ya ask me, and I hear'd some other fellers mumblin' when he did that thur thing. And some of them thur women-folk began lookin' at each other, shakin' their heads in disbelief and jest whisperin' up a storm like a bunch of hen chickens.

Then Reverend Coy stands up and solemnly starts in walkin' to the pulpit, using both hands to clinch the Bible to his chest with a genuine grief-stricken look on his face since he knew Tom so well and all, when out from the road I hear this here bellowing. I peep around the door a bit, stretchin' my neck to see what was goin' on, and low-and-behold I see Clyde T. Monroe running down the road as fast as his legs can carry him. His knees was churnin' high and his feet was plowin' up dust with his arms pumpin' like the wheels of a locomotive. His chest was stuck out and his long, skinny neck was noddin' his head with ever flyin' step he took. His head, arms and legs were all working together like a well moving machine."

Mr. Bushy was trying to hold back some deep laughter.

"That old black mountain dust was flyin' everwhere. He had on his black Sunday-go-ta-meetin' clothes and his Sunday hat was pulled low on his head so's not to fall off his head.

"At first I thought he was runnin' to make it to his brother's buryin' on time, but in jest two shakes I spot old Bocephus the one-horned bull right behind 'em, an that bull was tearin' up jack. Old Bocephus belongs to Jet Pruiett, and that old bull is old as Methuselah an mean as Lucifer. Hits body is covered with shaggy, mangy fur and ever since he was a young'un he only had one horn, and that one horn grow'd right out in front of his face. In fact, Jet had to citch 'em ever onces't in a while and saw his horn off so the bad-tempered thing could see.

Now, afore I finish my tellin', I gotta tell ya this one thing bout Jet Pruiett and ol' Bocephus the bull.

One night, way back yonder, after an evenin' of courtin' his sweetheart Grace, Jet was walkin' home alone in the dark of night... ya know...one o' them thur nights when ya cain't see yur own hand in front of yur face, when off in the bushes he hears somethin' walkin' along follerin' him. Well, this goes on fur a good long while and then Jet hears this here deep purrin' noise so he stops and peers real careful-like and what do ya know but he sees these here glowin' yeller eyes of a black panther. Well, that big old black cat was a'slinkin' along in the bushes beside the path as it follered 'em. Well, Jet ain't got no place ta run so he jest keeps on walkin' an whistlin' tryin' ta act real calm-like an hopin' he can reach the big oak tree at the next turn in the path cuz that big oak tree ain't too far from his house and he's thinkin' maybe he could give some hollers and his Pa would come out and help him.

But, real quick-like, he hears that big old cat's purrin' turn inta a deep chested growl and Jet knows for sure that cat is hunkerin' down on his haunches getting' ready ta pounce when...out of nowhere burst his pappy's young bull Bocephus and that bull teared inta that cat with vengeance. Jet took off running and never looked back. The next day when Jet went out and checked on Bocephus, the bull was fine an dandy but that big cat was stomped inta a puddle. So...since that very day Jet never had the heart to get rid of old Bocephus. Even though, I do believe, he was the meanest bull I ever did see. Yep...he was the meanest."

"Well anyway," he continued, "One-horned Bocephus had, at one time, got himself caught in a rabbit trap an ended up with a gimp foot. So he weren't much of a fast runner, but hit looked like the old bull was gainin' on Clyde.

"In jest a few shakes Clyde turned the corner of the path and headed into the church house as he picks up a little speed an gains some distance between himself and that old bull.

"Up the steps Clyde charged and without missin' a lick, he dashed right in through the open church doors, up the aisle at full throttle with ol' Bocephus bringin' up the rear. Clyde headed straight fur the buryin' box holdin' his brothers body and jest as he reached that pine box he gives himself a leap, and up and over that pine box he sailed, right smack dab into Reverend Coy's arms and they both hit the floor with a loud *thud.*

"By this time, everone in that church house was standin' on thur feet with dumbfounded amazement on their faces and their eyes were bugged out like frogs.

"Now, old Bocephus didn't hesitate fur one second, he came thunderin' down that aisle like a steam engine an kept right on bellerin' like ah herd of buf'lo' down the aisle towards that pine box. The pounding of hooves and the bellers comin' out of that ol' bull echoed through that little church like a twister on the prairie as it shook the rafters and swayed the walls. Then the women-folk start in screaming and trying ta run fur the doors but thur husbands was holdin' 'em back against the pews, jest in case old Bocephus changed his mind and charged back out the door.

"Well, Bocephus stampeded right on towards Tom's piney box and then – it seemed kindly like it was in slow motion – he plowed inta that buryin' box, splinterin' it inta bits, then straightaway falls over dead right onta the floor an ah roaring, thunderous fart exploded from Bocephus' body like a shotgun an purt near shattered the winders. All them church folks gasped loudly an started in gaggin' and some of them delicate women fainted right over onta the floor. Tom's dead body rose out of that piney box in slow motion, hovered over dead Bocephus for a few seconds, comes down on the side of that old bull and skids onta the floor where it starts rollin' like an old tumble weed down the aisle towards the door. Hit musta rolled over twenty times afore hit came to a stop right at my feet.

"The whole church house got quiet as a bone-yard, and then a few women folk start in gaspin' at the awful happenin's during the service. All the young lads rushed over ta take a good gander at ol Tom's dead body, as did thur pappys. Even the young gal's pushed in ta have a good look-see. Within minutes, everbody was comin' toward the aisle ta take a good gander at poor ol' dead Tom.

"The young widder woman, Azalea Rose runs right down next to me, takes one look at her Tom's body and then *she* faints away onta the floor with a loud *kur-plunk*.

"Well I'm starin' down at dead Tom, when all of a sudden I see his eyeballs pop open and he starts in lookin' round. A couple of the yung'uns gasped and I heard a few woman-folk scream. Now, I ain't scared o' much a'tall, but that was spookin' me. My heart was right up in my ears beatin' out a steady rhythm on my eardrums and my eyes bugged out like frog eyes. Tom simply lays thur fur a minute or two then sits right up and says ta me, 'How-do, Mr. Bushy? Ya been kissin' any sweet hogs lately?'"

Mr. Bushy gave a deep-chested chuckle, cleared his throat and continued.

"Now, I know'd why he ask'd me that thur question in particular, cuz not too long ago Tom and some of his rapscallion cousins caught me sittin' under a big o' tree after one of them thur marryin' up shin-digs and I was sleepin' like a new born babe. So they poured molasses all over my face then pulled an old sow-hog over ta me and I waked up with that old sow-hog jest a'larppin' all that molasses off'en my face all the while I was dreamin' 'bout yor beautiful Aunt Maggie Mae."

Mr. Bushy stopped talking and gave a loud laugh.

"Well, seein' a dead body come back ta life is a mite strange, but I go ahead and reach on down and give Tom a hand-up. Then he gets to his feet, kindly shaky an all, an takes a slow gander 'round at all the folks and gives them all a big ear-ta-ear smile an says 'howdy, thank ye fur coming!' But when he spots old Clay Bloomers standin' right thur in front of that whole bunch o' church folk, Tom points a shakin' finger at old Clay and shouts out: 'YOU!'

"'You hit me on the head after I climbed out of that thur tree.' Tom yells out, 'I was wantin' yur help and ya hit me on the head and ya thought ya kilt me, didn't ya? I'm gonna beat ya to a pulp is what I'm gonna do!'

"Well, I know'd he couldn't beat a five-year old to a pulp, cuz he could barely stand on his own two feet. But he takes off up the aisle real wobbly-like, havin' ta hold onto the end of each pew he's passin' as he tries his best ta get ta old Clay Bloomers. But jest as Tom takes a few steps, Clay jumped on top of dead Bocephus, whips out his pistol and points it straight at Tom an yells out, 'Hold et right ther'ah, Tom!'

"Then Azalea Rose comes to from her faint, and sees Tom headin' towards Clay and his pistol, so she jumps right up and plants herself between Tom and Clay an yells for Clay to 'Stop it and put that fool gun down.'

"'Ya bet'duh git out of the way, darlin',' Clay drawled. 'Tom, I'm gonna shoot ya dead an this time you will stay dead, and then I'm gonna take Azalea Rose away from this raggedy place.'

"The whole church let out a gasp – to think someone had such crazy notions about their mountain being a 'raggedy place' – and turned to each other with frowns and started murmuring and grumbling about the rude disrespect for their mountain, totally ignoring old Clay."

Mr. Bushy stopped telling for a few seconds and had a good laugh.

"Well, Old Clay raises his gun in the air and shot off two shots. *BANG BANG!* Right inta the roof of that church house. Real quick-like, everbody in the church house sucked in their breath and watched with anticipation fur lightening ta strike old Clay Bloomers fur disrepectin' the Lord's house and threats of killin' someone right in front of God himself and the Reverend. Although, at that point, I do believe Reverend Coy was still passed out under the pulpit with Clyde Monroe.

"'Ah said,' Clay shouted, 'Move aside, Azalea Rose darlin', Ah'm gonna shoot your'ah husband dead! An then the two of us are gonna be leavin' this place and goin' down ta Natchez ta live with civilized folk and raise us up a family.'

"Clay slowly stepped down off that old bull and stood right next ta its hind quarters as he lowered his gun and pointed it right at Azalea

Rose's heart. 'Move aside, darlin', or ah'm gonna shoot Tom right thru ya. Do ya he'ah me now, darlin'?'

"'You're my father's friend from many years ago,' Azalea Rose yelled at Clay. 'I don't love ya in the least and I never will. You're an old man!'

"'Oh, darlin', ya will come ta love me, an ya'll thank me 'til the day ya leave this earth for takin' ya away from this here'ah horrible place.'

"Azalea Rose stood right where she was, starin' at old Clay like she too was waitin' fur God's wrath ta fall upon 'em.

"And then…", Mr. Bushy snickered.

"And then the wrath came slippin' in with furious vengeance. Another thunderous fart exploded from old Bocephus' behind like ah double-barrel shot gun, and at that very minute Great Granny Bitsy, who was standin' in the front row in her place of honor, dropped her cigar and that gas from ol Bocephus' body turns into a ball of far and knocks Clay Bloomers down onta the floor beside Bocephus, who instantly let go a *third* rip-snortin' fart. And this one was so par'ful hit rolled that big old bull right over on top o' Clay Bloomers. Clay's gun goes off one last time afore he was crushed under that ol' bull, and that bullet shot a hole right through Delbert Monroe's hat and sent hit flying right out through the open winder."

Mr. Bushy slapped his knee in roaring laughter for almost a whole minute before continuing his story.

"After a bit of silence, ever last soul in that thur church starts in cheerin' an clappin' an thankin' the Good Lord on high for the favor.

"And that was the end of that old bull and old Clay Bloomers, since he was all crushed up and all. The undertaker hauled Clay's body off while the rest of us got some mules and a chain and helped Jet Pruiett tote his dead bull out of the church house. Then we all went on out to the cemetary an watched as Thomas T. Monro shoveled the dirt back inta that buryin' hole. When the last shovelfull was in, Thomas T. stood up straight as an arrow, lifted his hand to his forehead and gave a soldier's say-lute and said, 'Thank ye death fur not takin' me in, and ah thank the good Lord on high fur lettin' me stay on this here earth fur a while longer. I know this here hole will be here waitin' when I need it.' Then off we went to the church yard and had us a happy shin-dig instead of a sad one, seeing that Thomas T. Monroe was again amongst' the livin'. That young Doc Patton said sometimes a body will move even after hits dead and gone, as was the reason fur old Bocephus's fartin', but we all know'd hit was a favor from someone watchin' over Tom T Monroe. Doc Patton says Tom was jest in a co'mer, whatever that is."

Mr. Bushy's final words had not quite cleared his mouth when someone started banging loudly on the door and before André could get up out of his chair to see who it was, the door slammed open and in rushed Pete Turnkey. Pete Turnkey was the ticketmaster at the train depot, as well as André's part-time deputy.

"Sheriff," Pete blurted out. "I do believe we have Tillie Brown's killers. One of the barkeeps down at the Ruby Slipper came charging up to my ticket booth just a minute or so ago and says for me to come out and get you and get you quick. It seems two fellas from down around the bayous are sittin' at a table in the Ruby Slipper bragging about taking away one of Tillie's lives. That barkeep said their names are Girard something-or-other, and the other one is called Thomas Lafitte. He said they were braging about killing some other woman as well. Maybe we have our killers."

In through the door walked Benny.

"I'm going too!" Lily jumped up and said.

"No yor'ah not, Lily-Beth," André replied sternly as he turned and gave Lily one of his don't-argue-with-me-looks. "No tellin' what these two have up they'ah sleeves. Benny, you come on along with me and Deputy Pete. I'll send ya back home he'ah when its safe for'ah these women-folk ta go outside. Caitlin, you and Lily-Beth stay right he'ah and keep a watch out for those two men. Keep that rifle handy and all of ya stay right he'ah in this house! Don't even go out to the barn, even if it's burnin' down. Now that ther'ah is an order. Caitlin, you make sur'ah Lily-Beth does exactly what I said. Mr. Bushy, he'ahs yor gun, keep it on yor'ah lap. Any stangers come to the door'uh, Lily-Beth will tell ya if it's those bayou boys and if it is, it's time to do some shootin'. And, Tessa honey, I know I don't have ta worry about ya."

Tessa looked over at Lily and stuck her tongue out as soon as André turned his back.

"Let's go boys," he said. Out the door to their horses flew André, Benny and Deputy Pete.

As soon as they left, Tessa crawled onto Caitlin's lap with her face drained of all its color. Her bottom lip was quivering ever so slightly. She looked as if at any minute she would start crying.

"Well," Mr. Bushy said as he turned to Tessa and held out his arms, "Come over here Tessa lass. Ain't nothin' gonna hurt any of ya while I'm here. Come, let me tell ya'll another one of my tales."

Immediately, Tessa scrambled up onto Mr. Bushy's lap and snuggled her face right into his furry beard.

"Well, let's see me love, what tale should I be tellin'?" Mr. Bushy moved the rocking chair into motion and gave a deep sigh.

"Let me tell ya about the time I wrestled with a big o' bar until the wee hours of the night." Mr. Bushy started telling his tale in a soft, quiet voice to comfort and calm Tessa's fears and maybe put her to sleep for a bit.

"Late one afternoon I was jest sittin' on my porch rockin' in my rickety o' rockin' chair, enjoying the cool summer breeze as it softly blew across my face an chased all the worries of the world away, and listening to the sweet sounds of night coming on. The buzzin' of the Cicadas was sweepin' loud through the tree tops as June Bugs buzzed around my head and the bull frogs and cricket calls echoed up from the creek and ponds. I still remember that night as if it was yesterday. My soul was at peace with nature and my heart was filled right up with the soothing comfort of God's handiwork. Nothing was wrong in the world that night. Twilight started weavin' its way through the timbers as the shadows lengthened and daylight slipped on out on its way into the west. Red and pink clouds lit up the western sky with the promise of a beautiful new day at dawn. Bit by bit farflies began flashin' their lights, lookin' like tiny fairy lanterns flickerin' amongst the darkened greenery. The stealthy rustles of night creatures floated into my ears on the wings of the gentle breeze and the hauntin' calls of the Lake Loon softly echoed through the valley and up to my cabin door."

Mr. Bushy paused and looked down at Tessa, who was now sound asleep on his lap. Mr. Bushy had a special place in his heart for her. Granny Tomason says the reason is because many years ago, Mr. Bushy had lost his wife and his only little red-haired daughter in a house fire when he was out trapping and had not found out about it until days after his wife and little daughter were buried. When Tessa was born, Mr. Bushy immediately took on a strong parental attachment for her as if he felt a kindred spirit. For unknown reasons, Tessa was also drawn to Mr. Bushy. Whenever he came around she was in hog's heaven.

Giving his rocking chair another little push, Mr. Bushy continued with his mountain tale of strange happenings.

"Well, I was sittin' there jest relaxin' and enjoyin' the world when… all of a sudden…here comes Charlie Brigadoon tearin' through the trees yellin'; 'Grab yer gun, Bushy…grab yer gun!'. Now, old Charlie Brigadoon is this here long-tall lanky mountain feller who lives all by himself way up by Bluff Lookout in the Oh-zarks. He has a heart o' gold…ain't never hurt another feller in his life. And I've know'd him since I was jest a young fella startin' out livin' in these mountains.

I figgered he was really needin' some help iff'en he's askin' fur it. Ya see, Charlie ain't never asked nooo-body fur help as long as I know'd him. So…I jumps right up, snatches up my rifle and waits fur him ta tell me what ta shoot at. He's 'bout a hunert yards away from me so's I walk on out inta my yard and he bellows out: 'Turn 'round, Bushy…turn 'round!' and then… 'Whollop"…somethin' whacks me on my back and slammed me to the ground! Just a'fore I hit the ground I turn my head and see'd Brigadoon's pet bar, Aloysius Cornelius. Now…Aloysius Cornelius must be old as Saint Pet himself. He cain't get around none to fast and all his teeth and claws fell out years ago an ever time I see'd 'em, he's as gentle as a new born pup, but somethin' must'a happened to him that day cuz he was rarin' ta go."

Mr. Bushy stopped talking and gave out a deep chuckle.

"Well…I jumps right up and latched onto his neck and hung on fur dear life. Old Aloysius tries and tries ta give me a deadly swipe, but he jest cain't do it and by this time Charlie's right there beside me and he jumps onto Aloysius's back and there we go…rollin' 'round with that big o' bar and…we was havin' us a grand old time.

All three of us start in a'rollin' and a'tumblin' 'round in front of my cabin. That o' bar is jest growlin' and tryin' ever which way to get away from us, but me and old Charlie hang on like fleas on a dog.

Well, I work my way 'round and climb up on the back of that ol' bar in front of Charlie and as soon as I get a good grip on his fur Aloysius takes off running fur the creek!  By that time, me and Charlie both lost our rifles and are hangin' on enjoyin' the ride. Pretty soon, ol' Aloysius slows down to a crawl, but me and Charlie keep right on hangin' on and then we start in laughin'. It was kindly fun riding that ol' bar.

Well, pretty quick-like that bar comes upon a patch of wild strawberries and stops ta have a bite ta ear so's me and Charlie sit thur on his back and start in havin' a nice friendly talkin'."

'How ya been, Charlie?' I say.

'Well, cain't complain, Bushy, cain't complain. I been doin' some good trapping and getting' some *fine* hides ta take on up ta St. Louie. I was fixin' up some taters and biscuits when old Aloysius come'd 'round the side of my cabin jest a-bellern' like a bull and takes off runnin' down toward yor place. I know'd he would start in tearin' up yor cabin iff'en I didn't foller him down and warn ya. I'm much obliged to ya, Bushy. Much obliged. How ya been doin' ya self, Bushy?'

'Mighty fine, Charlie, mighty fine' I says, 'Can' complain. Life is good.'

Me and Charlie we keep on yakkin' fur what seems like hours on end with that old bar still rootin' 'round fur wild berries.

Then Aloysius starts in tryin' ta run again and he takes us on a jolly ride. He goes up and down them hills like he's huntin' fur somethin'. Finally, he starts in pantin' and drool is drippin' out of his mouth as he goes slower and slower until he's barely movin' a'tall. By that time he had circled on back ta the creek in front o' my cabin and walks smack dab inta the middle of hit an... 'plop'...down he goes inta that water. The only thin' stickin' out was his nose, which he had layin' on a big ol' rock, and his back. And there we sat...on top of that old bar with our feet and legs stuck inta that icy cold creek water. Charlie hops down off'en Aloysius's and bends down ta take a good look at 'em.

'Wellll, Bushy,' he says real slow-like, 'I'll be a dog-eared pup...I do deeee-clare...this ol' bar is sound asleep. And...I din't notice hit a'fore, but he smells like he done got inta my cornmash, and I'll be a hind-leg-of-a-hound-dog iff'en I know'd how he did that thur. He's as drunk as ol' Cooter Brown. I reckon we better let him sleep hit off. Humpf, I guess we don't have a choice, do we?'

'Nope, Charlie, I don't reckon we do.' I say, 'Let's go on up ta the porch and have us a nice sit-down, drink us some homemade sweet tea and have ah visit.'

'That thur sounds good ta me.' Charlie says.

So we pick up our rifles from the ground where we dropped 'em and go on back to the cabin ta have us a right nice sit-down fur a spell. We don't say nary a word ta each other, but hit was a nice sit-down and the sweet tea was might tasty. We sit thur a couple hours jest ah rockin' in them chairs and listenin' to the world go by. Then Charlie stands up, picks up his rifle and starts off up the mountain to his own cabin. He gets about a huner't feet away when he turns 'round an yells: 'Mightly fine visit Bushy, enjoyed the talkin...much obliged fur the sweet tea'.

Well, I give him a wave an jest keep sittin' there rockin'in my old rocker until I get on up and go on inside ta get me some shut-eye. I didn't even bother takin' my shoes off, I jest laid right down on my bed and a'fore I knew'd it, I was sound asleep.

Well, along 'bout five in the mornin'or so, when the sun is jest a'peekin' up over the horizon, somethin' strange wakes me up. I pop right up, peeped out my winder and low-an-behold, staring right back at me was this here little feller's face jest a grinnin'back at me and on his head sat this here little bowler hat. He had short red whiskers and his red mustache was curled inta a big handle-bar mustache stickin' way out beyond his ears. He was jest a'grinnin' from ear ta ear. Well, I jumps right up, grabbed my rifle and opens my door ta see iff'en he needs any help, and there he sat riding the biggest white horse I ever did see.

'Can I help ya, mister?' I say.'

'My name is Joseph David Prescott,' the little feller said, 'Just passin' through and saw your bear sitting on your tree stump over yonder and wondered if ya be wantin' ta sell 'em?

'What bar?' I say.

'Why, that bear sittin' over yonder on your tree stump.' He says and points down toward my creek.

Well, I turned my head towards the creek and sure nuf', there on one o' my tree stumps sat Aloysius Cornelius just as purty as ya please. He was sittin' thur lookin' at me and that thur little feller jest like a man would sit leaned against a tree stump. He had his legs crossed an I swear he had this here smile on his face.

Well, I tell the little feller Aloysius ain't my bar but I know'd who he belonged to. So I send 'em on up ta old Charlie's place and kindly tells him that old Charlie may not want ta sell his pet bar, but he insists on goin' on up thur and talkin to Charlie, so's that what he does. Not too long after he left, I hear Charlie coming down that mountain jest a'yellin' at the top of his lungs fur Aloysius Cornelius and when I go out on my porch and look over at the stump an all's I see is a young feller sitting thur with his back leaned against that stump smokin' on a pipe. He was all stretched out jest as comfy as can be. I look back at Charlie and he's still yelling over at that young feller and the young feller jest keeps on smokin' that thur pipe real lazy-like and then slowly he unwinds his long tall self up from the ground and walks over ta meet Charlie. Well…by that time I'm standin' at the bottom of my steps jest a'gawkin' like ah kid at the travelin' circus. I swear till this very day that young feller was not sittin' thur leanin' 'gainst my stump when I first looked out thur earlier when that little feller was there. Hit was Charlie's old bar!

Well I walk on down ta meet Charlie and that thur young feller and Charlie was talking real fast-like to the young feller. When I got close, Charlie stopped his yappin' and gave me a nod.

'Howdy' Charlie says

'How-do, Charlie.' I said, "who's this young feller here?'

'This here is Aloysius Cornelius.' He says, kindly sheepish-like.

'Aloysius Cornelius?' I asked, real muddled.

'Yep…that's what I said' Charlie answered.

Well, I'm jest as puzzled-up as a young-uns picture puzzle, but I go right on ahead and shake the young feller's hand and tells him 'How-do".

'How-do, Mr. Bushy,' the young feller says, 'mighty nice ta meet ya. I do hope ya had a pleasant evenin' last night. It was a mighty fine evenin' for a stroll, now wasn't it?'

I nodded my head and tell him I had a good 'nuf evenin', then him and old Charlie take off runnin' up Charlie's mountain.

Now…that thur was the strangest thing I ever did see in my whole life, and I've seen a lot o' stange happenin's on my mountain, but that thur was maybe the strangest. I never did see that little feller with the red mustache again and I ain't never seen that young Aloysius feller again neither. As a matter of fact, I ain't seen old Charlie in a month o' Sundays."

Mr. Bushy again starts scratching his beard as if in deep thought.

"Now, I was talkin' ta them thur Oh-zark hill folk about hit one time and they swore that old bar and that young Alysius feller be the same being. I don't rightly believe all them thur tales them folks tell me, but they said the American Indians call 'em Skin-walkers and these here Skin-walkers can change inta any ol' animal they want to be, anytime they want to. Like they can move thur skin around inta another being. And…the thin' that makes hit even more peculiar is… before I ever told 'em about that thur little feller on that big white horse, they told me evertime a Skin-walker changes, a white horse on a Leprechaun appears. Now, that thur is mighty irregular ta me. I reckon I ain't believin' that there particular tall tale. But that's jest the way hit happened and I ain't changed nary a word."

SLAM! The front burst open again, startling them all, and in walked André, Benny and Mr. Pete.

"We caught both of them!" Benny announced loudly.

"Shh," Mr. Bushy said quietly. "This here little gal is jest plum tuckered out and we don't want ta wake her up."

"Sorry," Benny whispered. "But we caught them both, and they confessed to trying to kill Tillie Brown a couple days back. They were sure she was dead until she chased them through the river bottom trying to get Lily and Ophelia away from them. They even confessed to taking Tillie's pouch of gold dust off her body, *and* snatching Gertie P. off Granny Wilkes porch the same day."

Benny started laughing as he continued telling about the capture and arrest of the two bayou boys.

"They even confessed to throwing Corn-Shuckin' John and Watermelon Willie off the raft, hoping the snakes would get them, or in hopes they would just drown. Didn't they, André?"

"Yes, they did," André said. "They confessed to everything, and even some things we didn't rightly know 'bout, but they swor'ah they did not kill Tillie the second time around. So we don't think we can charge 'em with that one. But we did arrest 'em for kidnapping you three gals and all the other things they confessed to us. I *can* say it will be a long time for'ah them in prison; maybe for'ah the rest of their lives."

Sighing with relief, Lily leaned her head back against the wall and enjoyed the satisfying sense of being free from fear.

# 12

## THE PRUIETT BOYS

It was another hot, muggy Saturday, and most of the people of Caruthersville had given up on finding the killer of Tillie Brown. Sheriff André had put a notice in the Caruthersville Herald letting everyone for miles around know there would be a one-dollar reward for the person – or persons – who could help lead to the arrest and conviction of the guilty parties.

As Sheriff André and Deputy Pete sat in their sweltering office drinking hot coffee and dreaming of diving into the cool waters of the Mississippi river, in through the door at a full run came Ott and Paul Pruiett.

Paul, the oldest, had a slight build and light, white-blond hair. Ott, who was not even a year younger than Paul, also had white-blond hair, but was taller and stockier than his older brother. Both boys were always punching or wrestling with each other, and if not with each other, it was with some of their many cousins living in the area.

Not stopping to say "Howdy" or "Excuse us", they raced in, flopped their bodies across André's desk with a loud *thud* loudly announced, "We found 'em, Sheriff, we found the killers!"

"Yep, Sheriff, we did. Do we get the dollar?"

"We already know what we're gonna spend it on. Ain't that right, Paul?"

"Yep, we do."

Ott started laughing and Paul joined in.

"We're gonna spend the whole dollar on a bag of candy at our Grandpappy's store. We're gonna have one hundred pieces of candy and we ain't sharing it with nooo-body 'cept Tom, Benny and Steve."

"Well," Ott scratched his head as if in deep thought, "maybe we'll give one piece each to Robbie and Frankie, if we have any left that is. But we ain't givin' any to the girls. They're mean'uns. Whenver our Ma and Steve's Ma makes us take a whoopin' them girls are snickerin' and laughin' the whole –"

"Well boys," André interuppted, in his slight Cajun accent. "First off, wipe off those dirt chunks ya got on my desk. Then tell us how ya solved this he'ah mystery."

Sheepishly Ott and Paul leaned over and wiped the dirt and dust off Sheriff André's desk with their shirttails and mumbled, "Oops, sorry Sheriff."

"Okay. What's yor'ah story?" Sheriff André grinned as he thought of Paul's expression of his sisters being their "burdens to bear".

Ott and Paul looked at each other and then leaned in close to André and Pete as Ott whispered in a sinister voice.

"Well, me and Paul went on over ta Hayti an was sittin' in front of the *Sugar Cake Bake Shop* waitin' for Georgie Dee ta meet us so we could go on down ta the river bottom and catch some snakes ta scare the girls with when we decided to sneak into that saloon called *The Broke Jug*. We slipped in and took us a seat on the floor back in one of them dark corners and sat there listenin' to all those fellas talking.

Well, there was this one fella sittin' at the bar named Pike something-or-other and he was bragging about stealing ah big o' black horse. He said that horse was the biggest horse he ever did see and it had muscles big as a barn, an that was when me and Paul looked at each other and knew right off he was talking 'bout Tillie Brown's horse Tally-Ho. He said he led that big horse all the way down to the river and was standing in the shallow water before he tried getting' on that big horse. But that horse startin' in buckin' and threw him off into the water and then the horse started raising up on its back legs an was gonna crush him with his front hooves when this Pike fella drew out his gun in a flash and shot that horse right through the heart! Then he said he had to roll real fast out of the way or that big horse would have fell right on top of him and squished him like a bug. Then he said he watched as the river came in and washed that big horse down the river.

Then he said he was so mad he went on back and found "that woman" in the field working in her garden and he decides to take his madness out on her, so he ends up getting' rid of her too! He said he didn't think that woman was so frail and all, seeing how strong she was, but he did her in and he's glad she's gone.

Well, by then me and Paul figured it all out. We figure "that woman" must be Tillie Brown and he thought she was tough as nails cuz she does all the work 'round her place and puts in her own garden an all every year. He must have taken her body on down to the river and dumped it in so it would look like she was with her horse when she died."

"That's right, Sheriff," Paul said. "Then me and Ott figured we better get on out of that saloon quick, cuz if Ma found out 'bout us being in there she would tan our hides. And anyway, after we left the saloon, Georgie Dee's Ma saw us and told us Georgie Dee had to go over to Kennet with his Pa ta pick up some cow manure. So here we are ready to collect that dollar. Ain't that right, Ott?"

"Yep, that's right as rain," Ott replied.

"Well…" Sheriff André drawled, "that dollar is only when yor'ah information leads to the arrest and conviction of the guilty party. That means the person has ta be caught and tried for the crime. So, I cain't give it to ya today, but we will investigate this information ya gave us. How about I give ya each a penny right now for all yor'ah information and then if this Pike fella is arrested and tried, I'll give ya the rest of the dollar?"

"Fair enough ta us, ain't it Paul?" Ott said with a big smile as he took the penny from André. "Come on Paul, let's go on over ta Grandpappy's store and buy us some candy. Come on, let's race!"

"Yippee!" Paul yelled as the two of them ran out the door.

André and Pete sat there for a minute as they watched Ott and Paul take off for Pruiett's General Store.

"Effie Mae sur'ah has her hands full with all them boys o' hers, don't she?"

"Yep, she certainly does," Pete replied.

"Well, I sur'ah do hope those burdensome sisters are the only burdens dey have ta bear in life," Sheriff André laughed.

Laughing, Deputy Pete agreed.

"How about we get on out of he'ah and take us a ride ov'ah ta *The Broke Jug* and see if we can find this he'ah Pike fella? Ya ev'ah heard of 'em, Pete?"

"Nope, can't say I have."

# 13

## MR. DT BROWN

Lily was helping Caitlin with supper when up onto the porch raced Ophelia, pushing her face against the screen door. "Lily, you home?"

"Yes, she is. Come on in, Ophelia," Caitlin called out. "You can help Lily sit the table for supper and then you can have a sit-down and eat with us.

"Hi, Ophelia!" Lily called out.

"Thank you, Mrs. Beaumont. Hi, Lily. Ma said I could stay if you didn't mind and I didn't ask. Now I can tell her you asked and I wasn't rude by asking myself over," Ophelia laughed.

"What's going on, Ophelia?" Lily stopped and looked at her friend's face. Ophelia was figetting with her hands.

"Well, you won't believe it," she said excitedly. "but my Pa knows a Mr. Brown! This Mr. Brown lives over in Piney. Pa said he has no idea if this Mr. Brown is related to Tillie Brown, but then again, maybe he is. Pa also said it would be okay for me to go down there with you if your folks don't care. After I told him about the impor- tance of finding one of Tillie's kin, he said we could ride one of our mules if we wanted to. I guess Pa met this Mr. Brown some years back when this fella was looking for work. Pa hired him to do some handy work at the store. He said Mr. Brown knew an awful lot about building and such, so he worked for Pa near on three years. I guess every Saturday Pa would ask Mr. Brown if he would like to come on over to our house to have some supper with us but Mr. Brown kindly refused, saying he had to get back to his home. He wasn't married and he didn't have any children, so Pa is thinking maybe he's Tillie's uncle, or older cousin or something like that. In fact, Pa said this Mr. Brown he knows came over here from Russia a long time ago."

"Wow," Lily replied, "May I go Caitlin? Maybe this Mr. Brown is a relative of Tillie's and we can give him the locket."

"Well," Caitlin said, pausing to think. "After we have supper, and only if you promise to come right home after your visit and be sure and make it home before dark."

"Yes?"

The old gentleman spoke softly as he opened the squeaky, wooden screen door. He was a tall, thin man with thick, white hair combed back neatly from his face and caught by a strip of black leather at the nap of his neck. It was not long and scraggly; it was short – just long enough for the strip of leather to catch it tightly. His spectacles were perched on the middle of his nose, making it possible for him to look over them as he looked down at the two young girls. His white suit was slightly too big as if he had at one time been a larger, muscular man. It was clean and neatly pressed, as was his shirt but both was slightly worn around the cuffs. He was a stately-looking gentleman, reminding Lily of a kind, old aristocrat from Europe. He stood slightly stoope, at the door of his house; he looked as if years of sorrow had worn him down. His face was lean, brown, and weathered with wrinkles from long labor in the sun. Pale, grey eyes looked out from beneath heavy, white eyebrows. Those eyes were strong and alert, not willing to back down from the unknown problems which may enter his life. Even though his eyes were penetrating, sorrow and sadness seemed to flow out into the realm of his vision. His hands were tanned and on the back of his hands the veins were raised unusually high. One finger was crooked, as if maybe it had been broken during his years of outdoor labor. Long, bronzed, gnarled fingers rested on the doorframe as he waited for an answer.

Lily shuffled her feet in hesitation, not wanting to venture where she knew she must go. Maybe it would be best if she and Ophelia walked away so as to not burden this stately old gentleman with more sorrow than he already carried.

"Are you related to Mr. Dannison T. Brown?" Lily asked softly.

"Yes miss, I am," he answered with a softly flowing foreign accent.

"Well, sir, I think we may have something belonging to you, if you are related to a Tillie Brown."

"I am Dannison T. Brown. I am Tillie's father," he said with a soft smile on his face as he leaned slightly forward with obvious interest. "And what might you have for me, young lady?"

"It is from your daughter Tillie, sir," Lily said with a shaky voice. "When she passed on, she gave it to me and asked me to find a relative to whom I could give to. So if Tillie is your daughter, you are the very person we have been looking for."

The old gentleman did not speak for a few minutes as he stood leaning against the door frame staring at Lily. His eyes filled with moisture as sorrow reached out and touched Lily's soul and pulled on her heart strings. Not knowing what to say, Lily nervously cleared her throat.

"If you rather, sir," Lily said quietly, holding out the locket to him as she and Ophelia began backing away from his door. "We can just leave this with you and not trouble you with anything more. We are so very sorry for arriving without warning."

As Lily and Ophelia turned to walk away, the old gentleman spoke in a low whisper.

"Stop, please. You are not an intrusion in my life. Please, come in. Come in."

Both girls stopped and looked back at Mr. Brown. A tender look had come across his face and his eyes had softened into a light blue-grey. Hesitantly the girls stopped and turned back toward the door as Mr. Brown walked out and held the door open for them to enter.

"Please, my dear young ladies, please do come in."

Mr. Brown's house was small, but neat. It was a small one story house with a small parlor, kitchen, and what looked like a bedroom off the back of the kitchen. In the parlor sat three chairs, a large, cushioned rocker and a small table holding a lantern. Red, white and blue handmade cushions were on the seats of each chair and on the parlor floor was a tattered red, white and blue braided rag rug. In the corner of the kitchen, next to the cook-stove lay a big, brown hound. When the girls entered the house, the hound started making a low rumble in its chest as it looked at Mr. Brown. Mr. Brown spoke to the dog in a language neither girl understood, and the hound lay its head back down but kept his eyes open and focused on the girls.

"Please have a seat, ladies."

"Thank you, sir," both girls replied.

Mr. Brown went into the kitchen, pumped water out of the pump in his dry sink and carried three glasses of water back to the parlor.

"I am sorry, young ladies, but I have no tea to offer you."

"That is quite all right, Mr. Brown. Water is just fine for such a hot, muggy day."

Mr. Brown sat in his rocking chair, took a sip of water and gently started rocking his chair.

"What might you have of my Tillie's?" he finally asked in a gentle tone.

Lily pulled Tillie's locket out of her pocket and carefully held it out for Mr. Brown to see.

Slowly he reached out and tenderly took the locket with his time-weathered hands, cupping it as if he had found a fragile treasure too delicate to touch. Mr. Brown lovingly nestled the locket in the palm of his hand and carefully pressed the latch. It opened with a tiny *click*. Tears began flowing down his weathered face as he stared at the little locket cradled in the palm of his large hand. He sat quietly staring at it for a bit, and then began rocking his chair slowly and talking to the picture in the locket.

"Ah," he whispered to himself loving tenderness. "My pretty little Tillie Natasha. What a blessed man I was to have experienced your escapades. You were a scamp, my beautiful child. But I would not have had it any other way. It is so good to see you again, my dear. And here you are also, my little Macy Kata-rina. What a kind and soft-souled child you were. How blessed I was to have all my girls. Ah..and you my beautiful, beautiful Katia, how I have missed you. I hope you don't mind, but I have named our newest baby Kisa Galina. I did not know what you and the girls named her, so I named her Kisa Galina, your beautiful mamochka's name. I could not bear to place the lonely word 'baby' on her marker."

For, what seemed like, a full half hour, Mr. Brown rocked gently in his rocking chair and stared at the locket. At times he would laugh softly to himself and at other times tears would roll down his wrinkled worn face.

Running a rough, weather-worn hand through his snowy-white hair, he looked up at Lily and Ophelia, as if finally remembering they were sitting there beside him.

"Please forgive my improper behavior, my dear girls. It was very rude of me to ignore you and travel back into my memories. I am so sorry; seeing this locket and holding my girls in my hands swept the past once again into my heart with such lovely memories and I could not stop myself from dwelling on them. It has been such a very long, long time since I have seen all my girls together. I had almost forgotten how beautiful they were. But now the ghosts of yesterday have come sweeping into my soul. It all comes back to me now. My heart is filled with smells of Christmas dinner cooking as I envision my Katia and the girls frosting Christmas cookies, the Victrola playing as they danced and sang the songs of the American Christmas celebrations. Their laughter echoing through the house as they played their indoor games during the cold winter months. The dirt on Tillie and Macy's pretty little faces as they came inside after the long hot days of summer. But sadly until this very moment, as the years passed, their faces grew murky in my minds-eye, as if they were fading from my soul. Lately, when I have dreamed of them, it is as if they are waving and calling out to me, 'do svidaniya Papa, do svidaniya Papa'. That is 'goodbye Papa, goodbye Papa' in Russian."

Mr. Brown looked directly at Lily and said, "Before you handed me my Tillie's locket, my minds picture of them was vanishing. You have given me a pearl no amount of money could ever buy, my dear girls."

Mr. Brown cleared his throat before he continued speakling.

"But, come now, let us talk of happier times – let me tell you of my Katia. What a lovely young woman she was. She was the joy of my life from the first day I spotted her in the marketplace buying bread for her family. She was thirteen, and I was a very mature sixteen, or so I thought." Mr. Brown chuckled as he continued his story. "My heart stopped beating when I first saw her face. She asked me for a bukhanka khleba – a loaf of bread – but I just stood there staring at her like a big oaf. I could not move a muscle. Finally Pa-pa came over, shoved me aside and handed her a loaf of bread. Every day after that I watched for her, and each time I saw her I grew a little bolder until finally I was able to squeak out a stammering 'Privet' – Russian for 'hello'."

A hearty chuckle rose from deep inside Mr. Brown's chest.

"Ahhh… She was a pretty little thing the first day I saw her," he said with a smile. "She wore a blue dress and a little blue sweater. Covering her beautiful black hair was a little blue platok. I remember thinking how I would like to ask her to take her platok off so I could see her hair, but I could not do that. That would have been very improper."

Mr. Brown stopped and once again stared at the picture in the locket before continuing his story.

"Well, one day lead to the next until finally the beautiful Katia and I were married and moving to the *great* country of America to improve our lives and raise a family. It was a wonderful, blessed life we built in New Orleans. Finally, along came our little Tillie Natasha and then a few years later, along came our Macy Kata-rina and our lives were complete."

Lily and Ophelia sat staring at Mr. Brown. They had never heard anyone speak with a Russian accent and Mr. Brown's story was getting more interesting by the moment. Never in their entire life would they have thought the rough Tillie Brown they knew would be related to this stately gentleman.

"Well, that is until the War Between the States broke out, and everything changed."

He continued with sadness in his voice.

"As the soldiers advanced on our home, we managed to escape, but three days later I was captured as I went into Natchez in search of food for my girls. I was carried away without being able to let my Katia know where they were taking me, and by the time I was released from prison, my girls had all vanished. I searched everywhere and finally found they had gone to a distant relative's farm in Reed, Mississippi. When I arrived there, I was told that my Katia died giving birth to another baby girl, and they told me the lie that after she died, my Tillie and Macy ran away and they knew nothing of their whereabouts. The Gomers had buried my Katia and our baby girl in an old, abandoned cemetery by the Mississippi river. I went to that cemetery and found it to be full of tall grass and snakes. Finally I was able to locate their grave marker and became very angry. The only way I found the final resting place for my Katia was a ragged piece of wood with the name Katia and the word 'baby' burned into the wood cross. I worked hard for two years and saved every penny I could manage to save. After two years, with the help of a few friends, I was able to unearth their burial boxes and bring them to the church cemetery here in Piney. Then I set out to find my Tillie and little Macy Kata-rina. After many months of searching, I came upon an orphan's home in Natchez and was told the Gomers had taken my girls there and dumped them onto the steps of the orphan home. My little Macy Kata-rina died there at the orphan home from the influenza and was buried in the orphan's cemetery. Once again, I saved my pennies and finally moved her so she can sleep beside her Mamochka and baby Kisa Galina."

Mr. Brown gave a huge sigh, looked at Lily and Ophelia and said, "Now, tell me of my wild and rowdy Tillie Natasha and the life she created for herself along this mighty Mississippi River."

Lily and Ophelia looked at each other with anguished eyes.

"What shall I say?" Lily's eyes spoke silently to Ophelia.

"Don't tell him all the details," Ophelia's eyes spoke back to Lily. "Elaborate on the positive."

Lily cleared her throat before she started speaking softly to Mr. Brown.

"Well, Mr. Brown, we really didn't know Tillie in a personal way. We knew of her and saw her quite a few times around town and on the river boats as they passed Caruthersville. But what we do know of Tillie is that she was very resourceful. She never married, but was able to take care of herself. She had a small house down by the Mississippi, she owned two horses and she was able to travel up and down the river on the riverboats whenever she wanted. Quite a few times I saw her standing on the riverboat deck watching the townsfolk as the boat passed by. I have no idea where she went each time she went up or down the river, but she seemed to be enjoying herself. We have heard she met many, many well-known people on those river boats and she knew how to present herself and make the impression she wanted to make. She owned a beautiful, exotic parrot, which she named Duck, and she taught him to talk. At one time, she told me how she and her mother had hidden a lot of coins and jewelry at the house they lived in while living on the relative's farm and when she left the orphanage she went and retrieved the coins and jewelry. I took it for granted that was how she purchased her home and lived comfortably all these years. I do know one thing – Tillie enjoyed her life and she never let anyone tell her what to do or say.

"In regards to how she died, I will not lie to you. She was murdered and robbed of a pouch of gold she was carrying with her. She was not beaten or abused by the killers, so she did not suffer, they hit her in the head and that was it. All they took was a small pouch of gold. We found her body, and the body of Duck, her parrot, along the path in the river bottom. We found her just a short while after it happened so no animals or critters got to her body. We took her to our family barn so my brother-in-law, Sheriff André could take her into town and then investigate as to how she died.

"Well, when we went back out to the barn, her body and the parrot's body were both gone, and the next morning as Ophelia and I were going to Ophelia's house, we met Tillie on her big, black horse up on the levee road. It seems as if she wasn't really dead after all. Well, one thing led to another and after a few days, someone found her body along with her horses's body floating in the Mississippi."

Mr. Brown shook his head as he once again spoke. "Why would anyone murder my Tillie Natasha for a pouch of gold? Were the killers caught? What happened to them? Does the Sheriff know who did this or did they get away with it? How did Tillie Natasha give you this locket before she died if she was murdered? Please tell me, I do not understand these things."

Lily's heart dropped into her stomach as she thought to herself, "Okay, how am I going to tell him that we met his daughter's ghost?"

Gulping down a swallow, Lily took a deep breath and hesitantly began telling Mr. Brown her story.

"Well, sir," She said and then stopped a moment. "It was like this: late one night Ophelia came to our house and knocked on my bedroom window and told me she thought she had seen a body out in the path leading though the woods to the river. So I got out of bed and we both went to investigate—seeing that I didn't really believe her and all, since I had never heard of a body being left along that path. But when we got there, sure enough, it was Tillie and her parrot. Now, I don't know if you believe in haints or ghosts, but we do, and sure enough, there was Tillie and her parrot's haint sitting on a branch right above our heads. Tillie started in talking to us and telling us her story of what she thought had happened to her and Duck, her parrot started in squawking about killers and such, then Tillie told me to take the locket off her neck and give it to the first relative of hers I come upon."

Lily repeated the story Tillie had told them – leaving out the part about her "pinching" Mr. Bushy's hides. Instead, she told Mr. Brown that Tillie was watching the thieves and Mr. Bushy and that she was sure Tillie was waiting for a chance to help Mr. Bushy.

When she finished her tale, Mr. Brown looked at Lily with a grin on his face and chuckled.

"Now Miss Lily, you don't have to sugar-coat this story for me. I know my Tillie-girl; if she was following this Mr. Bushy, I am sure she was up to some kind of mischief. Even as a small child she was very resourceful and did not hesitate to use her imagination in getting what she wanted or needed. Now, tell me the true story and please do not leave out any details. I delight in hearing of my Tillie's escapades! Tell me about her exciting life on the Mississippi. I was born a poor boy in Russia. I do not mind that my daughter had to work or wrangle to make a living."

Mr. Brown's was speaking with gusto and his face had a look of delight as he leaned slightly forward in his chair, anxious to hear about Tillie's life. "Tell me all of her adventures you may know of. Tell me how she lived her life bursting with excitement and adventure. I imagine my Tillie had many a fight in her life. She could tussle with the best of them even as a small child. She delighted in a great challenge. I am quite sure she gave all those wealthy gamblers and men along that mighty Mississippi a run for their money. At times I have sat back and imagined her brawling with a grizzly bear and winning. There have been times when my Tillie-girl would come to me in a dream and I was able to get a glimpse of the life she was living and after each of those times I would say to myself, 'Oh my. My Katia must be horrified if she is watching our Tillie Natasha."

Mr. Brown gave another deep-chested chuckle and continued telling his story of Tillie's escapades as a child.

"The life of the elite was not the life for my Tillie-girl. She was a girl born to live the rough-and-tumble life of the wild western states.

Once when my Tillie was about five years old, I had an important meeting with some wealthy investors in San Francisco, California, so Katia and I decided to take both of our little ones on the train journey and show them some of the wild west country along the way. Well after seeing a few native Indians from our train window, our five-year-old little Tillie tried to run away and join up with the Indians. She pinched some money from my pocket while we were sleeping and tried to pay the conductor to stop the train so she could get off and pay a tribe of Amerian Indians to let her join them. When the conductor said he could not do that, Tillie tried jumping off the train while it was in motion. The poor man was highly upset at such a thing from a small child, and when he picked her up, she began kicking and screaming and flapping her arms around as she tried escaping his tight hold. Well the unfortunate gentleman finally managed to get her back to our private car where he firmly declared she needed to be put under lock and key and maybe, he said, we should just throw the key away. Furthermore, he firmly stated he would never do such a thing to the native Indians. He also stated that, in his opinion, the native Indians did not deserve such horrible punishment by having her living among them. He was quite sure they would pack her up and toss her onto the first train they could find. The unhappy fellow's clothing was disheveled, his hat was gone and the next day it was quite apparent he had picked up a black eye and lost one earpiece from his spectacles. His spectacles were askew and he was none too friendly with us."

With a big grin on his face, Mr. Brown chuckled and continued his story.

"Along with having to keep a close watch on her, we had to try and comfort her by assuring her she would find another adventure quickly once we reached San Francisco. And sure enough, once we arrived in San Francisco, she decided she wanted to look just like the little Chinese children running errands for their parents, so we bought her a small, black wig which had a long straight braid hanging down her back and some clothing to match the other children.

She was as happy as a pig-in-slop—as you Americans say—for the rest of our stay in the city. On the return journey home, she decided she wanted to be the conductor on the train so she spent every day going up and down the aisles asking people for their tickets and wanting to know their names and where they 'hailed from' and just where were they going and why were they going there. Seeing that she insisted on being in the passenger cars, each day we left our private car and rode in the passenger cars until nightfall.

The first conductor we had was a very kind, grandfatherly gentleman and he found an old conductor hat and gave it to her as a gift. She was so excited about that hat she jumped up onto the unfortunate conductor's back and hugged him about the neck for a bit. Most people on the train were very kind and went along with her, but some were not so kind, and the last conductor we had was so very glad when we departed from his train that he and some of the passengers clapped when we disembarked.

"So I know what she was like. Please tell me of everything you know about her and her great adventures in this country."

Laugher seemed to echo off the walls of the small room when Mr. Brown finished his tale of Tillie and her adventurous personality as a small child.

Lily and Ophelia looked at Mr. Brown with wonder. They had never met a person who did not want their child to live with an abundance of money or did not mind that their daughter experienced outrageous, dangerous adventures.

"Okay," Lily said as she looked at Mr. Brown with curiosity. "Tillie had a very interesting life that was for sure. The first time she passed on, she was following Mr. Bushy around trying to pinch some of his hides. Mr. Bushy is a mountain man and he traps everything from beavers to bears for their hides. He and Tillie have a love/hate friendship. She follows him and tries to pinch his hides and he watches for her and stops her before she can rob him blind. Other times, when they ran into each other she will fix him some grub and talk the night away about the mountains and everything happening along the river.

So, sometimes it's hard to tell if they are good friends or battling enemies."

Lily continued telling Mr. Brown everything she and Ophelia knew about Tillie and then she told him how very sorry they were that he had lost all of his loved ones so tragically.

"My dear young ladies," he said softly. "By bringing me my Tillie's locket and talking to me about her life along the river, you have gifted me with another treasure for my heart to hold on to. You will never know how soft my heart feels at this moment. I now have all the answers to the questions I pondered for such a long time. Now I only have to wait for our God to take me home so I can once again see all my precious girls."

Lily and Ophelia stood up to leave, and Mr. Brown rose with them. He walked over and gave them both a heartfelt hug as tears once again rolled down his face.

Speaking with his soft foreign accent, he whispered to them quietly.

"I have very little in this life, but what I have left, when I leave this life, is yours. I will make sure my dear friend Kip Knudson knows what I wish to have done." Mr. Brown opened his door and walked out, holding the door open for Lily and Ophelia.

"Good-bye, Mr. Brown," both girls smiled as they walked off the porch toward Ophelia's old mule.

"Good day, my young ladies. You have been a gift sent to me from our most high God."

# 14

---

## THE CARUTHERSVILLE TRAIN DEPOT

---

Lily and Ophelia ambled along the road on their way to the train depot in Caruthersville just to watch the chaos they know would be taking place. As they walked, they shuffled up dust and kicked dirt clumps out of their way. The weather was pleasant; a warm breeze cooled away the heat of the sun. The hot heat of noon was past and the cooler air of evening was coming in off the river. Off in the distance, they heard the echo of a whistling train – the last train of the day approached the little, sleepy town nestled along the mighty Mississippi River.

As they stepped onto the platform, the vendors already had their whiskey barrels and food carts as close to the tracks as possible without actually falling off the edge onto the tracks. Cowboys were lined up holding tightly to their horses, readying themselves for the fight which was sure to ensue when they tried getting their horses aboard the stock car. Pete Turnkey was sitting at his ticket window with droopy eyes, as if the free-for-all was not worth a bother.

"Hi, Mr. Pete" Lily yelled out loudly.

Pete jerked his head up and looked around trying to spot the person who had called out his name.

"Oh!" Pete jumped with surprise. "Hello, Lily-Beth how ya doing?"

"Hello, Mr. Pete!" Ophelia called out.

"Hello back at you, Miz. Ophelia Knudson," Pete said. "How's your Ma and Pa?"

"They're doing just fine, Mr. Pete."

Pete Turnkey had, at one time, been in love with Ophelia's mother back when he first arrived from New York City, but when Kip Knudson drifted into town, all Corina's feelings for Pete left – if she ever had any. All she could see was the tall, blond, curly-headed, blue-eyed Kip Knudson, and all Kip Knudson could see was the pretty face of Corina Crawford. They married one month after meeting, moved into a farmhouse and quickly had six children.

"What excitement is going on in the lives of the Quinn family now-a-days, Miz Lily?"

"Well," Lily answered, "Not much really. It was pretty sad with Tillie Brown dying and all. We were hoping she would be alive and kicking. Ophelia and I are powerful glad you and André caught that Pike Herman. It's no wonder his wife took off and left him. He was one mean fella, wasn't he? Did you get to meet his wife? Was she all beat up too?"

"It was mighty sad, yes indeed, mighty sad," Pete answered gloomily. "Tillie Brown was a mysterious woman, that was for sure, and it's mighty sorrowful when a soul passes over for no other reason than greed from some low-life humans. No, we didn't get to meet Mrs. Herman. She had already packed up and gone by the time we picked Pike up from his house. He kept on saying he didn't kill Tillie Brown, and when the Judge Snow asked him who he killed if it wasn't Tillie Brown, he wouldn't say one word. So, Judge Snow said he didn't have any other choice but to sentence him for Tillie Brown's death seeing that he killed her horse and so many people heard him talking about getting "that crazy woman" and dumping her in the river. If you're gonna commit a crime, its best if you keep it to yourself. Sheriff André wasn't real satisfied on the outcome. Nope he wasn't, he's quite sure there's more to Pike Herman than what he's telling. In fact, he's gonna do some checking on old Pike Herman's wife just to see what she knows; if he can find out where she went. But…" he paused. "Judge Snow made the final decision, so that's the end of the case. Considering the place he's going, Pike Herman will have to answer to a higher power than old Judge Snow."

*Clickety-clack! Clickety-clack!*

*Clang! Clang! Clang!*

With screaming wheels, the huge locomotive brought the train to a stop. The rumbling noise from the engine vibrated the platform. Lily and Ophelia walked a few steps closer and watched as mayham covered the train platform like always. Passengers got off the train and were greeted by their loved ones with merriment and those leaving were being hugged with parting tears.

Alighting from one of the private cars was a small-built woman, eloquently outfitted in a beautiful, violet voile dress and a matching hat with plumes of dark, purple feathers flowing over one side. She had long, white, leather gloves covering her hands and lower arms. She lifted her skirt a bit as she stepped down from the car, enabling Lily and Ophelia to get a glimpse of her beautiful black satin slippers neatly laced up to her ankles.

Hanging over her arm was a dark violet, ruffled parasol along and a small, ruffled handbag. Both the parasol and the handbag were the same shimmering violet color of her dress. Her dark hair was swept under a large, violet, feather-plumed hat with tendrils of curly hair cascading along the sides of her face and neck.

Holding onto her right arm was a handsome, black-haired gentleman dressed as stylish as she.

"I wonder who they are," Ophelia whispered to Lily.

"I have no idea, but if they lived here in Caruthersville we certainly would know who they are."

When the woman looked over and spotted Lily and Ophelia gaping impolitely at them, she nonchalantly eased down the glove on her left arm revealing a tatoo of a beautiful parrot, and then just as slowly drew it back up.

As the couple drew near, the woman stopped, turned her head toward Lily and softly whispered with a smile, "I am going to get my Pa-pa."

The End

# FUN FACTS

Some facts are true and some facts contain a bit of legend.

<u>"Drunk as Cooter Brown"</u> – (true)

> Cooter Brown is an infamous character in Southern folklore. Legend says that he lived on the Mason-Dixie line — the border between the North and South during the Civil War. To avoid the drafted by the Union Army and the Confederate Army, Cooter decided to stay drunk throughout the entire war, making him ineligible for battle. His ruse worked.

<u>John "Liver-Eating" Johnson,</u> b.1824- d.1900 (mostly true - some folklore)

> Facts of John "Liver Eating"Johnson are said to be true. Some facts have never been proven. But it is an interesting story, and maybe they are true. Look it up!

<u>William Henry "Bully" Hayes,</u> b.1827 – d. 1877 (true)

> An American-born pirate, Bully Hayes was notorious for "blackbirding" many men to form his crew.

<u>The Battle of Chickamauga,</u> September 19-20, 1863 (true)

> Fought in Tennessee, the Battle of Chickamauga was one of the bloodiest battles of the Civil War.

The sinking of _The Monmouth_ October 31, 1837 (true)

On October 31, 1837, _The Monmouth_ sank in the Mississippi River, taking with it many Creek Indians.

The mailing of small children – (true)

The actual practice of mailing small children and babies did not start until approximately 1913, and ended in approximately 1915. The first child mailed in the U.S. was an unnamed boy in Batavia, Ohio, in mid-January 1913. The son of Mr. and Mrs. Jesse Beauge of Glen Este, Ohio was carried by rural delivery carrier Vernon Little to his grandmother, Mrs. Louis Beague, about a mile away. The boy's parents paid 15 cents for the stamps and even insured their son for $50.

On January 27, 1913 Mr. and Mrs. J.W. Savis of Pine Hollow, Pennsylvania entrusted their daughter to rural carrier James Byerly out of Sharpsville, Pennsylvania, who delivered her safely that afternoon to relatives in Clay Hollow. The daughter cost her parents 45 cents to send.

A year later, the longest trip of a child mailed through parcel post was made by six-year-old Edna Neff. She traveled from her mother's home in Pensacola, Florida to her father's home in Christainsburg, Virginia. There is little information on the specifics of Edna's trip other than her weight, recorded as just under the 50-pound limit resulting in a trip cost of 15 cents in parcel post stamps. She was mailed by train.

1915 was a banner year for mailing children. Unburdened by regulations now on the books against mailing children, more trips were made that year. In March, rural carrier Charles Hayes of Tarkin, Missouri carried the daughter of Mr. and Mrs. Albert Combs by parcel post for 10-cents. Hayes delivered her to her grandmother, Mrs. C.H. Combs, whose home was also on his route. That September, three-year-old Maud Smith made her parcel post journey when she traveled from her grandparent's home to her mother's, Mrs. Celina Smith, of Jackson, Kentucky. A local newspaper noted that this particular trip was being investigated by the postal officials. Superintendent John Clark of the Cincinnati division of the Railway Mail Service asked the Caney, Kentucky postmaster to explain why he allowed the child onto the train as parcel post in clear violation of postal rules. Perhaps the public notice of the investigation is what made this trip the final case of child mailing. Postmaster General Burleson issued directions to the nation's postmasters, stating all humans were barred from the mail.

Coming in 2016
"Lily and the Ghost of Peg-Leg Paddy McGee"

32041542R00119

Made in the USA
San Bernardino, CA
26 March 2016